SEVEN STITCHES

SEVEN STITCHES

RUTH TENZER FELDMAN

OOLIGAN PRESS
PORTLAND, OREGON

Seven Stitches
© 2016 Ruth Tenzer Feldman

ISBN13: 978-1-932010-88-6

Ooligan Press
Portland State University
Post Office Box 751, Portland, Oregon 97207
503.725.9748
ooligan@ooliganpress.pdx.edu
www.ooliganpress.pdx.edu

Library of Congress Cataloging-in-Publication Data
available upon request from publisher.

Cover design by Leigh Thomas and Andrea McDonald
Cover photo © tmc_photos, used with permission
Interior design by Cade Hoover

References to website URLs were accurate at the time of writing. Neither the author nor Ooligan Press is responsible for URLs that have changed or expired since the manuscript was prepared.

Printed in the United States of America on 30% post-consumer recycled stock.

For my mother, Sophie, who was and is.

"Hope" is the thing with feathers—
That perches in the soul—
And sings the tune without the words—
And never stops—at all—
And sweetest—in the Gale—is heard—
And sore must be the storm—
That could abash the little Bird
That kept so many warm—
I've heard it in the chillest land—
And on the strangest Sea—
Yet—never—in Extremity,
It asked a crumb—of me.

—Emily Elizabeth Dickinson (1830–1886)

PROLOGUE

The aroma of burnt sugar comforts Serakh, daughter of Asher, easing the stress of another journey through the *olam*. Alone, she leans against a tiled wall in a long, narrow passageway. Sunlight from latticed windows speckles the stone floor under her sandaled feet and warms her toes. Despite the task she knows she must soon face, she feels welcomed.

A man's deep voice pierces the air with the Muslim call to prayer from a mosque's towering minaret. Bowing her head, Serakh acknowledges the greatness of The One who has guided her travel over the centuries. She smiles, remembering her true youth, when twelve tribes of Ishmael and twelve tribes of Israel shared the dunes and wadis of home.

A lion's roar answers the muezzin's call to prayer. Startled, Serakh races to a window and presses her face against the lattice. She scans a broad expanse of walkways and gardens bounded by massive stone walls that form a courtyard of enormous proportions. A second roar echoes from a massive church arched in the Byzantine style, one of several structures within the courtyard. Four tall men with swords at their sides stride along a nearby path, the plumes of their elaborate turbans bowing in the breeze.

Now she knows. Serakh has traveled to the great city of Istanbul before. Surely she must be in *Yeni Saray*, the place some call Topkapı Palace, a complex of buildings that houses the sultan and thousands who do his bidding. But which sultan? When has she arrived? And why? Serakh rolls her shoulders and prepares for the task that will surely reveal itself.

The muezzin and the lion end their duet. Women's voices funnel down the passageway from the maze of rooms that house the sultan's female captives and concubines—his harem. Serakh tightens her sandals and tiptoes toward the sound.

Ten steps later, she stops in front of a rectangular niche half hidden by a pile of richly woven carpets stacked as high as her waist. She hears a sharp intake of breath and then, in a child's voice, an ancient lament meaning, "Upon my life!" She understands what follows as: "Ayele will be furious."

Serakh peeks around the pile. A wisp of a girl, no more than nine or ten, with a pale complexion and a mass of dark red curls, sits by a basket of silken threads. A square of tapestry dropped in mid-stitch rests on her lap. She dabs a bleeding finger with the hem of her plain cotton shift.

"Peace be unto you," Serakh says softly by way of introduction. Her words carry with them Serakh's gift of communication so that a listener who speaks any language can understand.

Scrambling to her feet, the girl stabs the air with her embroidery scissors. "Get away from me, or you will answer to Ayele! Do not dare tell anyone I am here!"

Serakh steps back, her gold-flecked hazel eyes half-lidded, her body offering no sign of threat. "What troubles you besides your pricked finger?"

"You don't know?" The girl glares at Serakh, her face betraying fear under a mask of ferocity.

"I am new here." Serakh hopes the answer will suffice. The One often left much to be discovered during every journey through the *olam*.

10

The girl cocks her head. Her lips quiver.

Serakh studies the girl's clean clothes and freshly washed hair. "Surely someone provides for you. Where is your mistress?"

The girl swings her arms wide, her scissors barely missing Serakh's shoulder. "My mistress? They came in the night and put a bag over her head. You could hear her screams all over the harem. They tied a stone to her and drowned her in the Bosporus. Someone was tired of her. When Ayele gets tired of me, he'll sell me or banish me to the streets. I would rather drown."

Serakh struggles to keep her voice lullaby-soft. "Ayele?"

The girl frowns in confusion. "Everyone knows Ayele. Even the newest girls."

Footsteps shuffle along the passageway. "Say no more, Izabel."

A tall black man enters the niche, his complexion several shades darker and less bronze than her own. He is robed and turbaned in the style of the wealthy and powerful. His gray eyebrows confess to old age. His features are thin, spare, as if The One has fashioned his face with a deficiency of clay.

"Stand behind me, child," he says with a gentleness that might have been genuine.

Izabel does so without hesitation, pocketing her scissors and keeping her bloody finger away from his robes.

"I am Ayele, second in command among the eunuchs responsible for the sultan's women. How can it be that you do not know me?"

Serakh offers her customary explanation. "I come from the East."

Ayele touches the small dagger tucked into the embroidered sash at his waist. "Many who serve the sultan, may he live forever, come from distant lands. Whose slave are you? Are you the concubine of an officer? Or a spy?"

"I am here to help Izabel," Serakh says, certain now that this must be the reason The One had guided her to this spot on the *olam*. "I mean no harm to you or to any in the harem."

Ayele steps closer. He smells of bergamot and rosewater. With one swift motion, he pulls off Serakh's headscarf, revealing stark white hair that cascades to her waist in a thick braid. "Open your mouth," he commands. "Show me your teeth."

For the sake of Izabel, Serakh does his bidding.

Ayele nods his approval. "You have strong teeth and exotic eyes, but hair the color of milk. Our chief of silversmiths enjoys such freaks of nature. He would pay more if your skin were as light as your hair, but I will offer a discount."

Serakh covers her head again. She smoothes her robe. "I am not for sale," she says, although she knows Ayele would think this a brazen lie. He would see her as a female without a protector, available for a price.

Ayele crouches down and puts his hands on Izabel's waist. "Go back to your embroidery. We have a tapestry order to fill."

"I pricked my finger." Izabel shows him her injury.

Ayele pronounces the finger nearly healed. "We must all be useful, little Izabel, in one way or another."

With her clean hand, Izabel holds up a square of linen embroidered in an intricate design of green, gold, and silver threads. "I promise I will always be useful. See? I am working on a pattern to match your talisman. It's a gift for you."

Ayele smiles. "One day you will be very valuable." He clasps Serakh's arm, his grip firm and unforgiving. "As for you, woman, come with me."

When they are out of Izabel's sight, Ayele unsheathes the dagger. His eyes soften with regret. "These are dangerous times in the harem, and you are a stranger here. You cannot be trusted."

Has he changed his mind about selling her to the silversmith? Will he simply slit her throat? Serakh shoves the old man and pushes herself backward. Ayele grunts, straining, and holds fast. He raises his dagger. Serakh twists away from the blade.

Jerking free, Serakh races down the passageway, too focused on flight to notice if Ayele is following. She turns a corner and searches for a hiding place in a cavernous room filled only with rugs, mirrors, low tables, and decorative pillows. Nothing offers shelter.

Serakh closes her eyes and fills her lungs. She prepares herself to step once more into the *olam* to meet another girl. Serakh knows that the girl will possess one of the ancient threads and will be named for a Miryam. The girl and Izabel will be linked in ways that Serakh has yet to discover. Invoking a Hebrew name for The One, Serakh lets herself vanish in a flash of blue.

CHAPTER ONE

I wrapped two of Rose's fresh-baked biscuits in a dishtowel and raced back upstairs in my nightgown to my mother's room. Jessa and I were a gluesome twosome most Saturday mornings, a mother-daughter binary sharing biscuits in Jessa's bed.

I opened my mother's bedroom door. Jessa's bed was its usual self. Jessa says it's a waste of time to make your bed except to change linens. Desks should be organized. So should bathrooms, closets, kitchen shelves, Chicken Hacienda, and the goat shed. Beds—hers was "the Jessa nest" and mine "Meryem's mess"—can be any way you want.

The note taped to Jessa's headboard read:

QUICK TRIP. HOME SOON.

♥ J

A look outside showed Jessa's car juicing up on morning sun, so she'd biked or walked somewhere. Or maybe she took the streetcar. She might be at the farmers market buying something luscious. Or at The Anthony smoothing things over between Auntie An and Grandma. She might be home any minute.

I snuggled into the Jessa nest, unwrapped the biscuits to breathe in their buttery aroma, and then wrapped them up again. I waited. Four minutes. Five.

Still, fresh-baked biscuits demand immediate consumption. I sat by Jessa's desk, switched on our PerSafe receiver and thumbed her code. Three seconds later, the PerSafe flashed her coordinates: 45°43' 19" N, 123°56' 02" W.

Manzanita—one hundred fifty kilometers away.

Cyber hiccup, I thought. *My mother wouldn't go to the coast without me.* I vid-voiced her.

"Good morning, lovey!" Jessa sparkled in the sunlight, her magenta hair looking extra purple, shinier than mine.

"Are you really in Manzanita?"

She laughed. "Yup. Just south of Neahkahnie Mountain. Sorry. It's for work, lovey. Boring, boring, boring. I'll be home late this afternoon. We'll do something fun then."

Manzanita is never boring. I waved a biscuit in front of the screen. "You're missing fresh-baked biscuits," I said, which was easier to manage than telling Jessa she should have invited me. We could have been a gluesome twosome on the coast. I took a bite. "Yum!"

Jessa scrunched her face. "I sacrifice for science. Save a biscuit for me."

I took another bite. "Maybe. Is that a guy I hear in the background?"

Jessa looked to her left, then back at me, all smiles. "Yusuf is a colleague from Istanbul. He...well, you might say he's in charge of our fieldwork this morning. He's going to have dinner with us. Tell Rose, okay? Whatever she makes will be delicious."

I brushed a crumb from my lips. "Can't your work wait until Monday?"

"Listen, biscuit breath, Yusuf says we're ready. I have to go. See you in a bit. Love you."

I frowned and clicked off, not bothering to say love you too, or good-bye. She was having fun on the beach. I was stuck at home. Unfair.

I wedged my feet into flip-flops and wrapped Jessa's biscuit to take to Munchkina and Chewsette. My goats loved treats. My goats didn't sneak off without me. My goats cherished my company.

I was walking to the goat shed out back when the neighborhood dogs started barking like crazy. My legs felt wobbly, as if they had delinked from my brain. My flip-flops vibrated against the soles of my feet.

United Newsfeed Emergency Alert System

Pacific Northwest Seismic Network

2058.03.09.1647 GMT

RED ALERT. RED ALERT. RED ALERT. RED ALERT.

8.9 magnitude earthquake, Cascadia subduction zone. Epicenter 20.6 km west of Reedsport, Oregon. Severe damage expected for western regions of Oregon, Washington, and Northern California. Massive tsunami expected to make US landfall by 1706 GMT. Activate evacuation and casualty prevention measures. Tune to SatSync 47.3 for updates every 90 seconds.

CHAPTER TWO

"Why am I lying under the kitchen table?" I asked Rose. "Where did you put my feet?"

My body seemed glued to the floor, and my tongue felt thick and sticky, as if I'd slept for a thousand years. Nothing hurt, and yet everything felt wrong. My legs tingled.

Rose sat next to me with two flashlights, one on, the other off. The room smelled of bleach and blood. The palm of her hand rested on my forehead. She looked tired, her face paler than usual. Long strands of brown and gray hair had escaped from the bun at the nape of her neck.

"No fever," she told me. "That's a good sign." She popped the earbud that life-lined her to our emergency crank radio, and she adjusted the pillows under my legs.

"Your feet are attached to you, Meryem," she said. "You can't feel them because of the analgesic spray and pain killers. We have to keep them elevated until help comes. The medics will be here soon."

"What happened?"

"You walked through broken glass in your flip-flops, remember? During the earthquake. Don't worry. Everything will be fine."

Rose's voice was steady, matter-of-fact. She could have been telling me how to make tomato relish. Jessa says that Rose was more than qualified to care for me, but her soft brown eyes and open, generous face were why Jessa hired her. Rose looks trustworthy. Which is why I believed her then.

"I'm not worried. Just whoozy. Was it The Big One?"

She held my head and brought a straw to my lips. "Pretty big," she said. "Take a sip. You need to stay hydrated. I gave you a sedative too. I might have gone a bit overboard."

The water tasted wonderful. "How big?"

"The decorative window shattered, and some other windows as well, but the house is basically sound. We have emergency supplies, so there's no need to get upset."

An image took shape in my brain, a vague recollection of Chewsette nearly buried under rubble, her back leg twisted at a sickening angle. I reached for Rose's hand. "Chewsette. We have to get to the goat shed."

"I know, Meryem, but let's concentrate on you. Are you hungry? No? Then get some more rest."

Rose hummed a Russian lullaby from when I was little—and from when she was little too. I closed my eyes and let the melody tuck me back into sleep.

Sometime later, she called my name. I climbed out of the haze.

"The medics are at the front door. I have to leave you here for a few minutes, but I'll be right back."

"Bon voyage," I said, which wasn't exactly what I meant.

The kitchen door closed. Noise leaked from Rose's earbuds. I pulled the radio closer and stuffed a bud in one ear.

The noise morphed into: "...listening to Oregon Public Broadcasting. The time is 7:42. I'm Nancy Beth Streitfelder, speaking to you from our emergency headquarters at radio station KOJD-FM John Day. We've reached Portland mayor Joule

Hammilason by satellite phone. Mayor Hammilason, welcome to OPB."

Rose's voice filtered through the kitchen door into my other ear. She was angry about something. Jessa calls it her thorny side. "I contacted MedAlert twenty-two hours ago," I heard her say. "What the hell took you so long? I'm nearly out of pain killers."

I couldn't hear what the medics were saying, but the mayor said, "…progress we've made over the past three decades to retrofit buildings, strengthen infrastructure, and prepare Oregonians. Had The Big One hit in 2020 or 2030, the situation would have been much worse."

Rose: "…the only drugs I had. What else do you expect?"

Nancy Beth: "…and so, with much of western Oregon experiencing the worst natural disaster in the recorded history of the Pacific Northwest, what can we expect in…?"

Rose: "Her mother is in Manzanita. Jessa Einhorn Zarfati. Of course, I haven't heard from her. Yes, I understand. You and I suspect that, but Meryem doesn't have to know. She's barely fifteen, for heavensake. How soon can you get her to the hospital?"

The mayor: "…been advised that the Sellwood Bridge, Tilikum Crossing, and the Morrison Bridge are structurally sound."

Rose: "You're kidding!"

The mayor: "The tank farm along the Willamette River suffered only one rupture, thanks to our soil stabilization project. Portland International Airport should be functional within the next month and…"

Rose: "There's a grandmother—Ly Tien Zarfati. She is the official next of kin. No, I haven't heard from her either. We're wasting time."

Nancy Beth: "…you tell us about the new Resilience Council, which you will be chairing?"

Rose: "Absolutely not! She's safer here than in a shelter. Meryem has been my responsibility since she was a baby. Don't you dare…"

Go, Rose.

The mayor: "…and the elected commission chairs of Multnomah

and Clackamas counties, with staff from our city, county, and state emergency management offices, and from FEMA."

Nancy Beth: "That's the Federal Emergency Management Agency. Are we operating under martial law?"

Rose: "I don't care about downed power lines or broken water mains or blocked roads. Her feet are torn to shreds."

They are? I tried to sit up and find them, but the room swirled around me, and my body refused to cooperate.

The mayor: "...can say that the Portland Metropolitan Area Resilience Council will exercise its emergency powers in order to preserve our safety and public order. We're working on the details. In the meantime, I urge patience and calm. I share your listeners' grief and fear, but I also know that Oregonians come from pioneer stock. We are resilient. We are..."

The door creaked open. I popped the earbud. Rose squatted next to me, back to her non-thorny self.

"Jantelle and Horatio are here to look at your feet," she said. "Stay still, and we'll slide you out on the quilt. Everything's going to be okay."

"I listened to the radio," I told her.

"We don't have the full story yet," Rose said.

Jantelle looked away.

"Jessa's not dead," I told them. "She can't be." The words spilled out of me. The room turned to ice. I started to shake.

Horatio took my hands. "You focus on me, little lady," he said. "Jantelle is going to unwrap and examine your feet and upload a medical scan to a special team of doctors in Bend. They'll tell us what to do next. This might hurt a bit. Go ahead and scream."

So I did.

CHAPTER THREE

Eleven months later.
Friday, February 14, 2059

I thanked Mr. Nabli for the box of Turkish delight because Jessa insists on showing appreciation for gifts. I would have preferred radish seeds. You can't plant candy.

"My pleasure, Meryem," he said. We seated ourselves on opposite sides of the dining room table, next to our weekly tray of tea and zucchini bread.

"None for me this time," he said. "It's the Muslim holy month of Ramadan. I fast from sunrise to sunset."

"Sorry," I said. I slid the tray to the end of the table and wondered for the sextillionth time why Jessa had told Rose to contact this man if anything happened. Two weeks after The Big One, she did.

Grandma was annoyed with Rose, as usual, but Grandma's lawyer assured us that Adnan Nabli came from a respectable law firm with offices in New York, Portland, and Istanbul. She was furious when she found out that Mr. Nabli was to be my temporary guardian, but the lawyers said all the papers were in order. Even in her absence, Jessa got her way.

Mr. Nabli extracted a vintage fountain pen and stack of papers from a courier bag made from upcycled Mylar survival blankets. "How are things?"

"Fine," I said, spouting the same answer to the same question I'd heard for months so we could get the damn paperwork over with. Fine—the other all-purpose four-letter F-word, suitable for all, especially useful in self-defense.

Mr. Nabli produced the usual sheaf of official-looking documents duly stamped and decorated with:

PORTLAND METROPOLITAN
AREA RESILIENCE COUNCIL

AUTHORIZED BY NATIONAL
DISASTER RECOVERY PLAN 2058-16A

STATE DISASTER
RECOVERY COORDINATION OFFICE

FEDERAL EMERGENCY
MANAGEMENT AGENCY, REGION X

"Fine as in genuinely better than last week, Meryem? Or fine as in shut up and let's get down to business?"

A laugh bubbled up inside and suffocated in my mouth.

Mr. Nabli handed me his pen. "I speak English as well as legalese. Do I detect a smile this week?"

"Fine as in the second sense," I admitted. Maybe he was being particularly friendly because this was the first time Rose wasn't meeting with us, and he wanted to put me at ease.

"Fair enough," he said. We got down to business. The first list claimed to contain all of the current non-credit occupants of 732-NW19-97209, meaning my house on Northwest 19th and Johnson.

According to the Council, the non-credit occupants were me and Rose plus now The Ladies—Auntie An and my grandmother—who'd been with us since right after The Big One. In legalese we were:

ZARFATI, MERYEM EINHORN, 15,
RESIDENT MINOR, TEMPORARY WARD OF
ADNAN NABLI, ATTORNEY

EINHORN, AN CHAU CLEMENT, 88,
GREAT-AUNT OF RESIDENT MINOR

ZARFATI, LY TIEN EINHORN, 85,
GRANDMOTHER OF RESIDENT MINOR

KROPOTKIN, HROUZA, 41,
RESIDENT HOUSEKEEPER

The only other document where I'd seen Rose's Russian name was her American passport. Calling Rose a resident housekeeper was like calling your right lung a resident organ. I couldn't imagine life without Rose. I could, however, imagine The Ladies returning to their condo as soon as it was rehabbed.

"Jessa should be on this list," I said. "She lives here."

Mr. Nabli got that sympathetic look. "I know. We've gone through this before. However, it is my responsibility to consider potential inheritance and insurance factors."

Blah, blah, blah. I added my mother's name as usual, and her current age.

Zarfati, Jessa Einhorn, 51, resident owner,
employed-PaleoGenetics, LLC.

Mr. Nabli smoothed his hair, which fell to his shoulders in a thick, black mane and smelled of coconuts. "I'm still trying to get credit-tenant funds for your grandmother and great-aunt, since they lodged here temporarily after earthquake-related displacement and in lieu of seeking Council-supervised shelter elsewhere. But the Council insists that family is family, and they don't qualify as credit tenants."

The Council. I was sick to death of the Council. They and FEMA still governed so much of our lives—where we could travel, what was available to eat, and who could shelter where. They tightened the water restrictions we'd had before The Big One and made it a crime to be out after midnight.

Mr. Nabli must have read my face. "Portland is still under a state of emergency, Meryem. We all have to do our part." He handed me the list of officially homeless Portlanders that the Council placed here after Rose and I agreed to have them. I had to ink my initials next to each one because Mr. Nabli said the house was presumptively mine during Jessa's absence. Presumptively, which is legalese for no one had bothered to check.

CHADWICK, PRISCILLA, 39, EMPLOYED—INTEL CORP.

CHADWICK, WINSLOW, 3, SON OF PRISCILLA CHADWICK

RIVERA, IGNATIUS, 64, VETERAN, UNEMPLOYED, MEDICAL DISABILITY

Mr. Nabli leaned closer. "Meryem, be honest. Have you had any problems with Mr. Rivera? Any at all? Feel free to tell me. Does he make you uncomfortable? The Council claims to be monitoring his intoxicant levels, but you never know."

"Ignatius is fine," I answered. "He says he's living in paradise."

A noise escaped Mr. Nabli—part snort, part chuckle. "Three meals a day and a large, airy bedroom in a clean residence. Mr. Rivera has never had it better. He's one lucky guy."

Lucky for now, I thought. *What happens when the emergency ends and the Council stops paying us?* I handed him Rose's accounting forms. Hard copy documents week after week for more than ten months now. Stacks of wasted paper, as obsolete as fracking pumps on a wind farm.

"I see you'll turn sixteen next week," he said. "February 18. Your date of birth is on all of my documents. Any celebration plans?" He read my look again. "Right. Not this year." Mr. Nabli cleared his throat. "One more item."

I knew what was coming. My mouth turned sour. I stood up and pushed my chair against the table. Meeting over.

"I'm drafting the missing persons documentation," he persisted. "On March 9, it will be one year since The Big One, and under the law…"

"Mr. Nabli," I said, trying to keep my voice strong and steady. "I spent all morning at RescueCommons examining drone images of the tsunami/coastal inundation zone. I found dental braces with three teeth attached. I've had enough of missing persons for one day."

His voice softened. "I know this is hard, Meryem. Believe me, I'm on your side. Let's wait to discuss this until after your birthday."

"Fine."

Mr. Nabli capped his precious pen and reached for his courier bag. "I can still arrange for someone to guard the house so you can attend the bicentennial events today. Leave it to Oregon to become a state on Valentine's Day."

I picked up his bike helmet. "Too much work."

He didn't argue. "Don't forget to set your Sentry Mat sensors after I leave. Safety is paramount, you know."

Paramount. I remembered Jessa pronouncing and defining the word in her homeschooling mode. *Pa-ra-mount. Of chief concern. We were sitting cross-legged on the floor. I was fan-folding a page from one of Grandma's vintage word-a-day calendars. "Let's see, lovey," she said. "When you grow up and become a sky diver, the state of your para-chute will be paramount."*

27

"Meryem? My bike helmet?"

"Sorry. I was someplace else." I handed Mr. Nabli his helmet and waved him on his way. Then I sat on the hallway stairs and leaned against the prayer rug that had hung on the wall there since Jessa brought it back from Istanbul when I was a baby. I slid a finger across my left forearm where my PerSafe chip nested between flexor and extensor muscles. Jessa's chip was just like mine, our private link that had been silent for so long.

Now that Mr. Nabli was gone, I'd thumb her PerSafe code and wait. So what if I was the only one left who still believed Jessa was out there somewhere. It wouldn't hurt to keep trying.

Which was so not true. I shuddered. Waiting and trying and nothing-nothing-nothing over and over hurt like hell, but I'd keep doing it anyway. If I stopped, she'd never come back.

CHAPTER FOUR

Two minutes later, I heaved my body toward the dining room. Rose was right. It wasn't wise to dwell on Jessa's absence when I was home alone. I ate a slice of zucchini bread, put away the rest, and focused on what had to be done before dinner.

Item One: Distribute Mr. Nabli's Turkish delight.

I left three random pieces on the table for Ignatius, Priscilla, and Winslow, and put four pieces of hazelnut-pistachio delight—Rose likes nuts—on Rose's desk. I took the rest upstairs.

Unlocking the door to the room that was mine before The Big One, I inhaled Grandma's lilac scent. When The Ladies descended on us after The Big One, I put most of my things in the storage closet on the third floor and borrowed Jessa's room. If we still had a full house when Jessa got back, I could bunk in with her or Rose.

I put two pieces of Turkish delight on a trunk made from a mahogany species (*Swietenia humilis*) that's gone extinct. Grandma kept an heirloom prayer shawl and other memorabilia inside. Her unicorn collection shared a shelf with a silver-framed photo of her, Grandpa, Jessa, and toddler me, and with Jessa's certificate from the Eliseus Project, dated 2042, Istanbul. The family story is that Jessa went to Turkey about a year before I was born, signed a compact to resurrect species to restore our biosphere, and fell in love with Istanbul. No one mentions whether she fell in love with a guy there as well.

I crossed to the bedroom Auntie An took over from Rose. Sage incense mixed with the stale flowers-and-cigars smell of weed. Auntie An's numerology, astrology, and palmistry books circled her bed. Two pieces of delight went on her end table next to three tubes of her special toothpaste and a faded photo of a black American solider in Vietnam.

Jessa's bed-and-bath suite still smelled a little like Jessa—*redolent of the Jessa nest* she would have said—citrusy with a hint of cardamom. My pillow and quilt augmented the bed, and my essentials crowded her closet. A copper-etched baby picture stood next to a photo of *Ectopistes migratorius*, her first resurrected species—a.k.a. the passenger pigeon. The last piece of the Turkish delight—rosewater flavor, because Jessa adores rosewater—went into a super-seal bag in her top drawer next to her favorite licorice whips.

Item Two: Query the PerSafe.

Cultivate helpful habits, Jessa always says, and my once-weekly ping was one of them. Too much of a battery drain if I tried every day, and we always liked Fridays. Plus today was Valentine's Day, and Jessa never let a Valentine's Day go by without doing some gluesome twosome bit.

I unscrewed the cap on Jessa's lotion—Crème Botanique—and breathed in her honey-orange scent. Fortified, I switched on the PerSafe receiver and thumbed my personal safety identification code to make sure everything was still working. My left forearm pinged the same way Jessa's must have before I'd vid-voiced her in Manzanita. Five seconds later, the PerSafe beeped then flashed my coordinates and medical assessment. Meryem Zarfati, here and healthy.

I thumbed Jessa's code, queried PerSafe, and waited. These things can take a while. One time Jessa freaked out when the system alerted her to something wrong with me and then glitched. The PerSafe took thirteen seconds—a cyberternity—before it registered my no-big-deal sneezing fit at the playground a few blocks away.

This time the PerSafe waited five seconds before it flashed the same message I'd gotten since The Big One: **NOT RESPONDING. CHECK PSIC AND TRANSMISSION DEVICE.** No beep. No coordinates. No health scan information. Nothing.

I paced the room and reminded myself that a lot could happen in eleven months. She and Yusuf Halab—he must have been the guy with her that morning because he disappeared from the Eliseus Project after The Big One—had been on the beach when I vid-voiced her. But what got to me was this: Jessa and Yusuf weren't on the roster of the 3,496 deaths reported in the tsunami/coastal inundation zone or the 672 quake-related deaths reported farther inland. The Digital Humanitarian Network listed them as missing.

Yusuf Halab didn't have a chip. All other known PerSafe chips had continued to function after The Big One, reporting injuries and deaths, but not Jessa's. Jessa—or at least her PerSafe chip—could be anywhere by now. Tsunamis travel in both directions. Debris from Japan's 2011 megaquake had washed up on the Oregon coast for eight years afterward. Maybe someone in Japan would find out something about Jessa. Chips don't just disappear. They have to be somewhere.

I rebooted the PerSafe receiver and re-entered Jessa's code. **NOT RESPONDING. CHECK PSIC AND TRANSMISSION DEVICE.**

A vivid blue light flashed behind me, like an electric arc in a malfunctioning circuit. Or maybe it was my optic nerves playing tricks. Or maybe I was really beginning to lose it.

I closed my eyes and rubbed my forehead. That's when I heard a voice behind me. Soft. Female. "Peace be unto you, Miryam Aharona."

My Hebrew name. The one my mother gave me.

My mother.

"Jessa?" I whirled around, ready for a miracle.

CHAPTER FIVE

Our eyes met. I sagged against Jessa's desk, my lungs deflating, my body turning to sludge. The person across the room had the same deep bronze complexion as Jessa's—mine too for that matter—but the resemblance ended there. A long white braid, not our magenta-dyed black tangles. She was more my age than Jessa's.

She was so not my mother.

"Peace be unto you," the person repeated.

Only then did it sink in. I had forgotten to set the Sentry Mat alarm. This was an intruder. A stranger. How did she know my Hebrew name? She'd breached my space and my privacy. My feet tingled. My head buzzed.

I thumbed the MyCom on my index finger to emergency alert with a ninety-second delay. I straightened my spine, inhaling deeply and exhaling slowly until I felt the pull in my navel. I had to take charge. I had to stay calm.

"Peace be unto you," I echoed. Jessa says that repeating friendly greetings shows positive intentions in any culture. I'd traveled with Jessa to several fossil digs. This wasn't the first tense situation.

I smiled.

The stranger did too. Her leather sandals and the precycled robes that draped from her shoulders to her ankles clashed with my hiking boots, body-hugging FemForm, and over-tee. She looked like a hologram from ancient Greece.

I glanced at the MyCom. Seventy-nine seconds until the silent alarm would send help here. No need to panic. "Who are you? What do you want?"

She rubbed the back of her neck. "My name is Serakh, daughter of Asher." The girl took two steps toward me.

"Don't come any closer," I warned, my breath quickening.

She glanced around the room and then settled her gaze on me. Golden hazel eyes, like my grandfather Aron. And his same creased eyelids. She seemed unsure of something. Or maybe she was blissed out on who knows what.

"I seek your help," she said.

"Stand still," I said.

She did.

I reached for the ScrutinEyes visor that Jessa keeps for emergencies. The intruder watched me adjust the visor on my forehead, key in Jessa's authorization code, initiate the scanner, and focus on her face for the two long seconds the visor required.

Alarm minus sixty-five seconds. I tried to keep my voice steady. "What was that blue flash?"

"I cannot explain the flash." She shifted her gaze to the MyCom on my finger and the lobe lockets twinkling from my ears. No sign of threatening behavior. Still, I wished our stun stick was within reach, instead of downstairs.

The ScrutinEyes took forever to start downloading information. Finally the visor registered results from the criminal matrix. No perps matched this girl's features. A good start.

"How can I help you…um…Serakh?" The ScrutinEyes shifted modes, dots dancing across the inside of the visor.

Forty-one seconds left.

She smoothed her braid. "I believe now that a bronze coin

must be why I have been guided to you. The coin bears the face of a young woman. I bestowed this coin upon your kinswoman. I wanted her to see that the baby she saved lived to beget children and children's children. Now we must use the coin to redeem a young girl from captivity."

"Sorry," I said. "I have no idea what you are talking about."

Zero hits on the social matrix, which made sense. This girl probably guarded her privacy like most of us did now, instead of what people gave away in the hashtag era when Jessa was a kid.

Twenty-nine seconds.

"Miryam Aharona, are you not a kinswoman of Miryam Tikvah, daughter of Henrik? In her place and time, she calls herself Hope."

Hope Friis Einhorn was Jessa's grandmother. My Hebrew name was for her and my grandfather Aron. She gave this house to Jessa before I was born.

My privacy was royally breached. But maybe this wasn't a coincidence. I had just tried to ping Jessa's PerSafe chip. Maybe this encounter on Valentine's Day had something to do with Jessa after all, as unlikely as that might be.

Seventeen seconds. Nothing on the education-employment matrix. Zip hits on the national service matrix, which meant that Serakh was some alien creature—hardly possible—or under eighteen.

"It is a blessing to be her kinswoman," she said.

The ScrutinEyes flashed **SEARCH COMPLETE**. Either she could afford to keep wiping her infoslate clean or she came from some nowhere speck and was such a nobody that she was off the infoslate entirely.

I countered Serakh's questions with ones of my own. "Did you come to Portland for today's celebration? Is this your costume for the parade?" That would explain why she was dumb enough to wear sandals in a postquake zone.

Her forehead creased.

"The bicentennial parade. Oregon statehood in 1859. Sound familiar?"

"I come from the East," she said, which explained a lot. People on the East Coast live in another world.

Eight seconds. Time to decide.

Jessa tells me to go with my gut. Curiosity beat out caution. I thumbed CANCEL.

"Miryam Aharona is my Hebrew name. I am Meryem Einhorn Zarfati, daughter of Jessa," I said, using the girl's style of speech. "Jessa is the daughter of Ly Tien and Aron."

Serakh put her palms together and bowed slightly. "You are a Miryam in the line of the blue thread," she said, which made no sense.

I took off the visor and stepped closer.

The girl exuded a faint aroma of goats. More questions crowded in. I figured the best way to get answers was the same way that Jessa taught me to gain the trust of any higher order creature. Use food.

"I've got hard-cooked eggs and fresh greens," I said. "Do you like radishes?"

She smiled. "I have a weakness for cucumbers."

"Me too," I said, which was true. I gestured toward the hall. "Downstairs and to the right. You first." It would be safer to stay behind her.

A minute later, Serakh stood at the entrance to our living room. She stared at my nutriculture wall, her mouth open, the perfect example of "transfixed." I remembered Jessa explaining that transfixed came from words meaning through and fastened. *Back in the Middle Ages, transfixed meant impaled, lovey. Jessa pretended to stab her chest. I giggled.*

"This is how we get fresh veggies in the winter," I said, walking to the nutriculture wall. Conversation might tease out what she knew about my family. "Three and a half meters by two meters. Fully irrigated." I picked two Persian cucumbers, handed her one, and took a bite of mine.

Serakh smiled as she chewed, then wiped her chin with the back of her hand. "This is the best cucumber I have partaken of since Egypt," she said.

Egypt? "Have another." I picked one and handed it to her. I pointed to the old wicker chair by the window. "Would you like a seat? Tell me more about yourself. How do you know about my family?"

Serakh dried her hands on her robes and eased into the chair. "I have a connection to you through the Miryams of the half tribe of Manasseh, son of Joseph."

It took me a moment, but then I caught her meaning. "The Josefsohns, right? They lived in this house about a hundred and fifty years ago. Miriam Josefsohn was my grandmother's great-grandmother, or something like that."

"I have been welcomed here before," she said.

"When?"

"You were not yet born."

Weird. "You must be a lot older than you look," I said.

No answer.

I studied her face. Maybe she'd had one of those rejuvenation treatments that cost a sextillion credits. Or maybe she was some sort of odd participant in Jessa's paleogenetics experiments with the Eliseus Project. My palms started to sweat.

"Do you know Jessa?"

Serakh's eyes shone. "She begat you and bestowed upon you the name Miryam. I know of Jessa."

"What!" I was at her side in a nanosecond, my heart beating triple time. "You waited until *now* to tell me? I've been pinging Jessa for months! Where's my mother? Is she okay?"

Serakh winced. "A thousand pardons," she said.

I backed off and gave this stupid person a chance to spit out what she should have told me the instant we met. "I don't care about pardons," I told her. "I want answers. Do you work in Jessa's lab? Did she send you a message?"

Serakh rubbed the back of her neck again.

"Please, tell me everything. I can handle it." I could barely breathe.

"Again, I seek your pardon," she said. "I do not know where your mother dwells at this very moment. I know only of the bronze coin, and I know of the garment of fringes bestowed upon the Miryams of your family. The garment has a long blue thread and the words *tzedek, tzedek tirdof.* They mean 'justice, justice you shall pursue.' You look of the age to have received this garment from Jessa."

My lungs shriveled. "You're talking about my grandmother's special *tallit*," I managed to mutter, using the Hebrew word for prayer shawl to show her I knew Hebrew too. "The one my grandmother got from my great-grandmother—from Miryam Tikvah. Hope. It belongs to my grandmother, not to Jessa or me."

Serakh frowned. "Let your grandmother bestow the *tallit* upon you. Let Jessa bestow the coin. Tell them there is nothing to fear."

The fullness behind my eyes warned I was close to losing it in front of a stranger. No way could I tell Serakh that I hadn't seen Jessa in an eternity.

"Fine." I focused on a crack in the floorboards.

"I have a great thirst from my journey," she said.

I blinked back tears. "I'll get us some filtered water."

"You are most kind."

As I waited in the kitchen for the water filter to do its thing, I decided to tell Serakh that she was welcome to stay until Grandma and Auntie An came home from the bicentennial celebration. Maybe they knew who she was. Plus Serakh said that she didn't know where Jessa was *at this very moment.* What about earlier?

When the pitcher was half full, I collected two glasses and strode to the living room. But by then Serakh was gone.

CHAPTER SIX

I grabbed my hoodie and work gloves, rearmed the Sentry Mat, and raced out the door. No sign of Serakh. Idiot! I never should have left her alone. What if she knew what happened to Jessa and was afraid to say?

I crossed the makeshift bridge over the debris trench dividing our front yard from what was left of 19th Avenue, and I headed to the apartment building on the corner—the closest place to hide. A cloudless sky that held no chance of the rain we needed at least offered better visibility. With her costume and hair, Serakh would be easy to spot.

The apartment shutters were locked shut, the Sentry Mat still alarmed. No way could Serakh have gotten inside. Neither could she have climbed the rubble blocking the rest of the street in such a short time.

Backtracking, I picked my way to what was left of the apartments on the other side of our house. A compliance officer with a stun stick and FEMA armband pointed to the DO NOT HABITATE tape circling the place. He slipped his filtration mask to his chin. "You can't come in here," he said.

I didn't bother to tell him that I'd seen plenty of scavengers in the building. "Did a girl go by a couple minutes ago? White hair, dark skin like mine. She's wearing a long robe and sandals."

He eyed me up and down. I let him. You have to pick your battles.

"Nah." He hitched up his belt. "Don't you live around here?"

I nudged a gnarl of wires with my hiking boots. "Stay safe," I said, spouting the Council's mantra. I headed to what was left of First Immanuel. The church's soup kitchen and meeting rooms were a decent place to hide.

The churchyard overflowed with tents, sleeping bags, and people. Placards leaning against the building read REMEMBER CALANTHA and DECENT HOUSING FOR ALL. I wove my way toward a woman distributing sandwiches near the side entrance.

That's when I heard Rose calling me.

"You're supposed to be meeting with Mr. Nabli," she said after she reached me. "What are you doing here of all places?"

"We finished early. I'm looking for someone." I described Serakh. "Did Jessa ever mention her?"

Rose shook her head. She adjusted the knitted cowl she wears outside nine months a year. Neither of us bothers with a filtration mask anymore. "Jessa did meet some odd ducks," she said. "Would you like me to help you look?"

I surveyed the crowd. "Forget it. She could be anywhere by now."

Rose touched my shoulder. "You must have really wanted to find this girl if you came so close to the soup kitchen."

My mind spiraled back to The Big One and Chewsette. My stomach lurched. I unzipped my hoodie and sucked in a breath.

"You okay, Meryem?"

When am I ever okay? "I thought you took The Ladies to the bicentennial celebration," I said. "How'd it go?"

"The usual speeches. A high school band played 'Oregon, My Oregon.' The compliance officers, police, and National Guard outnumbered the rest of us." She nodded toward the placards. "These protestors were there, but people seemed more interested in the Paul Bunyan cupcakes."

"The what?"

"You know that huge statue of Paul Bunyan from the 1959 centennial, the one in North Portland that toppled during The Big One? Well, someone made a mosaic of the statue out of five hundred cupcakes. It covered a quarter of Pioneer Square. I got The Ladies vanilla-frosted ones from his checkered shirt."

"Any complaints from them?"

"No more than the usual. They're sitting with a guy one of their good friends contacted for them. They have a live birthday surprise for you. He's scrawny, but he'll do."

"The guy?"

Rose brayed with laughter. "No, silly goose. Come. I'll show you."

The buck was the scraggiest goat I'd ever seen. More gray than cream, with splotches of moonspots across his back and watery blue eyes. The guy holding him was more colorful—reddish brown beard, wavy rhubarb-red hair, and blue-gray eyes—but just as skinny. Neither of them looked good for much of anything.

"The buck will service Munchkina," Rose explained to me after The Ladies hugged their hello. "When she kids this summer and freshens, we'll keep the doelings and have milk and cheese again. Great for us. Great for Munchkina." She leaned in and whispered, "We have to put up with the boy and the buck for a couple of days at most."

Goat Guy thrust his right hand at me. "Bandon Falconer," he said. His beard had captured specks of unknown origin. He smelled only a notch better than his goat, and his goat just plain stank.

I took off my gloves and shook hands anyway. "Hi, Brandon. Meryem Zarfati."

He tightened his grip. "It's Bandon, not Brandon, but I'm not named for Bandon, Oregon. You guys ask me that all the time. My folks named me after a Byzantine military unit, which fits now that I'm with Calantha Corps, although we're only out to conquer homelessness. Ever consider joining the Corps, Miriam?"

I eased my hand away from the source of information over-load. I knew very little about Calantha Corps. Before The Big One, Rose and I volunteered at the Oregon Food Bank, but that wasn't Bandon-not-Brandon's business.

"It's Meryem," I said, matching his correction with my own and stressing the two-syllable pronunciation. "M-E-R-Y-E-M. Turkish for Miriam. What's your goat's name?"

"Ah…Goat. He's not even mine. I borrowed him and brought him along as a favor to one of our donors. Frankly, I don't like goats."

No wonder the buck looked forlorn. Before I could set Bandon straight about kindness to domesticated animals, Grandma tugged on my hoodie.

"Be nice, Merry," she said through her filtration mask. Merry. Which is so not me now. "Bandon lives out near Gales Creek. He must have come thirty miles to bring you this goat."

Fifty-ish kilometers, translating from the old measurements. I figured Bandon would have trekked to the bicentennial anyway, judging from the signs in the churchyard. I wondered if The Ladies paid him for the goat's stud service.

Bandon collected his sleeping bag and backpack, leaving me to manage Goat. We started for home while Rose hung back to escort The Ladies at a slower pace.

"Slave shackles," he said, when he caught me looking at the black handcuffs hanging from his left wrist. "I wore them for the demon-stration. Human trafficking in the US is a multi-billion-dollar in-dustry. Victims wind up on the street, or get taken from the street. There'd be a 30 percent reduction in human trafficking if we pro-vided decent shelter for the homeless community. You'd think the progressive state of Oregon could have done that before The Big One, but no. No money then, or so they said. When this state of emergency is over, they'll claim there's no money again. Calantha Corps is going to change that."

I kept my lips zipped—no need to encourage him—and turned back to help Rose. The Ladies were a head shorter than Rose, half her size, and ten times less steady. Goat Guy followed.

Auntie An lowered her filtration mask. "Do you like bok choy, young man?"

"It's one of my favorite cabbages," he said, all proper and polite.

"Excellent! Rose, make the bok choy tonight. I told you to buy some, remember?"

"Of course," Rose said. "Now please keep your mask on until we get home. There are still toxic particulates in the air." She suddenly looked exhausted, her skin taking on an ashen hue.

"You could camp with your friends at First Immanuel," I told Bandon, hoping he'd get the hint. "We'll take care of Goat and bring him back tomorrow."

Bandon smiled. "No need. Rose says you house a formerly homeless guy under the Council's credit-tenant program. I'll stay with him."

"The homeless guy has a name," I snapped. "Mr. Rivera. He's entitled to his own room."

Bandon saluted. "You are absolutely right. I'll sleep on your couch." He looked at the goat and then back at me. "Does Tillamook work for you?"

"Pardon?"

"Tillamook. Our Oregon headquarters is out by Tillamook State Forest due to unfortunate circumstances involving your mayor. We've been there since September—the great unwatched, beyond the urban growth boundary, outside the box of the overregulated and the underserved. I'll call the goat Tillamook, okay?"

I shrugged. Mayor Hammilason, the Council, and FEMA had gotten us through the worst after The Big One, even if I wished they'd lighten up now.

"I take that as a yes," he said.

Even though Bandon was staying only one night, Rose and The Ladies treated him like a new boarder. Rose lent him a pair of slip-ons, the kind she and The Ladies wore around the house. She told him to leave his shoes at the door so he wouldn't track dirt inside.

Bandon's shoes looked like they'd been through their own footwear subduction zone, the leather frayed and the heels listing toward each other. "Doc Martens last forever," he told me. "These were my dad's." Then his face closed down, a look I took to mean, "Don't ask," so I didn't. He stared at the hiking boots still on my feet.

"Meryem and Ignatius are the exceptions," Rose said, thankfully without explanation.

I wasn't in the mood to explain either. I looked up at the DuroPlastic that still covered the place on the stair landing where our huge decorative window had shattered during The Big One. My feet tingled.

Twenty minutes later, I rubbed an old sock along Tillamook's neck and presented the sock to Munchkina. She wagged her tail unenthusiastically.

Rose patted Munchkina's back. "She's been erratic coming into heat with Chewsette gone. Maybe tomorrow. Maybe the next day."

The last thing I wanted was a slogan-spouting goat guy eating our food, using our precious water, and adding to the tension. "He looks puny and kind of stupid," I said, mostly meaning Tillamook. "Suppose she rejects him?"

Rose started to lead Tillamook to his glass-free makeshift shelter in the basement. "She won't. He's male."

"Got it," I said, feeling my face relax into the first real smile this Valentine's Day. At least Bandon wasn't as strange as Serakh, with her talk about my family, a bronze coin, and Grandma's prayer shawl. Maybe The Ladies knew about her. Maybe she had something to do with Jessa after all.

CHAPTER SEVEN

By the time Bandon joined us for dinner, the slave shackles had disappeared from his wrist, and he'd washed off most of the goat stench. I cringed at how much of our water quota he wasted. Priscilla was feeding Winslow upstairs, and Ignatius was out, so it was the five of us around the large dining room table.

Rose had on the same hemp jumpsuit she always wore on Fridays. I hadn't changed clothes either. Why deal with more laundry? The Ladies, however, had dressed for company—Grandma in a navy linen turn-of-the-century pantsuit and Auntie An in a flowing red-and-orange silk caftan. They sat on either side of Bandon and showed him Rose's challah.

"It's Shabbat," Auntie An said. She put on a cutesy face and batted mascara-ed lashes on epicanthic eyelids a shade darker than mine. "Don't I look Jewish?"

Bandon looked confused. Auntie An beamed at finding another surprised victim. Why people still think all Jews are as white as Rose, I'll never know.

"Our biological mother was Vietnamese," she explained,

launching into Einhorn-Zarfati geneology. "Our father was a black American soldier in Vietnam. It's a sad story."

Bandon nodded, but Auntie An wasn't done, not by a long shot.

"After the war, we were adopted by Hope and Kenneth Einhorn, a Jewish couple from California," she said. "My sister here married a Turkish-American Jew, Aron Zarfati. Merry's grandfather. He died several years ago, which is when I moved in with her. I've lived in this house most of my life, even after Meryem's mother moved in here and Meryem was born."

"Are you Jewish too?" Bandon asked Rose.

"My parents were Russian Orthodox," she said. "I am nothing."

Which isn't exactly true. Jessa says that Rose believes in the god of work.

"Who knows where Merry's father came from, but it doesn't matter," Auntie An continued. "She looks so much like her mother. She's a beautiful blend, don't you think? Especially the magenta hair."

My cheeks burned. Most of the kids I knew were blend. Plus my hair color was my own business.

"Let's light the Shabbat candles," Grandma said. "Merry, show Bandon our special method."

"Seismitis. Unusual behavior following an earthquake," I explained, air-quoting the definition. "There were a lot of fires after The Big One."

Instead of lighting our two candles with a match and letting their wicks burn, I thumbed an image of two lit candles in brass candlesticks on the MyCom and then connected the MyCom to the display glass on the table. We sang the candle-lighting blessing—all of us except Bandon.

My grandmother passed around plumped-up raisins in a porcelain teacup. With edible plates still in short supply, we used the old family china. Auntie An sang the blessing over wine. "The fruit of the vine," she told Bandon.

"No wine," Rose said. "Ignatius shouldn't be around alcohol."

I slipped off the lace cloth covering the challah. We recited the blessing, tore off chunks, and started on dinner: Rose's rice and pinto beans with braised bok choy and ground hazelnuts.

Bandon said little and ate a lot, obviously enjoying Rose's cooking as much as I did. The Ladies ate the bok choy and rice and left most of the rest.

Grandma told Bandon to call her Ly Tien as if she expected he'd be more than an overnight goat escort.

"You may call me Auntie An," my great-aunt said, careful to pronounce her name "on-tee-on" the way she liked it.

"Munchkina should be in heat tomorrow," I said, collecting the dinner plates. "Then Bandon and Tillamook will be on their way." The Ladies would be on their way soon too, once their condo unit was certified for habitation. At least I hoped so.

Bandon nodded. "I don't want the Resilience Council to know I'm in Portland. They wouldn't be as welcoming as you are." I hadn't noticed I was. He asked me if I spoke Vietnamese, and I told him no. I didn't bother to explain that I'd wanted to learn it for my educational competency requirements, but Grandma insisted that in America you have to learn Spanish. Auntie An nagged at me to study Chinese. I took Spanish.

Most nights Rose and The Ladies and I played Trivial Pursuit off-line, meaning we used Grandma's seventy-fifth anniversary edition of the actual board game. Ignatius never joined us, and neither did Priscilla. It was a way to pass the time, a click more enjoyable than folding laundry.

With Bandon around, we didn't bother with a game. Rose gave him a tour of the nutriculture wall, which got him out from underfoot while I cleaned up in the kitchen. The Ladies stayed in the kitchen with me, sipping their tea there because Auntie An thought the nutriculture wall had ruined "her" living room.

"After Mr. Nabli left, I had a visitor," I told them, in case they knew her. "I think her name is Sarah something." Serakh sounded weird. Maybe I'd heard it wrong. "She might be a distant relative, but she left before I could find out." I didn't tell The Ladies about how she appeared out of nowhere. They'd have freaked out about my not arming the Sentry Mat.

My grandmother wiped her lips. "There's a cousin Sarah on

your grandfather's side, may he rest in peace. Was it one of Lina's children?"

"I don't think so, Grandma." I wiped down the counter. "She talked about Jessa giving me your prayer shawl and a bronze coin."

Something shattered. I turned to see Auntie An's teacup in pieces on the kitchen floor. Auntie An was staring at the shards of ceramic and muttering something in Vietnamese.

My stomach cramped. "What's wrong?"

The Ladies volleyed in Vietnamese, gesturing in full argumentation mode.

I folded my arms across my chest. "If this is about me, I deserve to know."

They ignored me. I grabbed Grandma's hands and locked eyes with her. "Tell me. Please."

"I am so sorry," Grandma whispered. "My sister insists this is the right time. Maybe so." She took a breath. "Your visitor's name is Serakh."

I crouched in front of her, still holding her hands. "Serakh, right. Who is she? Why did she come?"

Grandma leaned closer, her breath smelling of dinner and ginger. "Merry, my sweet blossom, Mama Two—you know Mama Two, our American mother? From the Josefsohn side of the family?"

"Miriam Hope Einhorn. Of course, I do." I freed Grandma's hands. She touched my face, her fingertips cold against my cheek.

"A few months before she died, Mama Two gave us the prayer shawl and told us about Serakh. I always doubted Mama Two's story. I rely on facts and history, not magic. And we were adopted, so I thought that maybe the natural line of Miriams was over. But An Chau always believed."

Auntie An extracted one of her ancient cotton handkerchiefs from her caftan pocket and started to cry, tears streaking the rouge on her cheeks.

"Believed in what, Grandma?"

"I decided to tell you and Jessa when you were fifteen," she said.

47

"But after your birthday, weeks went by. Then came The Big One. Too late."

"It's not too late," I said, totally confused.

Grandma's lips quivered. "An Chau warned me many times this year, but I refused to listen. We should have prepared you. I am so sorry."

"Sorry for what?"

Auntie An moaned. Grandma kissed my cheek. "Someone out there needs you, sweet blossom. Serakh has come to take you away."

CHAPTER EIGHT

Rose's laughter floated in from the living room. Grandma and Auntie An stared at me, waiting for my response. Bewildered, I parked in a chair and faced them. "Serakh didn't say anything about a trip, and on top of that she ran away."

Auntie An shook her head. "Serakh did not run away. She vanished. Vanished is different."

"Nobody vanishes," I said. Except Jessa.

Auntie An stabbed the air. "You are just like your mother. You think I am a crazy lady with crazy red-dyed hair and crazy red lipstick, but I am eighty-eight now, a powerful number. You should listen to me."

I practically snorted in frustration. "I'm listening. I'm listening. Tell me about Serakh."

Grandma ran her fingers through tufts of gray hair. "My sister says that your birthday is auspicious this year. We'll give you the prayer shawl then, but we don't know where the bronze coin is." She slapped the table. "Now we have a guest. After the boy leaves tomorrow, we will talk to you and Rose."

That was it. You can push my grandmother only so far. Jessa got her snuggly side from my grandfather. She got her backbone from Grandma.

The Ladies retreated to the living room. I flung saucer shards into the recycler. When I'd calmed down enough, I joined the others, sat in the wicker chair that Serakh had used that afternoon, and pretended to be interested in a conversation about political pressure and social safety nets.

"The Resilience Council has made good progress in the past few months," Rose was saying. "Particularly in manufacturing, banking, and commercial sectors. I wish they would do more for the rest of us, but that will come."

"I doubt it," Bandon argued. "Income disparity and the economic divide are worse now than when Martin Luther King Jr. was alive a hundred years ago. If the government can feed, house, and care for the poor and homeless after The Big One, then the government should be able to continue once this state of emergency is over."

Rose studied her fingernails. "It's not that simple."

"No, it's not simple," he said. "But it's about time!"

I stared at the nutriculture wall and wondered what to believe from The Ladies, one with a passion for unicorns and the other trusting in palmistry, astrology, and numbers. Impatience ate at me. As soon as there was a break in the conversation, I asked, "Do you think tomorrow is an auspicious day for Munchkina to mate?" I tried to sound casual.

"I have no idea," Bandon said, stating the obvious.

Rose rubbed a callus on her thumb. "She's likely to be in full heat, auspicious day or not."

Grandma gave me her you-know-that's-nonsense look, but Auntie An grabbed my hand. "Let's check."

Perfect! As soon as we sat at the dining room table, she extracted a small, well-thumbed book from her pocket. "When was Munchkina born?"

"May 22, 2055," I said. "She and Chewsette were twins."

Auntie An licked her index finger and turned the pages.

"Tomorrow is 20590215," she said, putting the year first. "Munchkina's natal date is 20550522. What is the period between fertility?"

"About every twenty to twenty-two days for Munchkina."

"Ah, here we are." Auntie An squinted at signs and numbers that made no sense to me. A minute later, she said, "It will be a doubly auspicious day. She will get pregnant."

Auntie An took a deep breath and exhaled. "You realize it was your grandmother who arranged this business with your goat. When I lived here, we had a lovely flower garden in the backyard, not a farm. You don't need a farm in the middle of a city."

"Yes, you've told me that," I said, straining to be polite. "Several times."

She patted her hair. "I like Bandon, don't you? He is serious about the world, but with a playful spirit. You should get to know him."

I had zip interest in Goat Guy, but nodded anyway. "By the way, is my birthday an auspicious date to find that bronze coin? Do you know anything about it?"

She beamed. "Mama Two—you know, that's my American mother?"

I beamed back. One painful lesson I'd learned since The Ladies had moved in with us is that they ramble. If you try to focus them, they only get annoyed and start over. Counterproductive. "Yes," I said. "And Mama One was your birth mother in Vietnam."

"Now they are together in the world beyond, a world that presents itself in signs and symbols to the wise and the watchful."

I smiled encouragingly.

"Mama Two had two special coins, Merry. I wanted the bronze one with the picture of the girl on it. The other was silver with a man's face. When Ly Tien and I each celebrated becoming a *bat mitzvah*, Mama Two divided the pearl necklace that belonged to her mother and grandmother. She restrung the pearls with jade beads in between so there was enough for two necklaces, one for my sister, one for me. I wore a traditional Vietnamese outfit for my *bat mitzvah*—so pretty. Your grandmother wore an American dress. She has never respected our heritage as much as she should."

I bit the inside of my bottom lip.

Auntie An sighed. "Be that as it may, Mama Two kept both coins. She put them in a beautiful wooden box and gave them to Jessa when Jessa graduated from the university. She gave many things to Jessa, even those she shouldn't have."

My patience snapped. I wasn't about to listen yet again to Auntie An complaining about how Jessa inherited the house. "Where are the coins now?"

Auntie An pocketed her book. "Maybe your mother sold them. She was never sentimental, except when it came to Ly Tien's unicorns."

There was no way that Jessa would sell those coins. They had to be in the house somewhere. The Ladies had to be exaggerating about Serakh taking me away, but the coins were real. If Serakh came back, maybe I could use the bronze coin to bargain with her for information about Jessa.

"Thanks, Auntie An," I managed. "I'll look for the coins after Bandon leaves."

"He is too skinny, but we can fatten him up," she said, as we headed back to the living room. "Find out his natal date."

I had no intention of fattening up Bandon or asking about his birthday. And I wasn't in the mood to waste time listening to him fulminate against a world I was powerless to change.

"Good night, all," I said, interrupting the conversation. "I'll check on Munchkina and the chickens before I go upstairs."

Bandon shifted modes in a nanosecond. "Wait up, Meryem. I'll help you."

"No thanks. I don't need help," I said.

He grabbed his shoes. "I'll come anyway and stay out of your hair." He followed me to the back door. "Especially the magenta parts."

I rolled my eyes.

Bandon raised his arms in mock surrender. "I was only being friendly. My goat and your goat do their thing, and I am out of here. Rose found a place for me by the back stairs because the homeless guy—Mr. Rivera—he isn't around to ask about my staying with him. You're right about not presuming on his hospitality."

I punched the disarm code. "Fine," I said.

We walked to Chicken Hacienda in silence, but he started up again while I scattered feed. "What are their names? They have names, right? Tell me about your chickens."

"This one's Tillie, and next to her is Louise," I said, succumbing to an unusual attack of motor-mouth. "They're Buff Orpingtons, very easy to manage. Yetta over there is a Black Star. She's my favorite—bossy, but not as aggressive as a true Rhode Island Red."

Bandon eyed the enclosure. "Quite a setup."

I wiped down the feed bucket. "Chickens should live in a shelter that's clean and warm with good ventilation and a decent amount of space."

"Lucky chickens. We all should."

I shook my head, not wanting to hear another lecture. Instead he said, "Rose told me you used to have another goat. What happened to that one?"

"Chewsette died. I don't want to talk about her."

"Got it."

Fifteen minutes later, I was back in Jessa's room, more than ready to check off another day. I took a sponge bath and daubed Rose's calendula and lavender oil on my feet. Even with the prosthetic toe in place and most of the glass removed, I still wore silicone pads when I wasn't wearing thick socks. I needed a cushion against any sudden stab of pain.

I set SomniSoothe to my favorite sleep-inducing smell-sound combination—tulips and gentle rain—and burrowed under the quilts. Still, I couldn't stop thinking about Chewsette. *Rose was cradling me on her lap the day after the medics came. "There's a soup kitchen at First Immanuel," she said. "We owe it to Chewsette to end her misery. Her wound isn't infected yet, and she has lived a healthy life. There are people in the city now who are desperate for food. Can you be that brave?" It didn't matter whether I was brave or not. Rose had*

already made up her mind. I cursed her when she took Chewsette away.
Cursed her, and cursed her again and again.

I staggered out of bed, opened the window, and let the night air comfort me. "I am so sorry, Rose," I whispered. "I didn't mean what I said." Then, remembering Serakh's odd expression, I added, "a thousand pardons."

CHAPTER NINE

Bucks in rut top the stink scale, light-years ahead of dead skunk. When Rose and I offered Munchkina another whiff of the Tillamook rag early the next morning, she was ready.

Apparently Bandon had never seen the tongue-blubbering, urine-licking antics of bucks wanting sex. "I have nothing to do with our goats," he said, blushing.

"Obviously." I steadied Munchkina.

Tillamook was larger than Munchkina and mounted her easily. After the first time, he walked around her and repeated the process twice, until Rose decided he was done.

"Munchkina should be in heat through most of today," she told us. "Let's try again after lunch. Two bites of the apple are better than one."

"So that's what you call it," Bandon said. I rolled my eyes.

At breakfast, he ate four biscuits and three helpings of granola, as if filling Auntie An's prescription to fatten up. After Rose left to escort The Ladies to Saturday morning services, he cleared the table, his retro denim jeans riding low on his hips. Why was I even looking?

"We have a few hours until Tillamook and Munchkina do their thing again," he said. "I see a pair of Skliders by the back door. Show me how you get the Sklide board to split in two when you want to move your feet separately. I never got the hang of it."

I wiped the counter. "I haven't Sklided since The Big One."

"You might as well start now. Let's have fun."

"Fun?" I pointed to our to-do list by the refrigerator. "Rose and I run a credit-tenant residence and deal with The Ladies, who are twice as demanding as our three tenants combined. We have Munchkina and the chickens, the two pear trees, a nutriculture wall, and a vegetable garden. Plus I analyze drone images of quake damage for RescueCommons twice a week and take EduComps courses for homeschooling credits."

Bandon reached for the last of the biscuits. "Okay, forget fun, Madam Taskmaster. Or should I say Taskmistress? I am at your service."

His breezy manner bordered on sarcasm, but I'll take help when I can get it. "Our housebot needs a new visual tracker to be operational again, and we don't use the Sweeper Swarms around food." I handed him our old broom. "You can start by sweeping the kitchen floor."

Brandon grasped the wooden handle. "Consider it done. Any other chores?"

I pointed to the list. "Take your pick. Plus right before lunch I have to escort The Ladies back from services at Havurah Shalom."

He smiled at me for no reason at all. "The Ladies must be pretty religious."

"Sort of," I said, without stopping to think. "They insist on reciting the mourner's *kaddish* for Jessa every Saturday."

"The what?"

"*Kaddish*. It's a prayer you say for the dead."

"And you'd rather say a prayer for the missing?"

Anger flared. "Don't you zucker me, Bandon Falconer. It's none of your business."

Bandon propped the broom against the kitchen table and put

his hands on my shoulders, which was altogether too much touching for a guy I'd known less than twenty-four hours. Still, I didn't move away.

"Hey, private is private. I'm not zuckering you. But it's not all Zuckerberg's fault that his Facebook and Twitter and all the old social media stuff came back to bite us. People need to share things, especially when they're hurting. Rose told me about your mother. I'm truly sorry. Friends?"

In an unguarded moment, I sputtered, "Did she say that Jessa's dead and I'm the only one who…?" I stared at the floor.

"Maybe all of them are wrong."

"I have to deal with the laundry," I said. And I left.

Half an hour later, I was stripping the bed in Jessa's room and trying not to think about *kaddish*, when I heard knocking on the open door. Ignatius stood ramrod straight, in sad contrast to his sagging face and gray stubble. "Permission to enter, Miss Meryem?"

"Permission granted," I said, because Ignatius was steadier when we talked to him like we were still fighting the Caliphists before the Damascus Accord.

"I am ready to go on half-rations," he announced.

"There's enough food to go around," I said. "Do we have a situation?"

"Yes, Miss Meryem. Rose says we won't be certain about Munchkina's pregnancy for three more weeks. Rose wants Tillamook to stay until then."

I saw where this was heading. "So Bandon is angling to stay, and eat into our food credits, and mess with our water quota, and share your room? That's unfair."

Ignatius cleared his throat. "That's not how we see it."

We? "Go on," I said.

"Bandon is with Calantha Corps, and the Corps is on our side. That's what I hear on the street, Miss Meryem. They are fighting so the poor and homeless are treated decently after FEMA finishes its tour of earthquake duty. I would be honored to share rations with Bandon and have him bunk in with me. Rose will assign him duties."

I rubbed my forehead. It wouldn't be so bad as long as Goat Guy stayed out of my way. "Tell Rose I agree for Munchkina's sake, and I'm sure we can manage to feed you and Bandon."

After Ignatius left, I sat on the half-stripped bed and switched the MyCom to query mode. Aussie Jack—my favorite vocal feed— enlightened me about Calantha Corps in his Australian baritone as I finished with the bed. He said the Corps was a national activist movement founded in 2052 and explained their mission to ensure affordable and sustainable housing for everyone nationwide by 2076.

While I stuffed sheets into our old washer-dryer and set the filter to recycle Load One's water for Load Two, Aussie Jack cited popularity statistics. "According to the MyOpinion poll on January 15, 2059, 65.7 percent of all registered voters under age thirty and living west of Chicago favor Corps policies," he said. "And 47.3 percent liken Corps actions to those of the Occupy Movement. Slightly more than 14.8 percent of voters…"

The MyCom dinged. 12:15. Time to escort The Ladies home after services. I cut off Aussie Jack now that I was 94.1 percent sure that Bandon could tell me anything else I wanted to know. And more.

Rain, sweet rain, was falling, the first in six days. I hoped the air over the Cascades was cold enough to lay down the snowpack we'd desperately need by August. The debris trench exuded a burning-circuits smell rather than its usual rot. I didn't check why—I had my fill of examining debris for RescueCommons—but I did stay an extra meter away.

Setting the MyCom to whisper in my ear, I queried about Serakh. Aussie Jack had a raft of references to Serakh, daughter of Asher, including passages in the Torah (Genesis 46:17 and Numbers 26:46) and one from another biblical text—First Chronicles, chapter 7, verse 30. One folktale claimed she traveled with Elijah the Prophet. Aussie Jack didn't come up with significant links between Serakh and prayer shawls or bronze coins. Clearly, I had queried some biblical character and not the person who spoke in riddles, ate my cucumbers, and ran away.

I walked down 19th to the neighborhood's majestic western red cedar and resisted the urge to pull off bark strips the way I did when I was little. Faded ribbons and plastic flowers embellished its multiple trunks and branches. Jessa once told me that this species wasn't a true cedar, but an *arborvitae*, a tree of life. I inhaled the tree's welcoming scent and blinked back tears. No way would I set foot in the synagogue down the block with all those mourners inside. Pity Palace. The tree and I were survivors. Jessa was too— which is why I couldn't recite *kaddish* with The Ladies. You never knew who, after all these Saturdays, was still alive.

CHAPTER TEN

"You've been crying," Grandma said.

I wiped my cheek. "It's the rain. What would you two like for lunch? There's egg salad, but we also have sardines in tomato sauce."

My grandmother slipped her hand into the crook of my right elbow. "Egg salad. Rose knows I prefer sardines in olive oil."

Auntie An claimed my left elbow. "Sardines taste better in tomato sauce. Rose's egg salad has too much mayonnaise."

I changed the subject. "How were services?"

"Rabbi Judith invited you to the youth group meeting on Thursday," came Auntie An's nudge on my left. "You haven't gone in months. I told her you'd call."

"We're not saying *kaddish* next Saturday," I heard from Grandma on my right, "since Jewish tradition calls for saying *kaddish* for the first eleven months afterward and then just once a year on the anniversary of the person's passing. You should come to services next week. Everyone misses you."

From the left: "It's such a spiritual uplift, don't you think?"

And the right: "The congregation is planning a memorial

Shabbat service the day before Resilience Day. Of course, you'll come then. It would be an insult not to."

The Ladies walked more slowly than usual, with me as their captive audience. In the twenty minutes it took to go three blocks, I got an earful that added up to: Get on with life. Admit your mother is dead.

Saturdays suck.

Goat Guy, who would now spend weeks underfoot, was lounging on the couch eating a cucumber. I showed him our Council-approved list of credit-tenant rights and responsibilities.

"No smoking, vaping, alcoholic beverages, opioids, or incense," I said. "No loud noise before 7 a.m. and after 10 p.m. No unnecessary drain on power or water supplies. By law, we are required to provide a lock for each bedroom door. You and Ignatius will have to work that out."

He sat up and studied the list. "Daily access to two thousand calories of nutritious food, including fifty grams of protein. At least three liters of filtered water. Twenty-five liters of unfiltered hot water. Unlimited harmonica playing."

"What?"

He touched the harmonica sticking out of his back pocket and gave me an angelic smirk. "Lighten up, M-E-R-Y-E-M," he said. "What's for lunch?"

After the quickest lunch I could manage, I buried myself in gardening. February was the new March due to global warming, and I was determined to weed and work the soil and get in a row of beets.

Three mind-numbing hours later, I washed up and helped Rose with dinner. "Why'd you change your mind about Bandon?" I said, slicing carrots for vegetable and barley stew. "The house is overcrowded already. If Munchkina isn't pregnant, we can find another buck next month."

Rose wiped her hands on her apron. "He seems reliable. It's a chance to get extra work done. We can't afford to pay anyone to fix the basement shelves and clear the rest of the rubble. I've already discussed it with The Ladies. Besides, he's good company for you, someone closer to your age than Winslow."

"The last thing we need is more company." I carried out a frenzied assault on a helpless carrot.

"You haven't taken an hour to enjoy yourself since Jessa…" Rose cleared her throat. "It's all been arranged. Ignatius is happy to have him stay."

"I'm flat-out bushed," I said. "I'll grab a peanut butter sandwich and eat upstairs. Bandon will entertain The Ladies. It's the least he can do."

My feet complained half the night, but at least Saturday was over, the forty-ninth Saturday since I had vid-voiced Jessa and hadn't said good-bye. Would I ever stop counting?

The Chadwicks came downstairs at their usual 8:45 on Sunday morning for biscuits and soft-boiled eggs before church. Mother and son shared the same wispy blonde hair and deep blue eyes—exemplars of an increasingly rare gene pool, at least in Portland.

Winslow was already busy with the *Daisies vs. Dinos* game on his mini-MyCom. "Did Louise lay my egg?" he asked, his tiny fingers tapping the screen.

"Absolutely," I assured him as I packed apple slices for his mid-morning snack. His device matched one in a drone image I'd seen at RescueCommons, a mini-MyCom caught in an uprooted Douglas fir. Where was that child?

"Look what Mommy made for me." Winslow paused his game and pushed up the left sleeve of his over-tee. A fake tattoo of Louise covered his forearm. He pointed to what looked like two tiny fake pearls siliconed by her legs. "And see? Eggs! Just like Mommy's."

Priscilla raised her arm, revealing a genuine pearl-studded tattoo of gardenias circling her wrist. "His is Etch-a-Derm," she said. "Hypoallergenic. It'll fade in a week."

Winslow beamed. "Mommy says I can have another one after we go back home."

"You are so lucky," I said. "You don't know how lucky you are."

By the time The Ladies showed up for breakfast—who knows where Bandon and Ignatius were—Rose and I had divided the day's chores. Cleaning the eco-roof was one.

"Let's ask Bandon if he wouldn't mind going up there with you," Rose said.

"I can do the eco-roof myself," I told her.

"Two on the roof. House rules." Rose gave me her "don't argue" look. I didn't.

Grandma spooned yogurt on her fruit compote. "While you're on the third floor without the Chadwicks, look for Jessa's box of coins."

Before I could answer, Auntie An practically flew over to Bandon, who was coming down the stairs. "Good morning," she chirped. "You aren't afraid of heights, are you?"

"Pardon?" He had on another wrinkled tee and those same low-riding jeans with a harmonica shoved in his back pocket.

"Heights." Auntie An pointed skyward. "You wouldn't mind going up on the roof with Merry, would you? And then you two can go on a treasure hunt."

I clenched my jaw.

Bandon stroked his beard and smiled at me. "Sounds great." He headed for the breakfast buffet. "What are we hunting for?"

"It's not real treasure," I said.

Auntie An puffed up as if I'd offended her. "Of course it is. My American mother—Mama Two…?" Bandon nodded. "She gave Merry's mother two very valuable coins about thirty years ago, but they've disappeared," Auntie An continued. "This house has so many charming nooks and crannies. I love every square foot of this place."

"Check the old dumbwaiter by the servants' stairs," Grandma added. "That was one of Jessa's favorite hiding places when she was little and visited here."

Bandon scrunched his eyebrows.

"It's a tiny elevator for sending food up from the kitchen,"

Auntie An explained. "The main staircase only goes to the second floor. Servants lived on the third floor, so they took the back stairs."

I pointed to Bandon. "Don't you start on me about the landed gentry and the privileged rich."

He laughed. "I'll make an activist out of you yet."

An hour later, I crouched at the edge of the eco-roof. Bandon and I had polished the solar panels, and he was cleaning the gutters on his side of the roof.

The sky was overcast, the wind calm. In the relative quiet from the weekend ban on heavy construction, I could hear clucking from Chicken Hacienda and the *zee zee zee swee swee* of a Townsend's warbler in the neighbor's fir trees. I collected odd bits of plant matter from the drains and tossed them over the side of the house. They'd make good compost for the garden. I remembered how Jessa and I always cleaned the eco-roof together, a gruesome twosome giggling or singing or exploring our rooftop world.

"Hey, Meryem, do you want me to clean the landing pad for you?"

My memory shattered. "Don't bother," I said. "Residential drone deliveries haven't resumed yet."

I shifted my gaze to the patch of ground cover around me. Tiny spikes of moss mixed with the deep red leaves of *Sedum spurium*. Jessa's face returned, floating in front of me, her eyes wide in mock horror. *"Sedum spurium. Otherwise known as...dragon's blood!"*

"Whoa, Meryem, look at this. I can't believe it. The landslide on the West Hills is amazing from up here. Come on over. You can see better from this side."

"I'll pass," I told him, my time with Jessa ruined. "I'm going back inside."

Bandon caught up with me at the bottom of the drop-down stairs to the roof. "I didn't mean to upset you. That was stupid, reminding you about The Big One." He seemed entirely sincere, a different person from the guy I'd met two days earlier.

I took off my gloves. "Let's forget about snooping around up here for Jessa's coins. I'm not in the mood."

CHAPTER ELEVEN

When we told The Ladies that we hadn't found the coins on the third floor, Auntie An insisted on continuing the hunt. For a change Grandma agreed with her. I wasn't in the mood to argue about that either. Rose joined us as we checked the huge antique safe behind the paneling in the dining room. When I was little, I had worked the combination and hidden inside. I never did that again.

No beautiful box with coins, but we did find the graduation card my great-grandmother had given to Jessa. On the back of the card Jessa had scrawled "McPherson."

I stared at her faded handwriting. *"Hold your marker like this, lovey. That's right. Big capital M, little e. Excellent."*

"Earth to Meryem..." Rose touched my shoulder.

I came back to here and now.

"Mr. McPherson was Jessa's lawyer before she hired Mr. Nabli," Grandma said.

Auntie An shook her head. "His name was Mr. Kilmer."

"Jeff Kilmer was the engineer who quake-proofed this house,"

Rose said. "I know for sure. He was a lovely man. The retrofit cost Jessa a fortune, but you see it was worth it."

Auntie An folded her arms across her chest. "That was the least Jessa could do after she took this house away from me."

Grandma touched Auntie An's sleeve and said something in Vietnamese. Auntie An pulled away.

I glared at The Ladies, wishing they could vaporize, even just for a day—or a week. Besides, this was none of Bandon's business. Rose turned toward me. "So, Meryem? Who is this McPherson? Care to hazard a guess?"

"I'd better do the food budget so you can work on the accounts for Mr. Nabli," I said.

Bandon's eyebrows danced. "Need help? I'm good with figures." He grinned like Winslow, wanting to play.

"It's a one-person job. The next item on the list is mucking out Munchkina's shed."

Bandon pretended to vomit. "You really know how to hurt a guy. Show me what I have to do."

"She won't bite you," I told him.

"Small consolation," he said.

When I checked an hour later, Bandon was hanging with Munchkina in an acceptably clean shed. She was wagging her tail—maybe he smelled like Tillamook—and he was scratching behind her ears.

"I think she likes me," he said, a smear of something dark staining his jeans.

"I think I like you too," flew out of my mouth before I could catch it.

"Does that mean I get to scratch behind your ears?"

"Not a chance." A smile invaded my face.

He smiled back. "You and Munchkina have a certain charm, even though I'm usually more attracted to guys."

I picked at a nonexistent blotch in my over-tee so Bandon couldn't see my smile fade. For the first time in nearly a year, Bandon had the makings of someone who could be a friend and then some. Even if he was going to leave soon.

"Let's get you cleaned up, Goat Guy," I said.

At dinner, Bandon continued entertaining The Ladies, for which I was grateful. Grandma told him about her unicorn collection—not my favorite topic, but better than Grandma's usual swipes at Rose about meatless meals. Ignatius had joined us; the Chadwicks were away.

"You'd be fascinated by unicorns too if your name were Einhorn," she said. "*Einhorn* is German for unicorn." She launched into the *einhorn* legend in Germany, where her adoptive father's family came from.

Bandon buttered his fourth roll, not that I was counting. "Well, no wonder."

"Einhorn is Jessa's middle name. The same for Merry here, only my granddaughter isn't interested in the unicorn culture."

I shrugged. How I felt about unicorns was my own business.

"I use Clement as my middle name," Auntie An said, vying with Grandma for Bandon's attention. "Giles Clement was our biological father. Papa One. They named me An, which stands for peace, and Chau, which means pearl, the name of Papa One's mother in Mississippi. But we never knew peace in Vietnam, and we never met Grandma Pearl."

Ignatius, who hardly talks at meals or deals with The Ladies, cleared his throat. "Your father must have been a fine soldier," he said.

Auntie An put her hand to her lips. Silence shrouded the dinner table.

Rose broke the mood with, "Anyone for Trivial Pursuit after dinner? Bandon and The Ladies against Meryem, Ignatius, and me."

I snuck a quick look at Ignatius, who hadn't played with us in all the months he'd been living here. He sat erect, staring at his fork.

"With Bandon that makes three against three," Rose added.

"Sure," Bandon said. "What shall we call our team, ladies? The Unbeatables?" I wondered if he knew that Grandma had been a history teacher at Clackamas Community College and was the best at the game.

The Unbeatables led, but then I got an easy question about the 2050 outcome of the Erase Race Project. "The Census Bureau officially stopped using race as a category," I answered. "Good-bye mixed-race and racially ambiguous. Hello blend."

"There's still economic injustice in this country for people of color," Bandon said. He had a point.

Auntie An touched Grandma's arm. "Remember what they used to call us when we were growing up? Half-breeds and worse. Nobody wanted us. Not black people, white people, or Asians."

Grandma nodded. "Now we are accepted as blends, but nobody wants us because we're old."

Auntie An laughed. I laughed too, pretending it was a joke, which I'm not sure it was.

Rose answered "William Gibson" to the arts and literature question: "Who is credited with coining the term cyberspace?"

Auntie An arched her eyebrows. "Did they have his books in Russia?"

Rose sighed. "I went to university there, An Chau. In Saint Petersburg. They have an extensive library."

Bandon stopped devouring a postdinner peanut butter sandwich long enough to say, "Ah, I knew you had a secret life, Rose. You're really a double agent."

She smiled. "I was a sociology major, that's all. Nothing exciting. The rest I keep to myself. So, whose turn is it?"

I was surprised Bandon got that much out of Rose. No one would have zuckered her in the hashtag era. She was more private than an underwear drawer.

Ignatius was the surprise expert on science and geography. We won after he answered: "When did the first Earthlings land on Mars?"—2029; and "What was the first nation to completely disappear due to global warming?"—Kiribati.

I slept surprisingly well. The Ladies argued less with Bandon around. Maybe that made the difference.

Monday got off to a good start too. Rose and I watched Mayor Hammilason's weekly briefing while we prepared breakfast and organized our week. The mayor wore his usual vintage cowboy shirt and jeans in man-of-the-people mode. His five polyplaits—a cross between Dutch braids and cornrows—looked newly twisted, and his beard was trimmed to the three-day look.

"We've made great progress toward our residential goal since last Monday," he announced. "Twenty-nine more single-family houses are ready for habitation, as well as The Anthony, leaving only three yellow-tagged multifamily high-rises in The Pearl District left to be rebuilt. On behalf of FEMA and the Resilience Council, I want to congratulate Columbia Construction for its restoration work."

"Yes!" I raised my whisk in victory. "Let's tell The Ladies when they come down for breakfast."

Rose wiped her hands on her apron. "Your grandmother and especially An Chau might not be eager to move back immediately. Let's wait for the right time. Maybe in another couple of weeks."

Still, the thought of The Ladies leaving soon put me in a better mood to work on my EduComps. Plus, as Jessa says, *"Switching your MyCom to query mode is no substitute for learning."* I unfolded the vid-screen on the dining room table and keyed in an EduComps lesson on probability for my advanced ecology course. Bandon sat next to me, chewing a postbreakfast apple-kale roll-up—the guy was always hungry. Ignatius had a point about half-rations.

"Schools reopened months ago," he said between bites.

I nodded. "We shifted to homeschooling when I was nine and started going on fossil digs with Jessa. Before The Big One, a bunch of us EduComps kids studied at Central Library, but now…Have you seen the library?"

"What's left of it. What happened to your friends?"

I focused on the screen. "Most of them left after The Big One. My best friend Amy fractured her leg during an aftershock, and her parents made the family move to Boston on practically the first commercial flight out of here."

"You could use a friend," he said. The knuckles of his index and middle fingers were scraped raw, probably from cleaning Munchkina's shed.

I touched Bandon's hand. That guy-skin-on-mine feeling reminded me how much I missed a guy from my EduComps group who now lived in Montana. "Rose has a great salve for bruises. I'll get you some."

"Sit still. I'm fine."

We worked for an hour on covariance equations for populations in a biome. As I was folding up the screen, Bandon said, "Rose told me your mom is a paleogeneticist. Are you following in her footsteps?"

Your mom *is*, not your mom *was*. I liked this guy. "Jessa resurrects extinct species. I want to save rare or endangered ones, like the Larch Mountain salamander. *Plethodon larselli*. It breathes through its skin and lives in old growth forests here."

"What's Jessa's favorite extinct animal?"

Passenger pigeons was a safe answer, but I had this weird urge to tell the truth. "Unicorns," I said.

Bandon sat back and stroked his beard. He seemed totally serious. "So it's not just an Einhorn thing."

My mouth motored on. "Jessa is convinced that unicorns must have existed, since there are unicorn stories in so many cultures."

I ignored the knot in my stomach and continued. "Unicorns are Jessa's passion."

I didn't mention that passion is a click higher than love, and love is what she's felt for me.

Three seconds of silence. Then Bandon said, "Unicorns, utopias. Your mom and I are both working against the odds. My passion is about making government work for the poorest and neediest among us. Today is Presidents' Day. Everyone shops, right?"

I studied Bandon's bruised knuckles. "Sure. The Ladies dragged Rose to the Nordstrom's sale. What does that have to do with anything?"

"My point exactly. You'd think we'd celebrate our founding principles during Washington's presidency. Or Lincoln's Emancipation Proclamation. Or the universal health care system that President Obama-Bernstein finally signed into law in '56 when she completed what her father started ages ago. Instead we go out and shop."

I shrugged. "What's wrong with shopping? You weren't here right after The Big One. Rose traded her mother's gold earrings for six batteries."

Bandon cleared his throat. "That's not what I mean. Where's our civic responsibility? Consumption used to mean a lung disease. Now it's a national pastime. If Americans put one-eighth of one percent of the money they spend on designer coffee mugs into social welfare programs, we could probably end homelessness tomorrow."

He squeezed my hand. "That's why I'm committed to Calantha Corps even though the task is overwhelming. I'm nineteen years old, Meryem, and I doubt whether we'll achieve a decent level of economic justice in my lifetime. I'll be a hundred and nineteen and still pushing for my utopia."

That's when his stomach growled. "Let us consume lunch," he said.

Mr. Utopia was back to his regular banter a few minutes later, waxing nostalgic with Rose about cane sugar tasting better than the beet sugar we often used. As he inhaled fried tempeh, Rose told him about the sugar beet trains in Russia and about her mother's recipe for borscht. Then, to my surprise, she told him about coming to the States.

"It was at the end of the hashtag era years ago," she said. "People on the streets put the tips of their fingers together and smiled at each other. I asked Jessa what does this mean. She told me it's a new gesture about privacy and one-to-one relationships, about not exposing yourself to one million of your closest friends."

Rose looked happier than I'd seen her in weeks. Months. "I would confuse your phrase 'give me the fingers' and 'give me the finger.' You can imagine my embarrassment."

Tempeh spewed from Bandon's mouth. "Too funny," he said, wiping up the mess. He made the old fingertips sign. "So, Meryem, speaking from me to you, what would you like for your birthday tomorrow?"

"I'm not doing the birthday bit this year," I said, trying to keep my voice steady.

"Priscilla already told Winslow," Rose said.

My lunch plate clattered into the sink. "Unfair, Rose."

She looked up from putting enzymes in the digester. "Perhaps," she admitted, and she spared me the lecture about embracing life after The Big One.

"Do it for Winslow," Bandon said. "Why disappoint a three-year-old?"

I was trapped.

CHAPTER TWELVE

I got up the next day feeling nothing sweet about being sixteen.

Since it was Tuesday I made breakfast—oatmeal and tofu bacon—while Rose vid-voiced her grief counselor. She always took a while to get organized after speaking with Dr. What's-Her-Face about Jessa. When Rose helped me tidy up later, her cheeks were blotchy and her eyelids swollen.

"Happy birthday," she whispered, hugging me so tightly that the lobe locket hanging from my right ear got caught in her hair.

After we untangled, I concentrated on cleaning the digester lid. "There's no more tofu bacon," I said. "I put the extra oatmeal on the counter." I didn't ask about the counseling session, and Rose didn't volunteer anything, because that's the way things worked best on Tuesday mornings. I didn't want to hear how she'd given up on Jessa.

Half an hour later, I climbed the stairs to the crowded studio apartment that passed for the RescueCommons office. I checked the missing persons update. Jessa Zarfati and Yusuf Halab were still listed. That made eighty-four known missing as of February 18, 2059, down from eighty-seven last Friday. Those three were confirmed dead, bringing the total to 3,499 in the tsunami/coastal inundation zone.

I snaked my way over to my usual cubicle, the one closest to the window, and draped my hoodie over the back of the chair. Judging from the rustle and clicks and two backs I could see, three of the other five cubicles were already in use. Semi-silence clung to the room the way it used to at Central Library—the sound of people concentrating on the task at hand.

I wedged my backpack under the desk and squeezed past someone's courier bag on my way to the sink, solar fridge, and food processor that served as a kitchen. Shander stood by the sink, surveying the room.

"Happy birthday." I lip-read Shander's words more than heard them. This was the quiet zone. If you wanted to talk, you convened in the bathroom or went downstairs.

Shander deposited a bar of dark chocolate in my hand and a kiss on my cheek. Ze—the pronoun Shander used—wore the same blue loose-fitting top and bottoms every week, graying hair tied in a simple ponytail. No makeup. No jewelry. No facial hair except eyebrows. I'd stopped trying to guess Shander's gender months ago, which is how ze seemed to like things. The urge to help find Jessa had brought me to RescueCommons as soon as my feet had recovered. Shander's pity-free kindness is why I stayed.

"Thanks," I mouthed. I pocketed the chocolate because there was no eating allowed in the cubicles. Shander gave me my assignment, and I settled into the routine. Adjust chair. Flex fingers. Set monitor. Match GPS coordinates with drone visuals. Check high-def and zooming features. Apply eye drops, blink twice. Take centering breath, insert ear plugs, set MyCom to soothing music to minimize auditory distractions. Stare at screen. Search for, identify, and log objects used by, or part of, a human being: hair clips; nose rings; condoms; bones.

The day's visuals encompassed a square kilometer of muddy landscape near Arch Cape. The Big One had caused the earth to drop 1.6 meters there, and then an eight-meter-high wall of water scoured what was left. Rescue crews had done the sickening work on the midden piles from hell, finding bodies under boats tossed onto hotel roofs or survivors in shock clinging to a floating staircase. The drone visuals for RescueCommons in these last few months looked like paradise by comparison.

I found nothing worth logging for the first half hour. Time for a break. Shander's rules. No one stares at the screen for more than thirty minutes at a time or for a total of one hundred twenty minutes within a twenty-four-hour period. Otherwise you start to miss things, and that's unacceptable.

I walked around the block, not noticing much of anything except the sunshine. Then it was back inside. Nothing worth logging for the second stretch either. Or the third. I ate my chocolate bar in the bathroom. Shander and a couple of other volunteers went to the forensics lab. That left me and a tall black guy I'd seen a few times. He looked a lot like the American soldier in the photo in Auntie An's room—my great-grandfather. He wore an oversized GuyForm, the usually snug unitard baggy and sagging, with the leggings cut off at the calves, revealing thick wool socks and sad-looking sandals. I couldn't help noticing the pink barrette stuck to one of the polyplaits near his left ear. He turned toward me and grinned.

"My little girl," he said, breaking the quiet workspace rule. "Gemmie. She likes to stick things in my hair." He stood and stretched. "I'm Mark Albermarle."

"Meryem Zarfati," I said. No one else was around, so the rule didn't matter.

"I hope our vid-link doesn't disturb you. It's just temporary." Mark pointed to a second screen next to the RescueCommons one. "Hey, Gemmie," he said. "This is Meryem from my office. Say hi."

A little girl's face filled the screen. She had my same skin color and brown eyes. Her black polyplaits—there looked to be at least nine—housed a menagerie of plastic animal barrettes. Judging from her missing front teeth, she was five or six. "Hi," she said. "Charles has a stomachache."

"Charles is our giraffe," Mark explained.

"Poor Charles," I told her, switching to the entertain-kid mode I'd mastered with Winslow. "Would you like me to give him a kiss?"

Gemmie's face disappeared, replaced by a close-up of a mutant blue giraffe with a white face and solar cell eyes, an oddly somber expression, and bright pink tuffs on its horns. I made a kissing sound. "Is that better?"

Gemmie's nose and mouth reappeared. "Charles says thank you."

"I have to get back to work, princess," Mark said. "You be good, and I'll see you in a little while. Love you."

The link went silent. Mark sighed, sounding as if the last thing he wanted was to leave Gemmie. His forehead creased. "Are you related to the Jessa Zarfati on the missing persons list?"

"My mother," I said.

"I am so sorry. I hope you find out soon."

My insides shriveled. As I walked back to my cubicle, I deflected questions about Jessa with ones of my own. "How about you? What brings you to RescueCommons?"

"Shander got me this job. I'm technically a supervisor, so I get paid. I didn't lose anybody in The Big One. It's me and Gemmie and Tesla for now. We manage."

I returned to staring at the screen for my last stint of the day. I got lucky, if that's what you could call it—something metallic half-buried in the muck.

Zoom in. Zoom in. Squint. Blink. Adjust color and contrast. Guess—a lobe locket. Estimate accuracy of guess—80 percent. Log coordinates for search teams.

Mark congratulated me. "There might still be DNA on the locket. This could give someone closure. You, maybe?"

"My mother doesn't wear lobe lockets," I said.

"I am so sorry," he repeated.

Everyone was "so sorry" to hear about Jessa. I hated that sentence.

As I passed the parking lot by the office, I saw a wreck of a vehicle that had to be at least twenty years old. A stuffed blue giraffe peeked over the steering wheel. It wasn't until I was around the corner that I realized Tesla was the name of Mark's minivan.

"Birthday festivities at 1:30," Rose announced. Priscilla had arranged to work from home, and she and Rose had scheduled festivities for Winslow's window of happy toddlertude, after lunch and before naptime.

Bandon and Ignatius were still away at 1:20. Rose rubbed the back of her neck.

"Ignatius sometimes forgets his limitations," she said. "I hope Bandon has enough sense to make sure they don't get in over their heads."

I wondered why she was worried about Ignatius and what she meant by such a private thing as his "limitations," but I didn't ask. Rose switched to smile mode. She set out a festive concoction of peanut butter, shredded wheat, and honey, along with a bowl of pre-quake jelly beans that have a half-life longer than strontium-90. Then she decorated my hair with silver glitter.

"Just like last year," she said. "Remember when you and Jessa dyed your hair magenta for Jessa's fiftieth birthday?"

How could I forget? There was Jessa again in mind-sight, laughing and sprinkling glitter all over us. *Behold the perfect pair. Paragons of purple pulchritude.* I'd redone the magenta last month on Jessa's birthday, thinking I'd feel better, but that only made things worse.

"Well, look who's here," Rose said, turning toward the front stairs. "Are you ready for a treat, Winslow?"

"Just a little," Priscilla mouthed.

Winslow stood with his chin barely reaching the table.

I crouched next to him. "What's your favorite flavor?"

"Orange," he confided in postlunch carrots-and-cheese breath. Judging from Winslow's KidForm, orange was his favorite color too.

"Perfect. Now I can decorate your cake." I put two orange jelly beans on a kid-sized portion of concoction for him and handed him his plate.

Priscilla touched her son's head. "Winslow, what do you say when someone serves you a treat?"

"Zaaaank you."

"You're welcome," I said. And I meant it. The delight on Winslow's face—a perfect antidote to the morning's intensity—made my birthday bearable.

Priscilla extracted a plastic-sealed device from the smock she wore over her FemForm. I knew from past encounters that her smock, which had more pockets than Jessa's specimen jacket, housed saniwipes, a first-aid kit, assorted nutritious snacks, and a spare MyCom battery. But this device had me flummoxed.

"Happy birthday," she said. "It's a visual tracker for your GR-17. I'll install it tonight, and you'll have a fully functioning housebot by tomorrow."

I couldn't believe her generosity. "Thanks! How did you get one of these?"

Priscilla flushed. "Don't ask. You've been über kind to Winslow and me. I'm ready to move back into my house next week, but I'll miss you."

Grandma arrived with Auntie An, who waltzed up to Winslow, bent down, and raised her right hand. "Gimme five," she said.

Winslow nodded. "You can have five because you are a grown-up." He stretched his arm toward the bowl of jelly beans.

Auntie An laughed. "I keep forgetting that young people don't do high fives anymore. Two jelly beans, please." She nibbled on them while chatting with Priscilla about a Chinese couple that had rented the third floor from her for a few years before Jessa moved in. "I am now fluent in Mandarin Chinese," she said. "It's such a useful language."

I was as surprised as Priscilla seemed to be. I knew Auntie An spoke Chinese, but I hadn't heard about the boarders before. I wondered what else I didn't know about her.

The Sentry Mat buzzed. Rose ushered in Mr. Nabli—which was another surprise—and everyone sang happy birthday. I let Winslow unwrap Mr. Nabli's gift while Mr. Nabli hovered over him. No wonder. The apple-sized ceramic bowl I later nestled in the palm of my hand looked like a family heirloom.

"It's exquisite," I said, admiring the deep red tulips on a blue-and-white background.

"It's a traditional design from Iznik, where they made ceramics for the sultans," he said. "Ms. Kropotkin informed me that you like tulips and that your mother hoped to take you to Istanbul someday."

Jessa's voice filled my head. *"You would adore Istanbul, lovey. The most amazing koi swim in the Byzantine's basilica cistern, deep underground in the heart of the city."*

"My husband Aron's family has ceramics from there as well," Grandma said. "Aron was born in Iznik before his family moved to Istanbul."

Jessa disappeared.

Mr. Nabli waved his hand toward Jessa's rug. "Might I remind you again that your Turkish prayer rug is particularly vulnerable to theft."

Rose squared her shoulders. "The rug has hung in that spot since Jessa brought it back fifteen years ago, and that's where Meryem and I want it to stay."

"The client is always right," he said. Mr. Nabli stood and smoothed his jacket. "Unfortunately, I have to get back to work. I…"

Which is when Ignatius and Bandon strode in from the kitchen.

"Well, it's about time," Rose said, smiling with relief.

Before I could make the introductions, Mr. Nabli turned to Ignatius. "I'm Adnan Nabli, Meryem's lawyer. You must be Mr. Rivera."

Ignatius stiffened. He jerked his head in what passed for a nod.

"And this is Bandon," Auntie An chirped. "He's visiting us from Gales Creek."

Bandon winced.

Mr. Nabli glared at Bandon. "Bandon Falconer," he said, the way you'd announce bubonic plague. That's when I remembered Bandon saying that the Resilience Council wasn't the welcoming sort. My stomach lurched. My brain shifted to red alert.

CHAPTER THIRTEEN

Auntie An smiled. "Yes, Mr. Nabli. Bandon Falconer. How did you know?"

Mr. Nabli ignored her. "So this is the famous Calantha Corps activist, the leader of the DC Six, with the Council's ten-kilometer exclusion order on his head."

Priscilla gasped. "Oh my God, what has he done?"

Bandon took a step toward Mr. Nabli. "Not enough yet," he said, his eyebrows creased, his face strained and tense.

"Mr. Falconer and his gang of five from their Washington, DC, national headquarters are known to activists in the homeless community as the DC Six," Mr. Nabli added. "The Council did nothing to stop their arrival last summer. But then the DC Six disrupted an important Council meeting with FEMA last September to demand that our crippled city use emergency funds to solve our homeless problem permanently. Our mayor asked them to leave. They refused. They assaulted a compliance officer. The National Guard escorted them from the city. Have I got that right, Mr. Falconer?"

"Not even half right."

Mr. Nabli turned to Rose. "Harboring Mr. Falconer could jeopardize your status as a credit-tenant household, Ms. Kropotkin. As Meryem's guardian, I strongly advise that you to ask him to leave."

"No one's harboring anybody," I said, stepping between Mr. Nabli and Bandon. "We didn't know about the exclusion order. Bandon brought a buck here to service Munchkina."

"This is my fault," Grandma announced. "I arranged for the goat."

"Naptime!" Priscilla grabbed Winslow and headed for the stairs.

Bandon pointed to Mr. Nabli. "You're a lawyer. You know the DC Six exclusion order wouldn't stand up in court. I have First Amendment guarantees of free speech and assembly. I'm exercising every citizen's right to express grievances against the government."

Mr. Nabli's chest doubled in size. "Don't talk to me about grievances, son."

"Don't you call me son."

Mr. Nabli stepped closer to Bandon. "You want to test this in court, Mr. Falconer? I can make one call right now and have you arrested, and we'll see what happens in court. Is that what you want?"

That's when Ignatius switched into combat mode, his hands curling into fists. Rose grabbed Ignatius's shirt. "Ignatius, please!" He froze.

Grandma shifted into take-charge mode. "Gentlemen," she shouted.

Everyone shut up.

Grandma pointed to what I imagined was a gigantic Stars and Stripes over our heads. "My sister and I were born in a war-torn country, and we had the good fortune to come to America. We are grateful to live in a place with a deep respect for the law and for the peaceful resolution of differences. Mr. Nabli is a guest in our house, and we are here to celebrate Meryem's birthday."

She smiled at everyone and passed the bowl of jelly beans to Bandon. I stifled an eye-roll at Grandma's dramatic performance, because part of me felt proud of her. Life couldn't have been easy for The Ladies as half-black Amerasians after the Vietnam War.

"Bandon is our guest too, Mr. Nabli," I added, trying to sound as self-assured as my grandmother.

"I'll pretend that Mr. Falconer and I have never met," he told me. "This time."

Bandon took a jelly bean. "Fair enough."

Rose escorted Mr. Nabli to the door. Bandon and Ignatius conferred, and then Bandon reached into his hoodie pocket. He extracted a small box wrapped in tissue paper. "Happy birthday, Meryem."

"No presents," I said.

"You'll like this one," Rose answered, coming in from the front hall. "Bandon and Ignatius worked really hard to find it, because it's officially unavailable in Portland."

"Close your eyes and open your hand," Bandon ordered.

I did.

"Now open your eyes."

Two small tubes of hand lotion nestled in my right palm. Crème Botanique. Jessa's honey-orange scent. I felt blissed out and sucker-punched at the same time. "Where did you get this?"

Bandon bowed and then waved toward Ignatius. "Two men on a mission. We make a great team." Ignatius sprouted a rare smile. "We have a bit of business to finish," Bandon added. "See you all at dinner."

"Now for your last present," Auntie An said after they'd gone and Rose had left for a much-needed break in her room. The Ladies sat me down on the living room couch.

"We've had enough surprises for one day," I said. "Can't this wait until tomorrow?"

Apparently not.

Grandma reached into the bag. "I'll do the honors."

The prayer shawl was more beautiful than I remembered,

lamb's-wool soft and utterly feminine with vivid orange and ochre flowers, purple grapes, and green vines embroidered against a creamy white background. Grandma ran her finger across a row of crimson lettering. "*Tzedek, tzedek tirdof,*" she said. "Justice, justice you shall pursue. A basic tenet of our faith."

As I touched the shawl, something eased inside me. "It's lovely. *Cảm ơn,*" I said, thanking The Ladies with one of the few Vietnamese phrases I knew to show I was truly grateful.

I stood up and wrapped the rectangular shawl around my shoulders, letting the white fringes at the narrow ends fall to my knees. The longer fringes at each corner were bound in complex knots. One long fringe included a single thread of the most amazing blue.

Grandma enveloped me in a full-on hug, her hair tickling my chin. "I wish Jessa could have given you this. She was a wonderful daughter and a wonderful mother. Did you know she was planning to take you to Istanbul for your sixteenth birthday?"

"No," I managed, before my voice died in my throat. I put the shawl back in its bag, thanked The Ladies again, and made up some chore I had to do. The animals. Yes, I had to check on the animals. The Ladies went upstairs for a nap.

Tillamook and Munchkina each got licorice-flavored jelly beans, and the chickens got shredded wheat crumbs. Unhappy birthday to me. The wind gusted, bringing with it a chilling rain. I tightened my hoodie and started for the house.

Which is when I froze. There she was. That Serakh person, dressed in her ridiculous Greek goddess outfit. Sitting on the back step, her chin in her hands, watching me.

"Stop barging in like that," I said, after I caught my breath. I felt more angry than surprised. "I don't know how you found out I have the shawl, and I don't care," I told her. "Go away."

I folded my arms across my chest. Rain seeped into my socks.

"Do you have the bronze coin?" Her voice was low-pitched, almost guttural, serious and not entirely friendly. Maybe she wasn't eager to see me either.

"No."

"Yet here I am again." She shivered, her headscarf drenched and clinging to the side of her face. "Let us enter your dwelling."

I was too wet to argue. Besides, Rose and The Ladies were home. Maybe this time I could get Serakh to stay long enough to meet them.

Serakh surveyed the kitchen. "Much of this room feels as I remember it." She reached for my hand, but I backed away. "Miryam Aharona, can you remove the medal ornament from your finger?"

"The MyCom? Of course, but why would I? And stop calling me by my Hebrew name. Call me Meryem."

She ran her fingers along the counter. "Let it be so. We will hide the ornament later. A headscarf will cover your hair and the ornaments on your ears. Are you ready to go?"

"Go where?"

"Away. Only for an instant."

I shook my head. "Away? You sound as obtuse as The Ladies. If you can't say what this is about and where you're taking me, then walk out like you did the last time. If I wanted a magical mystery tour, I'd watch the old Beatles vid from a hundred years ago."

I held open the back door.

"Istanbul," she said.

My heart pounded in my throat. There was Jessa, in mind-sight, standing behind Serakh—Jessa from two summers ago in her lab coat and headscarf vid-voicing me from Galata Bridge with the mosques and minarets of Istanbul in the background. My mother never missed my birthday, plus Grandma had said Jessa planned to take me to Istanbul when I turned sixteen.

I closed the door. "Istanbul. Really?"

"This is so."

"Will I see Jessa?" It wasn't entirely, absolutely, miraculously impossible, was it?

Serakh held her hands out, palms up. "I am guided as a servant of The One. I cannot say if our travels will take us to your mother. I hold in my heart a prayer that it will come to pass."

"We're going now?"

"Now." Serakh touched my arm. "When you return, it will be as if no time has passed. Please fetch the shawl."

The no-time thing made zero sense. Still, maybe Serakh was speaking metaphorically. Maybe she'd produce two MyFlight authorizations and whisk us to the airport. Maybe she had a ride waiting out front.

Serakh draped the prayer shawl over us as we stood by the kitchen table. "Wind the blue thread around your finger," she instructed.

Somehow it felt wrong to have the blue thread next to the MyCom. I reached across and wound the long strand of silk around my left index finger. For some strange reason, I was certain I'd see Jessa again.

A faint blue glow spread across my left hand. My PerSafe chip tingled in my forearm; the MyCom overloaded. Then the world erupted in bright blue. My body twisted and strained.

I heard myself scream. And then...

Black.

CHAPTER FOURTEEN

I opened my eyes inside Mr. Nabli's porcelain bowl. Painted tulips danced on a blue-and-white background. I blinked. Blinked again. The bowl turned into a small, tiled, three-sided room, about the size of Jessa's bathroom. My body sprawled on a thick woolen rug like the one that hung in my front hall.

"Rest a moment longer," I heard Serakh say. "Have no fear. Izabel has hidden us well."

I turned a throbbing head in the direction of the voice. Serakh sat less than a meter away, her back against a large rectangular wicker basket with a lid. She brought a small wooden bowl to my lips. "Drink this," she said. "It will revive you."

The pale liquid was cool and thick, sweet and delicious, like melted pistachio sherbet. I hadn't tasted anything so good since before The Big One.

When I finished, she asked, "Shall I help you to stand?"

She held me until my dizziness cleared. I tried to thumb my location, but the MyCom screen stayed blank. Fried. "Where am I?"

"In Istanbul. I do not lie." Serakh wiped the bowl with the hem of her robe. "We are in the time of the sultan Suleiman, son of Selim. Izabel tells me that the harem is in chaos. No one is to be trusted."

I massaged the knots in my shoulders. "Impossible. I know a bunch about Istanbul and the Ottoman Empire. Suleiman the Magnificent ruled in the fifteen hundreds."

Serakh put the bowl in the corner. "It is always hard the first time," she said. She attempted a comforting smile.

I was not comforted. "Look, I don't play cybersensory games, and I don't like people handing me a load of complete crud."

Her smile stayed put. "Let us put on the garments in this basket and see to Izabel. Soon you will be back in your place and time as if not one moment has passed."

This weird girl was toying with me. "I don't care how much time passes or who this Izabel is." I rubbed my temples. "What about Jessa? Is she here?"

Serakh stepped out of the little room and returned a few seconds later. "I do not see her. I do not think so."

Anger overwhelmed hope so quickly it startled me. "You don't *think* so? Just say it. You know nanosquat about my mother, don't you?"

"I know what?" Serakh's expression was an infuriating mix of patience and confusion.

I clenched my fists. "Jessa was on the coast when The Big One hit. I haven't heard from her since then, but she's not dead. She can't be. And then when you said Istanbul…and she went there a lot…and it's my birthday…and I thought maybe…"

Serakh had the nerve to smile again. "I have come to you on the day of your birth?"

I lunged for the prayer shawl that Serakh had slipped under her arm. She sidestepped, sending me crashing into the basket. Before I could get my bearings, she'd put the shawl on the rug behind us, planted her hands on my shoulders, and made me face her.

"You have come willingly, Meryem. I did not force you."

I glared at her. "Take me home. Now!"

"Do not rush to judgment against me. Perhaps The One will guide us to Jessa as well. First we must look to Izabel. She is a child, a slave with nothing to save her from death or corruption except her skill at needlework. She lives at the whim of a black eunuch who is himself a slave, although one of high status."

"Izabel is a slave?"

"Yes. If I release you, will you flee?"

With the MyCom fried, I had no idea how to get back home. So far I didn't seem to be in danger. Plus I was…curious. "No," I said. I took a cleansing breath and calmed down.

She let go. "A wise decision."

"What can I do? I can't speak Ottoman Turkish or Arabic," I explained, rubbing a sore spot on my shoulder. "I hardly know modern Turkish except for a few phrases. I can't use the MyCom translator. How can I talk to Izabel?"

"You and Izabel will understand each other as long as I am present," Serakh said, which made no sense. She lifted the basket lid, releasing the smell of lavender, roses, and sweat. "Your garments do not belong here. Your purple hair, ear discs, and hand ornament will frighten her. They must be hidden or removed." She looked at my over-tee and FemForm.

"I'm not taking my clothes off," I said. And it turned out I didn't have to, except for my hiking boots. The beige linen trousers she handed to me fit easily over my leggings and FemForm bottom, even with its bias-cut skirt that flared at mid-thigh.

The rest was no problem: a loose linen blouse to cover my FemForm top and over-tee, then a floral-patterned calf-length robe, a wide brocade sash, and a crimson silk headscarf that hid my hair. I put my lobe lockets and broken MyCom inside the hiking boots.

Serakh handed me a pair of red felt slippers, but they were too small to fit over the socks. "You must remove your foot coverings."

"The socks stay. No one will notice."

Serakh pointed to their neon yellow and red stripes.

"The robe will cover them," I said, which wasn't exactly true. "I can't walk otherwise." Which also wasn't exactly true, but no way was I going to take off my socks without a silicone pad to replace them. Too painful.

Serakh found a pair of larger slippers for me in the basket and then decked herself out in a similar costume. She studied my eyes. "Outside you would wear a veil, as is the custom with Muslim women here. But in the harem you are unveiled. They will see your eyelids. We will say that you are from the East."

"You told me that too. Is that what you always say?"

Serakh smoothed the scarf covering her braid. "I will answer you with honesty. I was a child in the high desert of Judea. You dwell in Port Land. These are to the west of this spot. But I have learned this: people believe that what lies to the east, where the day dawns while they are in darkness, is a very different world from their own. They are more willing to believe me."

Then she shrugged—a Bandon-like shrug, as if we were friends. She seemed so human, so regular. My anger fizzled. Serakh and I somehow belonged together, doing whatever we had to do, at least for now.

After Serakh left to get Izabel, I tiptoed through the arch and down a narrow passageway until I came to a lattice-covered window. My stomach somersaulted when I looked outside.

The scene could have come from a video that Jessa brought home one time: *Byzantium, Constantinople, Istanbul: 1,500 Years as the Eye of the World*. I'd bet a sextillion credits that Serakh and I really were in Topkapı Palace. There was no mistaking the huge Byzantine church in the courtyard. Crazy. Totally crazy.

I closed my eyes and tried to remember the name of the church. *Jessa was sitting next to me with a vid-screen on her lap. "They didn't turn this one into a mosque like they did to Hagia Sofia. See, lovey? It's called Hagia Eirene in Greek. Aya Irini in Turkish. They translate it as Saint Irene's, but Holy Peace is more accurate. One day I'll take you there."*

I was so focused on the world outside the window and inside my head that I didn't realize Serakh was back until I heard her say, "This is Lady Meryem, Izabel. She is from the East."

The little white girl with a mass of red curls and large blue-gray eyes could have been Bandon's kid sister. Izabel bowed her head and dropped into a sort of curtsy. Then she studied my face, her eyes widening in wonder. "Ayele told me all about your tribe," she said. "Do you have a talisman too? Did you travel here on a magic carpet?"

Forget tribes, talismans, and magic carpets. I stood there speechless, because Izabel spoke perfect English.

"The gift of communication, of mutual understanding," Serakh explained. "Izabel hears you in the words of her native tongue. She converses with you in what you will hear as your native tongue."

A muezzin's call to prayer echoed across the palace. Then, as if on cue, a lion roared, the sound so loud that I imagined I felt the lion's breath. Startled, I lost my balance and fell on my butt. Izabel giggled and then covered her mouth.

"It's all right," I said as I stood and straightened my robe. "I'm not angry. Are there lions nearby?"

"Yes, Lady Meryem. Next to that armory." She pointed to the church.

Izabel trained her eyes on me, and for one awkward moment I caught a wary look, as if she wanted to ScrutinEyes me without causing offense. Then she seemed to decide otherwise. "Ayele says that the lions call the animals to prayer. Do you want to see them, Lady Meryem? Ayele says that when he was a boy and tended the sultan's animals, a lady of your tribe came with her talisman. Ayele says that he even tended the horse with the neck as tall as a minaret."

"A giraffe," I told her. I took Izabel's hand as she walked with Serakh and me toward the niche with the wicker basket. My mind flashed to Gemmie's stuffed animal on the dashboard of Mark's minivan. Charles, the giraffe that needed a kiss. Was that only this morning?

"A giraffe! Yes!" Izabel's too-broad smile showed she was anxious to please. She reminded me of how hard I tried to convince Jessa that I would be thrilled, thrilled, thrilled to sort through genome scans if only she'd let me stay with her at the lab.

Izabel chirped away. "On special days the keepers parade the animals for us to see. Monkeys, and tigers, and horses with stripes."

We settled ourselves on the floor by the basket. "Zebras," I said. "Do you like animals?"

"Oh, very much, Lady Meryem. Ayele says that he will take me to their cages so I can draw them and then embroider them for customers. Peacocks even, and horses with one horn."

"Unicorns," I said, without thinking.

CHAPTER FIFTEEN

Here and now shifted to Jessa and then. *"Why not unicorns, lovey? We have narwhals, and greater one-horned rhinos, and whitemargin unicornfish—all alive today—plus the Siberian unicorn from thirty thousand years ago and a dozen different ceratopsians in the fossil record." Jessa was swirling her index finger in the unwashed pot Rose had just used to make lemon curd. Jessa held out a dollop for me. The lemon curd was perfect—puckery and sweet.*

I remembered shrugging then, a small lift of my shoulders, not wanting to contradict Jessa. Unicorns didn't exist. The Siberian unicorn—*Elasmotherium sibiricum*—looked more like a rhino than a horse. I'd checked Query. I knew.

"Scientists dream too." Jessa's finger disappeared into the pot again. "I'm not all gene splicings and petri dishes. I haven't given up on unicorns. Wouldn't your grandmother be amazed if I resurrected one?"

"Lady Meryem?"

Something tugged on my sleeve. Jessa dissolved into Izabel sitting in front of me, her forehead creased in confusion or fear. "Lady Meryem, why are you staring at me that way? What have I done wrong? I beg you to take me into your service. I will scrub your sleeping mat with fleabane, and wash your menstrual linens, and fetch you spun sugar. I will taste your food for poison and embroider the finest garments for you. I will never ever give you cause to beat me."

Beat her? I winced.

"Lady Meryem is not displeased," Serakh said. "She needs a moment to rest before she learns of your circumstances. Is that not so, Lady Meryem?"

"Yes," I managed. "Everything will be all right," I added, as much for my own reassurance.

"Tell Lady Meryem your story, child."

And she did. I heard about her mistress in the harem, Lady Kuratsa, who was a gift to the sultan from a warlord in the Circassian mountains and who was drowned in the Bosporus. Izabel explained that the sultan's wife, Hürrem, had also died—of natural causes, it seemed—and the women of the harem were now fighting for power. Izabel was afraid she'd be drowned too, or that her next mistress would, so she persuaded the black eunuch Ayele to protect her in exchange for her embroidering items he then sold.

All of this fit with what I knew about the Ottoman Empire. Hürrem Sultan was known in the West as Roxelana. If she had recently died, we would be some time in the 1550s. A black eunuch made sense because dark-skinned castrated males governed the harem, although they were still technically slaves. What I couldn't wrap my brain around was how I got here.

Izabel explained that of all the tasks she did for Lady Kuratsa, the worst was dyeing her mistress's hair every month. Izabel had to pulverize henna, mix it with lemon juice and cloves, and guard it overnight, then spend hours applying and waiting for the right tone and disposing of the muddy mess.

"If one tiny drop got on her ear, she lashed the soles of my feet," Izabel complained.

My own feet answered with a twitch. I sucked in my breath.

Izabel stopped talking and stared at my headscarf, fearful, I suppose, of what was underneath.

"I don't use henna," I said, deciding not to mention my henna-based botanical dye. I tightened my headscarf. Izabel would probably freak at my magenta frizz.

Serakh leaned forward. "Where is your family?"

Izabel's finger traced a pattern on the rug. "My brother Habib is here in the military school for the janissaries. When they gathered boys from Salonika for the sultan, Habib pleaded with them to take me because there was no one left. Mama and Papa and our two sisters died in a fire."

Salonika. I was pretty sure that was an old nickname for the Greek city of Thessaloniki.

"When was this?" Serakh asked.

"Four years ago. I was five and Habib ten. The rabbi's wife brought us cheese and a blanket. The janissaries were kind. They gave me to the sultan instead of selling me at the market."

"You're Jewish?"

"I was, Lady Meryem. As Jewish as Lady Esther, who used to bring beautiful goods to sell in the harem. Now the harem is a hornet's nest, and Lady Esther stays away. She must have many girls working for her. I wish I could..."

Izabel slapped her palms to her lips, as if she wanted to shove back inside all the words she'd let loose. "Lady Esther means nothing to me now. I am whatever you want me to be. I am yours."

"What I want is for you to be free," I told her. "Completely free to go anywhere. You shouldn't be anyone's slave."

Serakh shook her head.

Izabel turned pale. "No!" She lurched forward and kissed my feet, her red curls smothering my slippers. "If I am free and unprotected on the streets, I will die! Let me stay with you. I eat very little. I will offer myself to you in every way that pleases you!"

"Have no fear, child." Serakh moved to embrace Izabel. "Lady Meryem is here to help you."

Izabel squirmed out of Serakh's arms. "You promised! How can Lady Meryem save me if she refuses to be my mistress?"

"You don't understand," I said. "You shouldn't be anybody's property."

Izabel rested a hand on the embroidered sash at her waist. "Ayele was right. He is the only one who will have me, because I belonged to Lady Kuratsa and she lost favor. I am cursed!"

I reached for Izabel's arm. "That's not so. We're here to…ow!" I jerked back. Blood bubbled up from the soft flesh at the base of my thumb.

Izabel sprang for the archway, a large tapestry needle in her hand. "You lied to me! You said you would help me, and you won't. If you tell Ayele I was here, I will poke your eyes out."

"Wait!" I shouted as she raced away.

Serakh clamped her hand over my mouth. "We cannot be found here. We must trust in Ayele's goodness. Or his greed. Izabel's embroidery is worth more to him than her body for now. He has the power and skill to hide her in the palace. No one else will claim her."

After Serakh took her hand away, I pressed a cloth against the base of my thumb to stop the bleeding. "Nothing makes sense," I said, as much to myself as to Serakh.

Serakh began to take off her disguise. "Izabel is right, Meryem," she said, using my English name, which made her seem a little less strange. "There is much for Izabel to fear on the streets of Istanbul. We must secure a home for her. First we must redeem her from Ayele."

"You mean buy her like a piece of property?"

"We will abide by the customs in this spot on the *olam*."

"The what?"

"The *olam*. All of time and space. The One has guided me to you, because you are the possessor of the bronze coin."

She made me sound like a character in a fairy tale. "Suppose I can't find it."

"We will trust in The One. When you have removed the garments of this time and place, take up the prayer shawl and wrap the blue thread around your finger. I will bring you home."

CHAPTER SIXTEEN

A flash of blue light. Suffocating darkness. Pain. Then I was cradled in Serakh's lap on my kitchen floor.

"I once carried another Miryam to this very place," Serakh said. "Would you like help to sit at the table?"

I managed a head wobble that meant yes. It was still raining outside, and the kitchen looked exactly the way it had after my birthday fiasco. I rested a minute and then thumbed the MyCom, wondering what time it was. The screen stayed blank. Totally fried. Like me.

"However you did what you did, don't do it again," I whispered.

Serakh guided me to a chair. "Izabel needs you. After we redeem her with your bronze coin, we will find a place of safety for her. Then the intertwining will be at an end."

"None of this happened."

Serakh pointed to a dot of dried blood at the base of my thumb. "How did this come to be?"

I shook my head. My mouth turned sour. Needing to lie down again, I lurched to the living room couch and pillowed my head with the prayer shawl. I closed my eyes and groaned as pain spiked through my body. I heard Serakh say, "The next time it will be easier, after the coin is found. Peace be unto you."

Later, I smelled stale tobacco smoke and menthol cough drops. I opened my eyes to Ignatius standing over me. "Are you okay, Miss Meryem?"

"What time is it?"

"Fifteen hundred hours."

"Where is everybody?"

"Bandon is upstairs. Rose is out. I can't account for the others. Are you injured?"

"I'll be fine, Ignatius. Just give me a minute." I struggled to sit up and think straight. Fifteen hundred hours. Three o'clock. I'd gone out to feed the animals at two thirty.

I did the math. There must have been about ten minutes between the time that I saw Serakh on the back step and the time I wrapped my finger around the blue thread. Then afterward, I must have spent at least five minutes in the kitchen before I made it to the couch. I was zonked when Ignatius came, and my mouth felt scummy inside, so I must have been out for at least fifteen minutes. That accounted for all thirty minutes. Serakh had told me that the trip would take no time at all. So she was right. And that was impossible. My guts and brain were in violent disagreement.

"You don't look so good." Ignatius held out his forearm. "Let me help you upstairs."

Which he did. I buried my head in my pillow and set SomniSoothe to tulips and gentle rain. I ignored several knocks on my door. When I figured I was sufficiently solid, I went downstairs to help Rose with dinner. She took one look at me and dispensed an everything's-going to-be-okay hug.

"Your next birthday will be easier," she said. She handed me the potato masher. Potato-and-turnip smash for seven and a half people, counting Winslow—bicep city. Bandon came looking for predinner snacks. I offered to share my Larval Farm's dry roasted mealworms with him. He reached for the peanut butter.

Then, out of nowhere, he said, "Let's have birthday dessert at the Hoyt Street Café."

I didn't know whether to smile at Bandon's invitation or frown at his cavalier attitude, so my face stayed in neutral. "Aren't you the guy with an exclusion order hanging over your head?"

"Tonight I live dangerously. Besides, no one will recognize me in Ignatius's hoodie."

"I'll think about it."

Bandon dug out his harmonica and played the "Happy Birthday" song. By the time he was done, I was smiling.

"I gotta see a man about a disguise." He headed upstairs.

"I haven't said yes," I called after him. Yet.

"Said yes to what?" Priscilla arrived, GR-17 visual tracker in hand.

"Bandon and I might go out to the Hoyt Street Café for a little while," I explained, as we went to the dining room to repair the housebot.

"You could use a birthday break." Priscilla guided a blonde curl behind her ear. "Bandon's a sweet guy."

I felt my face grow warm. "He's not as much of a yutz as I thought at first."

Priscilla laughed. "My husband turned out to be high on the yutz scale. Maybe your mother had it right by not marrying at all."

"Could be," I said. "I never missed having a father around. When Jessa was away, I always had Rose."

Priscilla inserted the tracker. Ninety seconds later, I heard the old *za-bing* and then, "Good afternoon, Meryem and Unidentified Guest. All of my systems are fully operational. How may I assist you?"

Yes! "Gryffindor, go to the kitchen," I instructed. "Assist Rose."

The GR-17 scanned the room, swiveled 180 degrees, lurched once, and whirled toward the kitchen. Priscilla grinned. "Gryffindor?"

"Jessa named him that and programmed the British voice. When she was a kid, she was into Harry Potter." I told Priscilla that my MyCom was busted too. "I was outside with the animals, and then I went into the kitchen, and the MyCom overloaded all of a sudden," which was near enough to the truth, whatever the truth was. "Now I can't even force a reboot."

Priscilla frowned. "I'll fiddle with your MyCom after I put Winslow to bed."

After dinner, Bandon and I checked the animals. I told him we had to be back by nine—three hours before the Council's curfew—which gave us about forty-five minutes.

"By ten," he countered. "It'll take your mind off things."

Which was so not true. Suppose there was news about Jessa, and I wasn't home? It was hard enough going to RescueCommons, but at least there I had a chance of finding something of hers. "Nine thirty."

"Deal," he said.

We walked side by side in the night breeze. I looked up at the sky and wondered what had really happened to me after the birthday party. What else could it have been if not some kind of vivid daydream? People didn't disappear in a flash of light and reappear thousands of miles away and five hundred years in the past. The space-time continuum wasn't supposed to include my kitchen.

As we passed a cordoned-off building near 20th and Hoyt, Bandon broke the silence. "What's with that salamander you want to save?"

"Oh. Um. The Larch Mountain salamander. *Plethodon larselli.* Larch Mountain is in the Cascades. I used to hike there with Jessa."

"Was this *Plethodon* guy hurt by The Big One? Is it special?" Bandon looked interested. Or he was a good faker. Hard to tell.

I stopped and faced him. "No, it's going extinct because we're destroying the salamander's habitat. Every species in a biome is important. It's not a question of being special or extraordinary."

He grinned at me. "Everyone deserves a decent biome."

"You have a one-track mind, Bandon Falconer."

"At least two tracks," he said. "Apple pie is one of them."

The café was nearly empty. The MyMenu tablet featured

pixel-perfect images of butterscotch custard, cinnamon rolls, and apple pie, as well as a list of ice creams, sherbets, coffees, health drinks, and teas. I tapped mint tea and a slice of pie. Bandon tapped black coffee and another serving of pie. "I'm getting vanilla ice cream for my pie," he said. "How about you? Splurge. My treat."

"Just the pie," I said. "I already had pistachio sherbet today."

My stomach lurched.

Bandon looked puzzled. "When did you have sherbet, birthday girl? You're holding out on me."

"Just joking," I said. Suddenly queasy, I escaped to the bathroom. Leaning against the side of a toilet stall, I took one centering breath after another. Still shaking, I finger-combed my hair and armed myself with deflecting questions. No way was I going to talk about what happened—or didn't happen—with Serakh.

Pie and tea were waiting for me when I returned. "So, Bandon, tell me about Calantha Corps. How did you get involved?"

Bandon spooned a dollop of ice cream into his coffee. "You probably know that during Baltimore's homeless count in January of '52, they found Calantha Broadwell and her dad frozen to death."

I nodded, not mentioning that I'd only recently found out from Aussie Jack.

"She was seven, Meryem. He had wrapped her in his coat, and they were curled up in a cardboard box by the harbor. Even though Facebook and Twitter and all that stuff were gone by then, everyone with a newsfeed knew about Calantha by the next day."

"She must have had a horrible life."

Bandon attacked his pie. "I was twelve. I made my dad drive me to Baltimore, and we marched in a demonstration. There was this homeless woman, and I carried a sign for her. She gave me a potholder she'd made, and she told my dad that I had the calling, whatever that meant. Anyway, I still have the potholder."

He got quiet, collapsing in on himself. I sipped my tea.

Then he inhaled and began again. "By the end of March that year, they started Calantha Corps. I did stuff, not much because, I mean, I was only twelve. But then I got involved after my national service. Some of us from the DC headquarters figured we could make a change out here. You folks had so many emergency services after The Big One. There was so much money. We thought, hey, if you're rebuilding a society, then it might as well be a better one."

"The DC Six. Sounds notorious."

"Well, it isn't. We just won't let them forget that it shouldn't be business as usual after the emergency programs end. No more Calanthas. Ever."

He reached into the hoodie pocket and handed me a flyer. "But, hey, it's your birthday. I didn't mean to get political on you. Ignatius found this. There's a Sklider fest tomorrow at Waterfront Park. Rubble Rally. See? Let's go."

I shook my head. "Sorry. Too much to do."

"It's only for an hour, Meryem. Rose doesn't mind."

I squeezed my fork. "You checked with Rose first?"

Bandon shrugged. "It was Rose's idea. She says you used to love Skliding, and your feet can handle it now, whatever that means. Think of Rubble Rally as part of your birthday celebration."

I grabbed my jacket. "I'll think of it as a waste of time."

On the way home, I apologized for my snark at the café.

"Yeah, well, next time I'll have Rose speak for herself," Bandon said. "What happened to your MyCom?"

I cleared my throat and opted for a half-truth. "It was fine and then it just died. Priscilla works at Intel, so I figure she'll know what to do."

Apparently that's not what Priscilla thought. When Bandon and I got back, she had MyCom guts strewn across the kitchen table. She looked at me as if I were a space alien.

"I've never seen this kind of damage, Meryem. Where have you been?"

"At the Hoyt Street Café, remember? I said I'd be back around nine thirty."

She shook her head. "That's not what I meant. Your MyCom looks like it was subjected to a huge electromagnetic wave, or solar flare, or who knows what. Tell me exactly what happened. Where did you go today?"

CHAPTER SEVENTEEN

I stared at Priscilla, my guts in a tangle. I had the urge to say, "I was in Istanbul this afternoon, only it was five hundred years ago, and, well, you know, time flies when you're having fun."

Instead I managed, "There was a flash of blue light. And then… nothing really."

"Where did the flash come from?"

"Um…the MyCom, I think. So, is it totally ruined? Can you retrieve my personal data?"

Priscilla rubbed her forehead. "Was the flash emanating from the MyCom or somehow attracted to the MyCom from the atmosphere?"

I lowered myself onto a kitchen chair. "No idea." Which wasn't exactly true, but what else could I say? What else did I believe?

I felt Bandon's hand on my shoulder. "It's obvious, Priscilla. Meryem was thinking of my hugely magnetic personality, and her MyCom went bonkers." He glanced at his own device. "Mine seems to have survived."

Tension drained from my body, but Priscilla was not in joking mode. "I'm sorry. I don't think I can fix it without a better idea of what happened."

"If I knew more, I'd tell you," I lied. "Forget the personal data. How can I get another MyCom? I really depend on that thing."

Priscilla sighed. "I can't promise, but I'll see what I can do. Look, I'd better get back to Winslow. If you remember anything else, let me know."

"Sure. Will do."

As soon as Priscilla collected the MyCom bits and left, Bandon sat down across from me. "What's up, Meryem? You look fried."

"I don't want to talk about it," I said, putting a lid on the discussion. We were so quiet that you could hear the digester devouring the last of the dinner scraps.

Then he said, "Ignatius is letting me share his room, you know. I did ask politely. I'm right across the hall if you need me." We walked toward the stairs. "Sleep well," he said, giving me an earnest look. "I wouldn't want to jeopardize the quality of my breakfast."

It took me a moment to realize that Bandon was back to the banter that now felt like a life preserver. Easy talk. Nothing intense. I'd had enough of intense for one day.

"Oh, yeah." I stepped ahead of him and touched Jessa's rug on my way upstairs. "You'd better pray SomniSoothe does its job, or tomorrow you'll get barley groats with poached dirt."

His eyes widened in mock horror.

That night SomniSoothe failed to protect me from image after image of Izabel and Serakh in Istanbul. How could something so impossible seem so real?

Hours later, sweating, exhausted, I clapped on the light and staggered to Jessa's desk. With the MyCom busted, I resorted to a scrap of paper and an old marker. I shifted into calculation mode. How many slices of bread did we have left in the freezer? How many credits could we spare to splurge on more cardamom? How many barrels of rainwater would we need to conserve for garden use, assuming the rain stopped by June 15th like last year and didn't start again until Halloween, and the average daily high temperature climbed to last summer's scorching thirty-five degrees Celsius?

It was still dark outside when I heard the first rumble of construction that meant the seven-to-seven noise abatement was over for the night. Too late for sleep. I took a sponge bath, changed my clothes, joined Rose in the kitchen, and got the conversation going on the day's chores with another mind-diverting list.

The day started out well. Priscilla announced at breakfast that the MyCom was dead, but that she'd look for a refurbished one at Intel. Winslow promised to draw a picture of Louise while he was at the Intel Child Center. Rose and The Ladies went out together in an apparently decent mood. Bandon took Ignatius's breakfast up to him and reported back that the two of them were going to work on the basement shelves later. Until then, he'd help me with my EduComps lessons.

We were unfolding the screen on the dining room table when Bandon said, "What's with toothpaste around here? Rose asked me if I saw Ignatius hiding any in his room."

"The great fennel-flavored, fluoride-free toothpaste mystery," I told him, hoping sarcastic hyperbole would diminish its importance. "Rose goes way out of her way to get this special toothpaste, and Auntie An hoards it, and then suddenly it's gone. Auntie An accuses Ignatius of stealing the toothpaste and selling it on the street. One time she said that she stumbled and accidentally dropped a whole tube into the digester."

"Weird."

"That's Auntie An for you." I walked to the window to close the curtain, which was when I saw two compliance officers driving up the street. They stopped out front.

I whirled around to face Bandon. "You've been breached," I said, my breath coming fast.

"What?"

I pulled him out of his chair. "Mr. Nabli must have snitched. Or they got info from your credit charge last night."

"Who? Compliance officers? There's a law against randomly pulling personal information like that."

I grabbed his hand. "Not during a state of emergency, I bet. Get out of here. Hide in the old garage. It's boarded up on the outside, but you can squeeze into it from the basement, and Tillamook should keep them from looking too closely. Behind what's left of the shelves there's a door to the garage. I think it still opens."

The Sentry Mat buzzed.

"I'll stall them. Hurry! Get your shoes from the back door. There's glass down there."

The Sentry Mat buzzed again.

"Coming," I called.

CHAPTER EIGHTEEN

I took my time disarming the Sentry Mat, then slapped an inno-cent look on my face. "What can I do for you?"

A white guy with a shaved head and T-shaped, double-bit ax tattoo over his right ear waved a paper in front of the Sentry Mat's entry screen. His partner, an Asian woman, probably Chinese, said, "We're here at the request of the Resilience Council. May we come in, please?"

"My grandmother and housekeeper aren't home," I told them, in little-kid mode. "I'm not supposed to open the door to strangers."

"We'll be only a few minutes," the woman said. She looked at her MyCom. "There is a ScrutinEyes registered to a Jessa Einhorn Zarfati at this address. If you'd be more comfortable, we'll wait here until you can use the ScrutinEyes to verify our identities."

The perfect stall. "Good idea," I said. "I'll be right back."

I took my time bringing the ScrutinEyes downstairs and ad-justing its visor to scan the faces through the door's security win-dow. Seven precious minutes later, the guy (ScrutinEyesed as Alex Kingsdale, fifty-four, former Portland police lieutenant, and fanatic

Timbers soccer fan) paced in front of my nutriculture wall in the living room and looked ready to arrest every veggie in sight. The woman (ScrutinEyesed as Francine Chin, twenty-nine, part-time librarian, president of Canines for Kids, and mother of two minors) smiled in that "we're here to help" way. I wondered if she saw me as Asian too, because of my eyes, or black, because of my hair texture and skin color, or blend, because that's what I really was.

I smiled back. "Can I get you both a cup of coffee and a slice of homemade zucchini bread? It's very good."

Library Lady looked ready to say yes, but AxTat shook his head. He waved the paper in my face again.

"We have reason to believe that a Bandon Falconer is on the premises," AxTat warned, his eyes narrowing in a way that made me think Bigot was his middle name. "We have the right to escort him outside the ten-kilometer boundary of his exclusion order. My colleague will take the basement. You and I will start on the third floor. External surveillance has already taken care of the roof."

I shifted to concerned-citizen mode. "This is a credit-tenant residence with official boarders. You have no right to search their rooms."

Library Lady sighed. "The Council is still vested with emergency powers. I'm sure you understand." She walked toward the kitchen.

I crossed my arms over my chest. "The basement is filled with broken glass. There's nothing down there but a temporary shelter for a buck that's servicing my doe. Smell for yourself."

"I have to check just the same," Library Lady said. "Thanks for the warning."

AxTat touched his FEMA armband. "Let's go."

I left the ScrutinEyes visor on the dining room table, and we plodded up the servants' stairs to the third floor. I unlocked the two bedrooms and play area and watched AxTat eyeball every corner.

We headed for the second floor, which was when I remembered that Ignatius was still home. I glanced at the stun stick holstered on AxTat's hip and shivered.

I unlocked Auntie An's room and opened the door, letting the musky smell of weed waft into the hall. AxTat inhaled deeply, smiled, and took his time searching through her things. Ten minutes later, we walked through Grandma's room, where he stopped long enough to admire her unicorns. He got super thorough in Jessa's room, snooping in her bathroom and walk-in closet. I pocketed my fists to avoid slapping his hands away from my mother's clothes.

AxTat headed for Ignatius's room.

"That boarder isn't feeling well," I said, cutting in front of him before he could knock on the door. "We shouldn't disturb him."

"We are going to disturb him," AxTat said. "Now. No more stalling from the likes of you, understood?"

I turned my back on him. "Understood," I said, and then I knocked on Ignatius's door. "Mr. Rivera, there's a compliance officer here with me. He just wants to check your room for a minute. You haven't done anything wrong. Mind if we come in?"

No answer.

I knocked louder.

First a groan, then a pustule of expletives. The door opened halfway. Ignatius leaned out. "Gotta get to the latrine," he said.

The nanosecond after he left, I slipped into the room ahead of AxTat. Bandon's sleeping bag, backpack, fake shackles, and assorted clutter practically screamed, "Falconer is here!"

I stepped in front of Bandon's gear. "Satisfied?"

AxTat eyed the room slowly and nodded. "I think we're going to wrap this up real soon now," he said.

Ignatius wobbled back, bleary-eyed, in an old Army undershirt and sweatpants.

AxTat slid a finger across his stun stick. "You know a Bandon Falconer." More like a statement than a question.

Ignatius stood at attention. "Sir."

"That's not an answer, Mr. Rivera. These items by the dresser, they belong to you?"

Ignatius stared at the wall a meter above my head. "Corporal Ignatius Rivera, United States Army, RA768-47-1390."

"I'm not asking for name, rank, and serial number, soldier. I'm asking whether Falconer is staying here with you. A simple yes or no."

Ignatius continued to stare.

AxTat swooped around me, grabbed Bandon's backpack, and held it in front of Ignatius. "This doesn't look like yours, does it?"

"Please leave Mr. Rivera alone," I sputtered. "Those things are probably from his time on the street."

AxTat glared at me. "I'm not asking you." He rounded on Ignatius. "So, soldier?"

"Corporal Ignatius Rivera, United States Army, RA768-47-1390."

I couldn't tell whether Ignatius was toying with AxTat or imagining he was back on the battlefield. Sadness swept over me. "Honorable discharge," I added. "Check his record." My heart pounded in my throat.

AxTat tossed Bandon's backpack on the floor, rummaged through the closet, and checked under the mattress. Ignatius didn't budge.

"Hell with it," AxTat said finally as he strode past us into the hall.

"At ease," I whispered to Ignatius. "Good job, Corporal."

He winked at me, not as out of it as I'd feared. I winked back and mouthed, "Thank you."

I caught up with AxTat on the main stairs and unlocked the door to the library, now Rose's postquake room on the first floor. Three pairs of shoes were lined up under our books and infoscreens on Turkey and next to the large suitcase that contained all of her clothes. Her bed was jammed against the shelves housing our Golden Books Centennial collection. Jessa adored those books. *The Poky Little Puppy was 101 when you were born, lovey.* I used to wonder how he could still be a puppy.

When AxTat was done, we met Library Lady in the kitchen. "Nothing in the basement," she reported. "Except one stink-pot of a goat."

I aimed a smile at the kitchen floor.

They handed me a contact card and warned me that Bandon

might be dangerous. Once I was sure they'd gone, I opened the basement door and called to Bandon to come out of hiding. He emerged with a grin so broad that his beard practically tickled his ears.

Ebullient. A Jessa word. Bubbling over with enthusiasm. He waved to me. "Come down here. You've got to see what I found in the garage."

I hadn't been inside the garage since forever. Plus there was still a lot of broken glass. My feet tingled. "Describe it."

"You've got to see for yourself," he said. "Remember we were looking for your mom's coins? And we found that graduation card in the safe, but the coins weren't there?"

"So?"

"And your mom had written 'McPherson' on the card, and no one knew who or what McPherson was?"

"You're dragging this out, and it smells like Tillamook down here. Get to the point."

Bandon jerked his thumb toward the garage. "The point is I found McPherson."

CHAPTER NINETEEN

I scrambled to the bottom step. "McPherson? You found the guy?"

Bandon's eyebrows danced. "McPherson is a thing."

"Well, then, bring it over."

"No can do. McPherson is attached to the garage."

After I took Tillamook outside and tethered him to Chicken Hacienda, I followed Bandon past our bank of storage batteries and a gauntlet of basement debris. We squeezed through the partly opened door to the garage, and he pointed to a spot near four shriveled tires resting against a cracked cement wall. "McPherson."

I studied an old plaque at the base of the wall. White rime accented what was stamped into the thick metal:

W.G. MCPHERSON
CO
47 FIRST STREET
PORTLAND, ORE
NO 2

"It looks like a builder's plate," Bandon said.

My fingers slid over the lettering and the raised rectangular frame around the edges. Two triangular pieces sat on one side of the plaque opposite a small circular knob on the other side. Hinges. A door.

"It's the ashbin from when our fireplaces worked ages ago," I said. "They collected the ash in the chute down here."

We found a rag and an old oilcan to lubricate the hinges. The metal door screeched open. Whatever I imagined a grave might smell like at midnight—acrid and sinister—that's the odor that came whooshing out of the chute. Powdery gray ash assaulted my nose and eyes. Sneezing made things worse.

Bandon let out a triumphant "Yes!"

A leather bag the size of an apricot hung from a hook screwed into the chute. I reached for the bag and emptied its contents—Jessa's two coins—into my hand. The silver one looked ancient, with a man's face on one side and a cross of some sort on the other. The second coin—bronze—was larger and smooth on the back, with a profile of a young woman's face and bustline on the front. A strand of pearls and elaborate headscarf adorned her hair. Her earrings might have been a loop of pearls around a gemstone.

Serakh's coin.

I shivered.

Bandon grinned. "The Ladies will be ecstatic."

I stared at the girl's face. "Don't tell them. Or Rose. Don't say anything about this. I'm not ready."

"Ready for what?"

My pulse kicked into hyperdrive. "We're putting the bag back where we found it. My house, my rules."

"What's up, Meryem?" Bandon held out his hand. "You've been on edge since yesterday. Maybe I can help."

I turned away and hugged myself. "There's nothing you can do."

"Is it about your mom?"

"Just leave it, okay?"

"Whatever you say." Bandon wandered over to examine a vintage bicycle pump.

My pulse slowed. I recalculated. Better to have Serakh's coin upstairs than down here. I might want it in a hurry. If Serakh came back, I might be able to use it. Maybe her guide, whoever that was, had information about Jessa. I stuffed the coin inside the top of my FemForm, then closed the bag with the silver coin inside, rehung the bag, and shut the ashbin door.

Bandon and I dusted off and headed upstairs to the kitchen. Rose and The Ladies were there—the last people I wanted to see right then.

"We were surveying the damage in the basement and the garage," I said in answer to their questioning looks. Serakh's coin pressed against my left breast.

Rose brushed gray-white powder from my hair. "Did you find a vial of Mount St. Helens ash down there?" She laughed. "Remember when we got so worried about the St. Helens dome-building five years ago? Give me another volcanic eruption over an earthquake anytime."

Bandon cleared his throat. "Meryem and I were in the basement because I hid there when a couple of compliance officers came looking for me. Meryem saved my…derrière."

"Oh, you poor dear," Auntie An said, touching Bandon's arm. "What would have happened if they'd found you?"

Bandon reached for a piece of the pear leather that Rose kept in a jar on the kitchen counter. "They probably would have escorted me out of Portland and slapped me with a fine I wouldn't pay." He offered me a piece, but I shook my head. I had eaten way too much dried fruit in the first months after The Big One.

Grandma pressed her hands against the table the way she did when she was about to make a pronouncement—one that she'd stick to no matter what. "Young man," she said, "we appreciate your bringing the goat here and your assistance with home repairs, but we must be careful. Merry, fetch me that gizmo you left on the dining room table."

My stomach lurched. "The ScrutinEyes? Grandma, that's ridiculous."

Auntie An scowled and muttered something in Vietnamese.

Rose faced Grandma. "Ly Tien, don't you think this is overkill?"

Grandma's fingertips tapped the table. "This is none of your business. I have a responsibility to protect my granddaughter."

Rose's eyes flashed. She stormed out of the kitchen.

"It's okay," Bandon told me. "Honest. Go on, Meryem. Zucker me good."

Grandma arched her eyebrows in annoyance at the Z-word. Auntie An smirked.

"It's my mother's," I explained to Bandon. "I used it on the compliance officers to stall them."

Bandon smiled while I focused the ScrutinEyes on him for two seconds and waited for infobits to march across the inside of my visor. DATA RETRIEVAL: BANDON THEODOSIOS FALCONER...

"What is his natal date?"

"Auntie An!" My face grew warm.

"My natal date?" No longer needing to stand still, Bandon snagged another a piece of pear leather.

"She means your birthday," I said.

"Oh. September 10, 2039." Which confirmed what the ScrutinEyes had already streamed.

"Aha! 2039. The year of the goat in the Chinese calendar. Some say ram or sheep, but I prefer goat. September is the month of the rooster. Perfect." Auntie An patted Bandon's cheek. "What time of day?"

"I have no idea," he said.

Auntie An studied him. "Pity. Merry is pig-tiger-dragon, a compatible combination for you, if you treat her with great kindness."

Apparently for all her cryptic powers, Auntie An hadn't picked up that he was gay. Or maybe she'd chosen to ignore that fact.

Bandon laughed. "Definitely."

Auntie An took his hand. "Come sit with me in the living room while Merry tells my sister a shitload of information that is less important than your natal date. 'Shitload' is what young people used to say. Do they still say that now?"

Grandma stayed at the kitchen table, her arms crossed. I

summarized each feed as it streamed across the visor. "He's got a mother and younger brother in Bethesda, Maryland. An older sister works for a museum in New York City. His father died in a traffic accident in 2056."

I closed my eyes and pictured those run-down Doc Martens that Bandon cherished. No wonder.

"What else, Merry?"

I scanned the feed again. "There's a cat named Che Guevara. Fully vaccinated—that's Bandon, probably the cat too. No known allergies. He went to George Washington University for a semester, and did his year of national service working at a homeless shelter. And he won an award at the Appalachian Folk Music Festival in 2053."

The ScrutinEyes reached the criminal matrix. **20570413: CONVICTION/FINE—DISTURBING THE PEACE.**

My mouth turned sour. "Buffering," I said. "The feed must have gotten scrambled."

Grandma waited.

Two more hits streamed across the visor. **20570827: CONVICTION/FINE—VANDALISM. 20580103: CONVICTION/COMMUNITY SERVICE—DISTURBING THE PEACE.**

"Merry, is there anything about a criminal record?"

I didn't skip a beat. "No, Grandma." Who knew what she'd do if I told her the truth? Rose was right. Bandon was good company. He probably had a good explanation, plus he'd never gone to jail.

I clicked off the ScrutinEyes. "Let's save him from Auntie An. He's had more than enough scrutiny for one day."

"I'm glad to see you taking an interest in something other than chores," Grandma said, now in mellow mode. "Tomorrow you and Bandon should continue the hunt for Jessa's coins. They must be here somewhere."

I bit my lip.

CHAPTER TWENTY

Jessa used to play this game with me when I was little and bathed in the tub. I'd dunk my head underwater while she knocked on the tub or made noises. Everything sounded distorted, as if it came from an alien world.

That's how I felt for the rest of the day—underwater, only this time there was nothing fun about the experience. I stashed Jessa's ScrutinEyes behind the washing machine instead of returning it to Jessa's bedroom, in case Serakh suddenly appeared there. The more I thought about what had happened—or didn't happen—the more confused I became. So I kept busy, always managing to have Rose or Bandon nearby. Then I sat through dinner listening to conversations, still underwater.

"...isn't that right, Meryem?" Auntie An eyed me expectantly.

I looked up from my dessert, having no idea what she'd asked. Her dyed red hair reminded me of Izabel's dead mistress and the henna story. How could Izabel exist? How could she not exist?

Rose grabbed my hand. "You're putting chocolate pudding in your tea!"

I stared at the brown glob oozing down the inside of my teacup. "Go to bed, Merry," Grandma said. "You've pushed yourself too hard again."

I probably said something inane as I left the table and stopped to linger by Jessa's rug, studying its complex patterns of dragons and other strange animals in a forest of stylized flowers. *"Lovey, I bought this especially for you. Don't you wish we had a pet dragon?"* I touched an intricate design in the bottom corner, the one I'd seen Jessa touch again and again. This rug and I were waiting for Jessa's touch. We'd been waiting a long time.

I went upstairs, took a centering breath, and opened the door to Jessa's room. No Serakh. The underwater feeling drained away. I cuddled into a nightgown, put Rose's oil on my feet, adjusted my silicone footpads, and rubbed the red-rimmed circle that Serakh's coin had etched into my flesh. I scanned the coin's image into my vidscreen and set Query's response to written rather than Aussie Jack.

The download was enormous: The coin was actually a bronze portrait medal—all the rage in medieval Europe—that an Italian artist had made when the girl on the medal was eighteen. Her name was Gracia Nasi. Historians called her Gracia La Chica or simply La Chica—the little one—because her famous aunt, Doña Gracia Nasi, had the same name. Doña Gracia was an international banker with connections throughout Europe. The family were wealthy Sephardic Jews from Portugal who fled from the Inquisition to various European cities and came to Istanbul in the 1550s. Doña Gracia sponsored synagogues and helped resettle other Sephardic refugees—meaning those from Spain and nearby areas. Eventually Sephardic Jewish culture overshadowed the traditions of the Jews who had lived in Turkey for generations.

I ran my finger over Gracia's face and wondered if her family had known the Zarfatis, who were also Sephardic—they'd come from Córdoba, Spain—and had fled to Turkey. Were we related?

I tucked my prayer shawl and the portrait medal under my pillow, clapped out the light, and waited. I'd avoided meeting Serakh all day, but now, somehow, I felt compelled to confront her.

Sleep was out of the question. Wind screeched through loose bricks in the chimney. The top sheet grabbed at my feet. My quilt nearly smothered me. Suddenly I couldn't stay in bed another nanosecond.

I dressed in my FemForm, over-tee, and hiking boots, took the portrait medal and my prayer shawl, and headed downstairs in the dark. A moment later, I heard the click-click-whirr of the GR-17 shifting into operation mode after sensing motion and sound. I hurried to Gryffindor, pressed our code and IGNORE, and set the bot to restart in three hours, at exactly 4:33. Then I disarmed and unlocked the front door, made a cup of pudding-free tea, and sat at the dining room table.

"I have it," I told the darkness. "I have your damn coin. Whatever is happening to me, bring it on."

I sat. And sat. The old house creaked. The street outside was eerily quiet, thanks to the curfew. The sleep that was impossible in the Jessa nest crept up on me. I leaned over the table, pillowed my prayer shawl, and sank into oblivion.

Later, I smelled goats, sweeter than the Tillamook stink. I knew before I opened my eyes.

Serakh sat next to me with two cucumbers in her hand. "I have gleaned these from your wall," she said. She held a cucumber under my nose. "Have one."

I shook my head, oddly relieved to see her.

"Then I shall eat both and be grateful for your hospitality. When I am done and you are ready, let us cross."

I showed her Gracia's portrait medal. "I can't deal with your crazy crossing business. If I give this to you, will you tell me everything you know about Jessa?"

"I have told you all," she said. Which was basically nothing.

"How about The One, that guide of yours?"

Serakh licked her fingers. "You are entwined with Izabel. You possess something more that we need to redeem Izabel. I do not know what. I trust that there is something that Izabel will bestow upon you as well."

Her soft tone grated on me. I clenched my jaw. "Unless she can bestow Jessa on me, I'm not interested."

Serakh wiped her fingers on her robe. "Always the second time feels easier on the body but is harder on the mind. Yet that which we cannot explain fills the universe around us."

She sounded like Auntie An.

Serakh pointed to the prayer shawl I'd used as a pillow. "For the sake of Izabel and for Jessa and for your own sake, step into the *olam* with me. You will see once more what your mind refuses to accept. I have not asked you to believe, Meryem. I have asked you to take a step."

Take a step. I stared at Serakh's sandaled feet. Jessa used to quote from a famous French priest-paleontologist whenever someone asked her about unicorns: "*Instead of standing on the shore and proving to ourselves that the ocean cannot carry us, let us venture on its waters just to see.*"

Pierre Teilhard de Chardin. That was the man's name. Jessa admired his work. She would have stepped into the unknown just to see. I gave Gracia's portrait medal to Serakh and reached for the blue thread.

CHAPTER TWENTY-ONE

Aching, exhausted, I slouched against that same wicker basket in that same tulip-tiled space. Serakh crouched nearby as if she'd done this a sextillion times. Maybe she had.

"Let us approach Ayele," she said. "You will be my mistress, and I your slave. I will say that I have reported Izabel's worth and that you are ready to buy Izabel using this rare coin."

I struggled to sit up. "Now you're my slave, and I'm buying another slave? That's disgusting."

Serakh nodded. "It is the custom of this place and time, this spot in the *olam*. I will bargain, as in the marketplace, and pretend to fear your displeasure if I do not succeed. This will fit with what Ayele knows of mistresses and slaves."

I rubbed a stitch in my left side and rolled my shoulders, checking to see that my body was still in one piece, although my brain felt fractured. "Ayele?"

Serakh began to pull clothes out of the basket. "Remember? He is the black eunuch Izabel speaks of. He controls her fate. Izabel belongs to the sultan, and the sultan cares for her less than for the fleas on his dogs. If Ayele sells Izabel, no one will notice that she is gone. If we leave her in his care, he will soon fetch a high price for her from men who are not interested in her embroidery. Ayele relaxes alone in an anteroom to the harem. We must hurry."

How could this be happening...again?

Serakh raised a large rectangular scarf to my face. "We will hide your hair and cover your face with a veil in the style of rich and proper Muslim ladies in public."

In two minutes she had me dolled up even fancier than when we had met Izabel. I could barely see out of the veil that fluttered in front of my face, and my feet balked at the wooden platform sandals Serakh said only Muslim women were allowed to wear. "It makes them taller and keeps their feet from the filth on the streets," she explained. "Ayele will notice your sandals and think highly of you."

I insisted on keeping my socks—luckily a plain gray pair this time—and Serakh reluctantly agreed. She grabbed my wrist and rushed me down a long corridor, my feet complaining and those ridiculous sandals sliding on the polished floor. As we paused in an archway, she lifted my chin.

"Hold yourself erect. Do not look at Ayele directly. Show no interest in the transaction. At the end of the bargaining, nod your head as if you have procured a laying hen at a good price. Leave Izabel to me until we are well away."

I thought about Louise, Tillie, and Yetta, whose lives were more secure at Chicken Hacienda than this little girl in the sultan's palace. "Suppose he won't sell her? This is only a portrait medal. It's not a real a coin, you know."

Serakh frowned. "The One has guided me to you," she said, as if that would solve everything.

She didn't know the coin was a fake. What else had she gotten wrong? Who was she anyway? I grabbed Serakh's arm. "Wait a minute. You keep talking about taking orders from The One. Maybe I'd better speak to The One directly."

"Now?"

"Yes." I tried to sound sure of myself, which I wasn't. "Now. Or I'm not seeing Ayele."

"Let it be so." Serakh flexed her knees, bowed her head, and, in the softest of whispers, began to chant. The melody was unfamiliar, but the words sounded similar to Hebrew. Apparently she thought they didn't need translating. She looked at me once, as if expecting that I would be chanting too.

I bowed my head. My breath slowed, and I felt an odd sense of complete well-being—and of clarity. At Havurah Shalom, we prayed to The Eternal One, The Abundant One, The All-Merciful One, to all sorts of names.

"God," I said a moment later. "The One is God. You're praying to God."

She lifted her head toward me. "Have you spoken directly?"

"I suppose so," I said, putting my hand on my heart, feeling unsure and absolutely certain at the same time. "I'm ready."

A thin old man, darker-skinned than I, lounged on a pile of pillows next to a tray of fruit-colored squares. Marzipan. Jessa had told me that marzipan was centuries older than Turkish delight. She seemed so close I could almost smell her.

I fixed my eyes on the marzipan as Serakh's voice echoed in the tiled room. Ayele and Serakh bargained over Izabel the way Jessa had probably bargained in the Grand Bazaar for her prayer rug, or some white slaveholder had bargained over black children on the Mississippi side of my family. Bile rose in my throat.

At one point I heard Serakh say, "You have your pick of so many girls, and you will find another. Behold, this coin is from Ferrara and of great value. See how large it is, written in two languages, Latin and Hebrew. A marvel."

Ayele's ringed hand reached for another square of marzipan. "The coin is a trinket."

I swallowed the bitter taste rising from my guts. This wouldn't end well.

"The Jewess Esther brings such trinkets to the harem," he continued. "Even she would not dare to trade in a medal bearing the likeness of another Jewess. If the sultan, may his wealth increase a thousand-fold, saw this abomination, my head could wind up on a pike."

Serakh signaled to me that negotiations had reached an impasse. I turned on my heel, as best as I could in those sandals, and paraded through the archway. Serakh caught up with me and guided me through a maze of halls and rooms to the niche with our clothes basket.

I eased out of the sandals and rubbed my toes through my socks. "Now what?"

Serakh emptied the clothes on the rug. "We will turn to our own people, the Jews."

"You mean Lady Esther?"

Serakh traded my wooden platform sandals for felted slippers. "I have learned much since I saw you last. Esther Handali, the widow of Rabbi Eliya, had great influence with the sultan's wife. Now Hürrem Sultan is dead, and Esther does not trade with the women of the harem. We must seek Jews who have influence with the sultan. One of them will redeem Izabel for us."

She took off my veil. "Only Muslim women are allowed this in public. You will use a large scarf to cover your hair and part of your face. You will be my servant, and I your mistress."

"No. My black great-grandfather would turn over in his grave."

Serakh nodded. "Let it be so. We go as companions to Galata, on the north side of the water across from Topkapı Palace. The girl on the coin has arrived there from Ferrara with her new husband, Don Samuel, at a place they call Belvedere."

I rubbed my forehead, trying to remember what I'd read. "If Gracia and Don Samuel just came, it must be 1559 or 1560." Which made sense given the way everything looked and what Izabel had told us. If you could call any of this sense.

Serakh wrapped an ochre sash around the top of my trousers. "Let us hope that Gracia will be as welcoming as she is beautiful.

Cover yourself with this woolen outer garment as protection from the wind over the water. We travel by ferry across the Golden Horn inlet of the Bosporus, and then by foot or donkey cart to Belevdere."

No one stopped us as we walked under the cypress trees through Topkapı's main courtyard crowded with high-turbaned janissaries and men in a wild assortment of brightly colored robes and trousers. The air felt cool, with a nip that promised a chilly night, like Portland in late fall. Shifting breezes mixed the heady smell of late-blooming flowers and freshly baked bread with the musky scent of caged animals from the menagerie by St. Irene's Church. I thought of Izabel telling me about the sultan's unicorns and resolved to check out the menagerie later. Just to make sure. She couldn't have been right.

A kestrel perched on the stone wall circling us—a gorgeous bird, female, with light chestnut plumage and dark striping. Probably *Falco tinnunculus*. She must have been looking for mice or voles, and there would be hundreds in the area, living by the sultan's kitchens that Jessa said had fed thousands of people every day. If only the person holding my elbow were my mother!

As we paced through the courtyard, I caught sight of an odd rectangular marble fountain—more like an ornate spigot—set into a wall. Curious, I stepped away from Serakh and walked to the fountain. There was something odd about it. Austere. A swarm of houseflies buzzed nearby.

"Stay on the path next to me," Serakh called, her voice anxious.

I pointed to the fountain when I got back to her. "Are you supposed to wash your feet when you enter the courtyard?"

Serakh buried her face in my ear. "That is the fountain of the executioner. Say nothing more about it. Fix your gaze on the path as we walk though the front gate."

Those flies kept annoying me, and I smelled something rotten. I looked up, and that's when I saw them—three straw-stuffed heads skewered on pikes. Maggots feasted on decaying eyeballs. Putrescence oozed from withered lips.

Serakh wrenched my face toward hers. "Look at me," she

ordered. "Swallow. Breathe. Show no sign that you feel ill. The guards are watching us. Pretend that you see this every day, as many do when they pass between the city and the palace."

I gagged but managed to hold vomit inside my mouth.

"Brave girl. Now let us walk through the gate."

I willed myself to take fifteen steps outside before stumbling into an alley and spilling my guts into an open sewer. Afterward, I steadied myself and wiped my mouth with the back of my hand. Serakh reached into her robes and handed me several sprigs of lavender wrapped in cloth. "Cover your nose against the strong odors of the city."

I held her elbow as we picked our way down a winding street. Wooden buildings crowded in, their windows shuttered, and their second and sometimes third stories leaning over the first like overgrown shrubbery, blotting out the sun. Finally we reached an open area with a public fountain and mosque. A man was selling sesame-coated loops of dough stacked on a pole he carried over his shoulder.

Comfort food. My stomach quieted. "This is *simit*," I said. "It's a cross between a bagel and a pretzel. Jessa eats *simit* a lot when she's in Istanbul."

I rinsed my mouth in the fountain while Serakh bought us *simit* to share. "Let us be on our way," she said. "It is nearly midday, and I want to reach Belvedere before dusk."

I suppose I should have taken in everything around me, like the tourist I always wanted to be with Jessa. Instead I clutched the lavender to my face and focused on the path around my feet. A misstep could land me in a mound of dung or pool of slime. I rarely looked up, afraid of seeing another severed head.

Sounds threatened to overwhelm me. Braying, barking, screeching, and the yowl of cats, cats, and more cats. And then there were the people.

A woman's voice, rasping and urgent, "Spare me a coin, honorable lady, may Allah praise your kindness."

A man shouting, "Sheep heads. Sheep heads here. Hot from the spit."

Another man, his voice deep and threatening, "Tell her if she refuses to spread her legs again, I will sell her to the brothel. Let her rot in a cage for the sailors to use as they will."

Serakh must have read my face, because she whispered, "The gift of communication brings you pain. I can spare you until we are at Belvedere."

"What?"

"The languages. I can lift this burden for now. You understand the languages around you because you are in my presence. I have the power to withhold that understanding. Shall I do that, except between us?"

I nodded. Human speech—all but Serakh's—turned to gibberish. Relieved, I waded through a surround-sound of noise and lavender-buffered smells. Every few minutes, when the lavender began to be cloying, I eased the cloth from my nose. Once I was rewarded by the sweet pungent smell of cardamom, and Serakh explained that we were near the Spice Market. Mostly the air reeked of waste, worse than during the first horrific days after The Big One. Then we walked downhill through an arched gate in a massive stone wall, and suddenly it smelled as if I'd fallen into a composter of rotting fish.

"The docks," Serakh said. "From here we cross to Galata. There are fishermen in this section. The rougher sailors are further east, facing Asia across the Bosporus."

"The sailors with the caged women."

Serakh sighed. "I pray Izabel escapes that fate. Come, let us find passage."

I shuddered. If Bandon were with us, he would have reminded me that human trafficking was still a fact of life five hundred years later, even in Portland. My guts threatened to be sick again.

We crowded onto a wooden ferry that could comfortably hold eight and managed to squeeze in twenty. Two men with their heads wrapped in rags rather than turbans rowed us away from the dock and raised a tattered sail to catch the wind. I turned my back on the rest of the passengers and gulped in relatively fresh air.

Serakh touched my shoulder. "Meryem, this is the best time to care for our needs. I will hold the cloak for privacy while you relieve yourself. Then you will do the same for me."

"You're kidding," I said, although I could see she wasn't.

"You pretend not to be doing what you are doing," Serakh added. "Others will pretend not to see you doing this."

After a few minutes, modesty lost out to a bursting bladder. I handed my woolen cloak to Serakh. Afterward, I said, "And people fish here?"

"As they have for centuries," she said.

"Remind me to stick to *simit*." I looked back at Istanbul proper and remembered Jessa's photo of a similar skyline from a bridge yet to be built over the waterway I was on. She and I were seeing the same massive walls surrounding the city as they had for a thousand years. And there was Topkapı Palace with *Aya Irini*—St. Irene's—in the enormous courtyard, and the companion church—now the mosque *Aya Sofia*—on the other side of the palace wall. Time seemed to fold in on itself. Jessa felt almost as close to me as the last time I vid-voiced her before The Big One. I clutched at my cloak.

"There is Galata Tower," Serakh said, pointing to a tall round building not far from the giant shipyards on the opposite shore. "Do you see the repairs from the last time the ground shook?"

"An earthquake? When?"

Serakh shrugged. "I do not know. There have been many. The survivors rebuild. Is it not so in your time and place? Look there. Men with donkey carts wait by the dock. If we are fortunate, one will take us to Belvedere."

We were fortunate. Very. Neither the donkey nor the boy who drove her looked diseased or malnourished. Judging from what I'd learned from my zoology EduComps, this animal's smooth, dark gray coat and relatively large size meant the breed was Anatolian. The boy, maybe seven or eight years old, treated her more like a pet than a beast of burden. His eyes widened at the coins Serakh offered for his services, so she must have overpaid him, which made me feel even better.

I settled myself on a rug-covered bale of straw and hoped the fleas were busy elsewhere. "I'm ready to understand the languages now," I told Serakh, who sat across from me, her eyes closing, her knees nearly touching mine.

"Let it be so," she murmured. "The boy says the journey is about an hour. He is eager and pleasant. I hope that he will use my extra payment to purchase a sweetmeat for himself and a carrot for the animal."

"Serakh, have you been to this side of the Golden Horn before?" Thanks to Query and Jessa, I knew that Galata, or Pera as the Greeks called it, was settled mostly by foreigners from Western Europe—diplomats and business magnates from Genoa and Venice, and wealthy people like Gracia's family.

Serakh shook her head. "Always I have been on the other side, among the emperors or the sultans, and once in the time of Atatürk. But I have been to Ferrara at the marriage of Gracia. That is where I got the coin for Miryam Tikvah, the woman who calls herself Hope."

I stared at her. "So you went to Ferrara in the fifteen hundreds and got this portrait medal to give to my great-grandmother in the nineteen hundreds, and then you came to me in 2059 to get the medal back, and now you're going to show it to the same family you probably got it from in the first place. Have I got that right?"

"Exactly so." Serakh glanced at the boy. "We are safe for now. You may rest." She looked half asleep already.

Riding in the donkey cart, my body felt exhausted, but my brain buzzed on hyperdrive, trying to tease logic out of absurdity. I was going to meet a girl whose portrait was cast in bronze five hundred years ago and given to my family by the person who slouched across from me snoring.

CHAPTER
TWENTY-TWO

We headed uphill through streets wider and straighter than those across the water, and through market squares matching my image of medieval France or Italy, with an occasional mosque. After we passed through a large arched gate in the city wall, the street gave way to a dirt road with meadowland on each side and a forest in the distance.

Finally, the boy coaxed his donkey—the two seemed to travel by mutual agreement—to turn into a lane lined with evenly spaced cypress trees. Pebbles and marble chips covered the dirt, changing the cart's thump-bump feel to a smoother ride. After a few hundred meters I saw what lay ahead—Renaissance Italy! If I hadn't stayed awake during every creak and jounce of the ride, I would have sworn we'd traveled through the *olam* again.

I touched Serakh's knee. "Wake up. We're almost there. They live in a huge stone villa. It's gorgeous."

Serakh blinked into wakefulness as the boy stopped the cart by a massive wooden door wide enough for the cart to go through. The door had a smaller, human-sized door cut in the bottom. Serakh thanked the boy and sent him on his way. She didn't pull the bell cord until he'd disappeared around a curve in the drive.

The old man who opened the door could have stepped out of a Renaissance fair. He wore a square-topped, felted-wool hat instead of a turban. A brown velvet doublet hugged his chest and waist.

"I bid you welcome to Belvedere," he said, but his eyes registered annoyance. "The path by the fountain leads to the kitchen. There is a hearty broth today and bread, with the compliments of La Señora."

I knew from Query that the man meant Gracia's aunt, Doña Gracia Nasi, who reputedly fed dozens of poor people at her home every day.

Serakh brushed away a blade of straw that clung to her robes. "We are grateful for your hospitality, but we have not come for food. We are here to see La Señora on a matter of urgency."

After a dismissive look—probably at our dusty clothes and lack of jewelry—the man announced, "La Señora is not receiving visitors."

Serakh reached into her pouch. In a slow and ceremonious manner, she extracted Gracia's portrait medal and held her palm under the man's nose. "Please tell La Señora that a Jewish woman from Ferrara has arrived and must speak with her on behalf of a captive girl in need of her generosity."

The man stared at Gracia's likeness. "Yes, madam." He bowed slightly and ushered us into a small square room with wooden chairs and tables. Tapestries hung on the walls. The only evidence that we were in Galata and not Western Europe was a bouquet of deep red tulips in a porcelain vase that reminded me of the Iznik bowl Mr. Nabli had given me for my birthday.

The man left after telling us that someone would attend to our needs. I barely had time to adjust my scarf and settle in a straight-backed chair before he returned to watch over us as if we might steal the large brass candlesticks on the sideboard. Serakh sat silently, and I did the same. Two birds—larks, judging from their high-pitched trill—sang outside the open window.

A few minutes later, a middle-aged woman with an impressive collection of large metal keys hanging from her waist appeared in the doorway. Her white blouse, tight blue bodice, and full gray skirt would have been at home in one of the old paintings by Titian or Breugel that Jessa had insisted I study for an EduComps arts credit. From what I'd seen on Query, the woman standing before us wasn't Gracia's aunt.

"Thank you, Jacov," she said. "I will attend to our guests."

Serakh must have realized this as well. "Kindly inform your mistress that I am Serakh, daughter of Asher," she said. "We have met at the celebration of her niece's marriage to Don Samuel in Ferrara, where I received this coin. My traveling companion and I must speak with La Señora at once."

The keys woman sighed. "I regret that is not possible. La Señora suffers from an attack of catarrh, and the doctor has ordered a bloodletting. La Señora must not be disturbed."

Serakh's lips narrowed into a thin line. "I have learned many healing arts and will relieve the suffering of your mistress. I will go alone so as to disturb La Señora as little as possible."

Until now, Serakh had rarely let me out of her sight. I stifled my confusion as the three of us walked through the main hall and out into a garden overlooking the Bosporus about ten meters down the hillside. The keys woman led me to a sun-warmed marble bench under a grape arbor. I felt my shoulders relax and a slight smile crinkle my face. Better to be here than in someone's sick room.

"I could not chance your becoming ill with a disease not of your time and place," Serakh whispered. "I will return as soon as I have arranged for Izabel's redemption. While I am gone, you will lose the gift of communication. They are speaking Ladino. Do you know this language?"

I rubbed a spot where my scarf itched the side of my neck. "I know a few words from the Zarfati side of the family. I speak

Spanish pretty well, and it's not that different. Besides, no one's out here."

After Serakh left, I loosened my scarf, lifted my face toward the shafts of sunlight gliding between the grape leaves, and shut my eyes. The arbor felt peaceful, a safe place far from heads on pikes and threats to put women in cages. My shoulders relaxed as I listened to the larks in full song, accompanied by a screech of gulls. I imagined Tillie, Yetta, and Louise adding amiable clucks to the conversation, and I wondered whether Jessa had visited this part of Galata during her trips to Istanbul. She would have liked it here.

I didn't know how long I'd been resting with my eyes closed when I heard a female voice say something about *higos*. Or *figos*. Figs. I peered out from the vines. There she was, about five meters away, plucking the rosy brown fruit from its large-leafed tree and handing it an old woman carrying a woven basket.

My pulse double-timed. I'd seen this girl before. Same nose. Same mouth. Gracia. My family's bronze portrait medal had come to life.

CHAPTER TWENTY-THREE

I retreated to a more secluded spot where Gracia likely wouldn't notice me. She was shorter than I expected and even more beautiful. Skin a golden wheat color. Deep rich brown hair piled up under jeweled netting. Pearl droplet earrings the size of almonds. A silver-and-turquoise brocade gown scooped low and tight across breasts that looked like they needed more breathing space.

Keeping myself hidden, I strained to catch the conversation. Gracia was doing most of the talking. The older woman, less elegantly dressed, was nodding more in acknowledgment, it seemed, than with enthusiasm. Gracia said something about a jewel or brooch misplaced on her trip from Ferrara, then something about new linens for Don Samuel's bed, and then something about feeding a kitten.

The older woman stopped nodding. I caught the word *pulgas*. She made a hopping motion with her thumb and middle finger.

Fleas. Stray cats had fleas. From what I'd already seen, Istanbul was Cat City. Lots of fleas, lots of disease.

Gracia was insistent. The kitten would be hers. Carina had died on the long journey—whoever Carina was—and this poor kitten looked lonely. The old woman glanced skyward but said nothing. I imagined that the kitten would be subjected to the most thorough anti-*pulgas* campaign a cat could survive.

Gracia picked another handful of figs and rattled off more instructions. I remembered from Query that Gracia's aunt ruled her life. Gracia was the heiress to a huge fortune. She'd been born in Antwerp, her family already on the run from the Inquisition. She'd married her cousin, Don Samuel, in Ferrara to keep the money in the family. The Duke of Ferrara had practically held her captive—he wanted to somehow invalidate the marriage and get his hands on her fortune. The Nasi family asked the sultan to intervene so she could join them in Istanbul. No wonder Gracia wanted a kitten.

The older woman hefted the basket of figs and left. A late afternoon breeze caressed my face. Gracia hugged herself as she stood in profile—the same pose as on the portrait medal—and looked out over the Bosporus to the coast of Asia, as far to the east as she'd ever been.

Forlorn. That's the vocabulary word Jessa would have used. More than just unhappy. Gracia exuded sadness. For all her wealth and comfort, she seemed lonely. She seemed to be waiting for someone who would never come, and that's when I remembered that her mother had died when Gracia was fifteen or sixteen.

I took a breath. After all these months since The Big One, I was so tired of waiting for Jessa and wondering about my future. It couldn't hurt to tell Gracia what I knew about hers. She wouldn't die of bubonic plague from fleas or have to run for safety again—Query had told me that and a lot more.

Still, I couldn't just spring out of the grape arbor like some oracle and tell her. Ridiculous. She'd probably freak out.

And yet.

Gracia sighed and started walking toward the manor.

I tightened my scarf and stepped out into the full sunlight. Pretending my Spanish was better than I knew it was, I cleared my throat and managed to sputter, "*Señora?*"

Gracia shaded her eyes and looked at the arbor. I took another step toward her, only one, so she wouldn't run away.

I called again. "*Señora?*"

This time our eyes met. She stiffened. I put on my most welcoming face and explained that I meant no harm. I was Jewish too. My family came from Africa and from China—close enough to the truth—which explained my eyes and skin tone. She had nothing to fear.

Gracia folded her arms across her chest. She demanded to know what I was doing at Belvedere. Making do with so-so Spanish, I explained that Serakh and I were guests of La Señora. I was able to tell the future—not bothering to add that I was from the future. I said that she would live a long life.

"*Mi vida?*" She tilted her head to one side.

"*Si, señora.*" Your life.

She stared at me and then thrust out her right hand palm up, an unmistakable sign. She wanted me to tell her fortune.

Auntie An would have accepted a palmistry session in a nanosecond. I'd let her read my palms a couple of times, but I didn't believe a word she said. And I hadn't paid attention.

"*Por favor,*" Gracia pleaded, her eyes softening. She told me that she longed to know what would happen to her in this new place.

We sat on the marble bench under the arbor. Knowing next to nothing about palmistry, I cradled Gracia's right palm in my left hand and pretended to study her lifelines. Her smooth skin smelled of lavender and almonds. The barest tang of sweat and onions clung to her brocade gown.

I inhaled, collecting all I remembered from Query, and began. I told Gracia that Istanbul would be her home for the rest of her life. She would be safe here and keep her wealth. She would have a child with Don Samuel. She would be happy. I added the happiness part. It couldn't hurt.

Gracia asked whether she'd have a son or a daughter, and I told her a daughter. She frowned. No sons? I told her that I was reading her palm as best as I could.

She asked if her cousin Reyna would have sons. I couldn't remember anything about Reyna, except that she was La Señora's daughter. I said I would have to see Reyna's palm first.

Gracia seemed satisfied. She assured me that this bad news about no male heir for Don Samuel meant that the rest must be true.

Tears welled up. I wanted to say how sorry I was that her mother had died, but I couldn't bear to talk about mothers then, hers or mine.

There was a rustle of robes.

Serakh stepped slightly ahead of the keys woman and dropped into a curtsy in front of Gracia. "I am deeply honored to meet you. May The One grant you long life and good health."

My cheeks burned. I'd done none of that. When I met Gracia, I must have seemed ridiculous.

"This is a healer from the East, good lady," the keys woman said. Since Serakh was back, so was that magical communication. I understood every word. "She will be staying the night with her assistant. I see that you have already met, I trust under amicable circumstances. La Señora has requested your immediate company."

Gracia smiled at me. "I am eager to meet you again at dinner."

The keys woman pursed her lips. "Perhaps in the morning, good lady. I have arranged for our guests to dine in their room so that they might retire early from their long journey."

Gracia touched one of her pearl earrings, her face registering defeat. "Then I will have the pleasure of seeing you again tomorrow morning, Señora…?"

"Señorita Meryem Zarfati y Einhorn," I said, using Grandma's maiden name because I had no idea who my father was. "I assure you that everything I foretold will come to pass."

The keys woman arched an eyebrow and motioned for Gracia to precede us inside. She escorted Gracia toward the stairs, while a young girl about Izabel's age led Serakh and me to a cramped room with one shuttered window. The girl walked with mincing steps, as if her felt slippers were too small, and I wondered whether her tightly bound headscarf was a sign of modesty or an attempt to contain a rampant infestation of lice. Her cheeks were plump and her clothes reasonably clean for a servant or kitchen maid. Was she safe here? I reminded myself that life was harder in sixteenth-century Istanbul than in my time and place. And then I remembered Calantha.

Except for two brass candlesticks with fat, unlit candles, the room featured one of everything. One small bed under a velvet canopy. One carved mahogany table with a matching chair. One water pitcher and washbasin. One linen towel. One chamber pot. I would rather have slept on a blanket in the grape arbor.

Two more servants appeared, one to light the candles with a glowing charcoal in a brass container and the other to leave us dinner—two goblets of red wine, a rounded loaf of bread, and a small roasted fowl of some sort. Chicken? I preferred to think the poor dead bird was pigeon or quail, and besides, I was hungry.

"We are too well respected to be sent to the kitchen with the servants," Serakh said after they left, cocooning us for the night. "But we are not deemed worthy enough to be invited into the dining room with the family. No one will come until morning." She took off her headscarf and let her long white braid dangle down her back. "You look unhappy at our meal."

"No utensils."

Serakh wiggled her fingers. "I have ten. Perhaps they do not trust us with the family's carving implements. Or there is a shortage since Gracia and her husband and servants have arrived. Come, let us eat while the bird is warm and succulent."

I sat on the bed since there was only one chair. "What happened about redeeming Izabel?"

"La Señora will see to Izabel's welfare. Tomorrow we will secure her safety." Serakh pushed the table closer to me and lifted the pitcher of water. "Will you hold the washbasin for me?"

The heavy ceramic bowl sat solid against my forearms as Serakh poured water over one hand, then the other, and murmured a prayer as she wiped her hands on the towel. Then she set the pitcher down, took the basin, and held it toward me.

"Like Passover," I said, remembering the Passover seders I had attended with Jessa. When I was little, my job was to walk around the seder table from one Zarfati relative to the next with a pitcher of water, a basin, and a towel. Each relative would pour water over their hands and use the towel to dry. The last person would take the basin and towel and pass the pitcher to me, so I could wash too.

Serakh's eyebrows arched.

"You know about Passover, don't you?" I hugged the pitcher to my chest. "The exodus from slavery in Egypt? The ten plagues? Moses parting the Sea of Reeds? Wandering in the desert for forty years? You're Jewish, aren't you?"

Serakh smiled. "Yes. I am of the tribe of Asher. I know of this time. I remember the cucumbers of Egypt with great fondness. It was hard to convince the elders that Moshe was sent by The One to free us. I showed them where to find the bones of my uncle Joseph when we left."

"You were there?" Nothing should have surprised me about Serakh by now. But still, I felt dizzy.

Serakh grabbed the pitcher before it would have hit the floor. "I was there. I wandered with the others and with Miryam the prophetess. I stood before Moshe and the elders with the daughters of Zelophehad and Miriam, daughter of Julius."

I shook my head. Finally I said, "I've accepted that this...this travel...can happen, because it's happening. But...who are you?"

She put the pitcher on the table. "I am someone's daughter, as are you. I am of a tribe and a family. My father Asher is a brother to Joseph. The One has guided me ever since I told my grandfather Jacob that Joseph was alive in Egypt. Your blue thread comes from Joseph's tunic. I do not understand the gifts I have received, and I also accept this travel because it is happening."

"Who's Miriam, daughter of Julius?"

Serakh sat next to me on the bed. "This surely you know. Her dwelling is your dwelling. She is kinswoman to Miryam Tikvah, who is entwined with the child of Dolcette and Avram. I do not know what entwines you with Izabel. The One will show us."

I sat, silent, trying to take all this in. Julius's daughter had to be Miriam Josefsohn. And Miryam Tikvah was Miriam Hope Einhorn, my great-grandmother. Miriam to Miriam to me. Candlelight flickered across the wine goblets.

Serakh rose from the bed and wiggled her fingers at me again. "Come. Our dinner grows cold." The next thing I knew, Serakh was holding a morsel of white meat in front of my lips.

"I can feed myself," I said, reaching for the wine goblet.

"No doubt this is so. But there is a single towel. Why should we both soil our hands? Tell me the portions that you like, and we will share."

The room darkened as the sun set. The candles burned bright and clear—beeswax candles, the best kind. The wine was smooth, with an earthy flavor. I drained my goblet dry and had some of Serakh's. I let Serakh feed me bird bits; I fed her bits of bread in return.

We traded food stories. I told her how I'd fed broth to my grandmother when she came to live with us, because sanitation was sketchy right after The Big One, and she'd gotten sick. Serakh told me how she'd chewed bits of roasted goat before feeding them to her grandmother Zilpah. We ate and drank and talked, and then she helped me out of my clothes, including the FemForm, which felt like it had clung to my flesh since forever. I insisted on keeping on my socks.

We put our clothes in a pile with the prayer shawl folded on top. It felt weird to lie nearly naked in bed next to her, so I wrapped my large scarf around my middle. Serakh blew out the candles, and we nested under the covers in the dark.

A snippet of a Hebrew School story drifted across my brain. "Serakh, wasn't Zilpah Leah's slave? Didn't Leah give Zilpah to her husband, Jacob, and Zilpah's sons counted as Leah's? Wasn't Asher one of those sons?"

"This is so," Serakh murmured, half asleep. "My grandmother Zilpah was a trusted handmaiden. Leah treated her with kindness."

I stared at the ceiling. "My great-grandfather's ancestors were slaves. I don't know how they were treated, but they were still someone else's property, which is just plain wrong."

Serakh sighed. I rolled onto my stomach, scrunched down to let my feet hang over the bottom of the bed, and eased into sleep.

Later, I heard a loud gasp. My feet felt cold. I pulled myself into wakefulness.

Serakh was squatting on the floor by the end of our bed, my socks in her hand. Moonlight slipped through the shutters, highlighting my scars. "They have whipped your feet," she said when our eyes met. "I thought as much when you would not bare them in front of me. A thousand pardons, but I had to know. This is an abomination!"

"What? No, it's not like that." I reclaimed my socks and explained about The Big One, my flip-flops, broken glass, infected feet, and surgery. "They're much better now," I said. "I use silicone slipovers when I'm not wearing socks and hiking boots. Sometimes the pain goes away completely."

Serakh paced the small room. "I have been to places and times where people's feet are whipped or burned to force obedience. I have seen what happens to feet that are bound as a false sign of beauty and wealth, forcing women to take tiny, shuffling steps. Many of us are without power over our lives. I see injustice again and again. I can do so little, and the need is so great."

I thought about Bandon and the Calantha Corps utopia he believed in. "You sound like a guy I know," I told her as I eased back under the quilt.

She ran her fingers down her braid. "Our sages say that to save one life is to save the world."

"Well, at least we'll be saving Izabel's," I said.

"Let it be so," she answered.

CHAPTER TWENTY-FOUR

I asked about Izabel the next morning. Serakh and I were in the grape arbor, eating figs and sipping watery yogurt from handle-free cups. Apparently the family wasn't up yet, and the girl scrubbing a copper pot in the kitchen had been eager to give us food and get us out of the way.

"La Señora tells me that her nephew Don Joseph has influence with the grand vizier, Rüstem Pasha," Serakh said. "Also with the sultan's son, Selim."

Selim II, I thought. Named for his grandfather. "Don Joseph is Gracia's brother-in-law and her cousin," I said. "Selim will be the next sultan. There will be more infighting at the palace, and Suleiman's empire will weaken. I checked that out on Query."

Serakh frowned. "Query?"

"Sorry. Query is sort of a cyberbiomimetic know-it-all. It's got personalized connectivity, which means that…um…never mind. What does this have to do with Izabel?"

"Muslims may have Jewish servants here, but Jews are not allowed to have Muslim servants. Your Query knows this too?"

I shook my head. Probably so, but I hadn't checked.

A trace of satisfaction stole across Serakh's face. "Jews may have Jewish servants, if this is done delicately," she said. "Don Joseph will tell Rüstem Pasha that the Nasi household needs more servants because of Gracia's arrival. Izabel was born a Jew. Don Joseph will give a gift to Rüstem Pasha, and Rüstem Pasha will give Izabel to Don Joseph. We will go to the palace with Don Joseph to make sure that Ayele releases Izabel and not another girl in her place."

Butterflies hovered over the grape leaves. Larks sang. Serakh oozed contentment. I felt like slime. "He's buying Izabel and making her Gracia's slave for the rest of her life?"

Serakh reached for another slice of fig. "Izabel will serve in a wealthy Jewish household. Gracia might teach her to read. La Señora is a kind and generous person. Gracia will be pleased to have such a spirited girl as a helper and companion."

My jaw clenched. I put my cup on the bench, stood, and started to pace. "Hasn't anybody thought about what Izabel wants? Her parents die, and she's doomed to servitude forever?"

I fumed while Serakh finished her fig. Finally she said, "Meryem, it is the best I can do in this place and time. Izabel will be treated better than most."

"No. That's not good enough. At least Izabel's brother got to choose to go to military school. She has fewer options than Gracia's kitten."

Serakh looked at me, puzzled but not protesting. I took both of her hands in mine. "Your grandmother and my Mississippi relatives were slaves. We can do better than this. That's what the prayer shawl says. We are supposed to be pursuing justice. This isn't justice."

Serakh's eyes seemed to lose focus, as if she were weighing options. Then she said, "You are right. I will ask La Señora to provide a dowry for Izabel, so that the girl might marry a respectable man when the family decides it is time."

I dropped her hands and rubbed my forehead. "You don't get it, do you?"

Silence.

And that's when I felt Gracia's kitten twining around my legs. As I lifted her—no, him—I smelled rosewater and vinegar. I nestled him against my chest and turned toward the manor house. "I'm going to talk to Gracia."

"Wait, Meryem! You cannot rush inside. We are guests."

I clutched the kitten and headed inside. A moment later my eyes adjusted to the gloomy entrance hall.

"Gracia," I called out. "*Yo tengo el gato.*" Meaning, I hoped, I have the cat.

A door opened near the top of the stairs. Gracia stepped out, her long dark hair hanging halfway down the back of a white linen shift. I took the steps two at a time.

"You found Sansón," she said, cradling the kitten I transferred to her arms. "Thank you." She raised an index finger. "Wait here. I have something for you."

At least that's what I thought she said, given my rusty Spanish.

Serakh appeared in the entrance hall. She frowned and began to climb the stairs. Another servant girl poked her head out from a room downstairs and gasped. She rushed past Serakh, who caught her in mid-stride and told her Gracia was expecting us. The girl curtsied and retreated down the stairs.

Serakh—and her gift of communication—met me outside of Gracia's closed door. "I will help you to speak your piece," she said, her voice tinged with either resignation or respect.

A moment later, Gracia opened the door and then slid in front of it, closing the door behind her. "These are for you," she said, handing me a plum-sized bundle wrapped in embroidered cloth. "Pearl earrings. Slip them into your waistband and do not tell my aunt. I want to show my gratitude for your kindness in the garden."

I started to say this wasn't necessary, but Serakh shook her head, and this time I listened. Instead I gave a deep curtsy, making up for the one I'd neglected to do when we first met.

"Your cousin Don Joseph is buying you a young girl today," I told Gracia, with an emphasis on "buying."

"Don Joseph is most kind," she said. "I appreciate his hospitality at Belvedere."

I bit my lip, realizing too late that a rich girl from the Middle Ages wouldn't condemn servitude.

"No." I touched her sleeve. "This is not kind."

"No?" Gracia's eyebrows arched. Serakh shook her head again. My pulse ticked up.

"Forgive my…um…impertinence," I said. I had to try, and this was the only power I had. "What I mean is, it is very, very important that I read the young girl's palm first. Don Joseph might be making a huge mistake. This girl might not be the right one for you."

Gracia brushed a lock of hair from her cheek. "What would you have me do?"

The rest was easy. "Tell Don Joseph that you will accept this young girl—her name is Izabel—if I say that your fortunes…um… intertwine. Otherwise, he is to do with Izabel as I ask."

Gracia nodded. "Don Joseph is with his brother, my husband, on the jousting field—one of Don Joseph's indulgences. When they are through, I will speak with him." Gracia opened her door. "Until later. Peace be unto you."

"And unto you peace," Serakh said.

I felt anything but peaceful.

Thanks to Query, I had seen the one picture left in the ether of Don Joseph Nasi. He looked like a prince in a feathered hat and overblown Venetian high-styled clothes. As we waited in front of Belvedere for the coach that would take us to Topkapı, Gracia introduced Serakh and me to the man himself. I was ready to loathe the man, even if he had helped to preserve the family fortune. I wasn't prepared for the warmth that suddenly spiked inside me.

He was more handsome than his picture, in a thirty-something kind of way. He had shoulder-length curly black hair, a black mustache, and a narrow beard outlining a sculpted face and deep brown eyes. Despite his elegant clothes, he still smelled faintly—and seductively—of the horses he'd ridden while he and his brother tried to unseat themselves from their jousting saddles. All very knight-in-shining-armor.

Willing my hormones to shut up, I remembered Don Joseph's taste for servant-wenches and the vid-clip that Jessa once showed me on women in the 1960s protesting against "male chauvinist pigs." Don Joseph fit the pig role perfectly.

Gracia laid her hand on her cousin's arm and stood on tiptoe to whisper in his ear. He smiled and led her away. Gracia was blushing when she returned, but she told me that Don Joseph had agreed to have me read Izabel's future.

I curtsied again. "Thank you."

Hooves clattered on the gravel path. The coach rolled into view, its blue-and-gold passenger compartment balanced on a wood frame with a set of large, spoked wheels in back and smaller wheels in front under a bench for the driver. A pair of perfectly matched Arabians snorted in their harness.

"I bid you a safe journey," Gracia said, taking my hands in hers. "You are always welcome at Belvedere."

"I hope to meet you again," I said, because with Serakh who knew?

Don Joseph helped Serakh and me into the coach and settled us on velvet cushions opposite him. As the coach lurched forward, I lost my balance and tumbled between Don Joseph's knees, my chin hitting the codpiece covering his crotch. He murmured his polite concern for my welfare, but his face registered pleasure. Pig!

I adjusted my scarf, turned away, and looked out the tiny curtained window. We said nothing for a while as we jostled along in a ride no smoother than the one in the donkey cart and a lot tenser.

Don Joseph stroked his mustache as he broke the silence. "My cousin claims that you are an expert at palmistry, as true a teller of the future as Nostradamus. I do not believe in that French apothecary's tales, and I have no faith in yours."

He extracted a leather pouch from under his brocade jacket and poured several coins into his gloved hand. "Let us agree that this slave girl's palm will show a fine future at Belvedere."

Serakh's eyes narrowed in anger. Before she could say anything, I covered Don Joseph's hand in mine. Two could play this game, and I had the advantage of Query.

"Put your money away, sir," I said. "Take off your gloves—if you dare."

Don Joseph's face twisted into a sneer, the first real sneer I'd ever seen. He thrust his right hand, palm up, in front of my face.

"Give me your left," I said, trying to sound confident. "You must bare the one closer to your heart."

He did so—a small but reassuring victory. I leaned over that palm, pretending to study every line while silently thanking the cybergods for the historical infobits I was about to dispense. "You will prosper. The sultan's son Selim will become the next sultan. He will make you the Duke of Naxos, and you will control the wine trade throughout his empire."

The sneer died, replaced by a look of both satisfaction and awe. I couldn't resist adding one more infobit I'd read, although of dubious origin, possibly a lie. It didn't matter, as long as Don Joseph thought it might happen. "In gratitude, you will give Selim a young girl for his harem. She is your daughter by a woman other than your wife."

Serakh sucked in her breath. Don Joseph pulled away from me and closed his hand into a fist. "Enough," he said. "Perhaps I was mistaken as to your true gift."

"I will give Izabel the reading that you and she deserve," I said. No lie there.

Don Joseph patted my knee and settled back on his side of the coach. I stared out the window. A few minutes later, he reached across me and tied the window curtain closed. "Stay inside while I arrange for the crossing," he said.

I expected to be on one of those public ferries again, but I was wrong. As horses whinnied, men swore, and Serakh and I swayed, I realized we were going across the Golden Horn by barge.

The coach tilted. Serakh looked positively ill. Something splashed into the water. A boy cried out. Don Joseph shouted, "You idiot! Put another block under the wheel. One more mistake and you swim to shore."

I leaned back against the cushions and tried not to think about the coach sinking with Serakh and me trapped inside. Back in Portland, Rose and the others would be waiting for me, wondering what had happened. My PerSafe chip would be useless centuries before satellite technology. When would they give me up for dead? Even after the coach reached solid ground, I sank under thoughts of death by drowning. And tsunamis. And Jessa.

At the palace, Don Joseph left us and his horses in the care of his driver, a large man with a scowling face and a no-nonsense sword. Serakh managed to convince the driver to let us visit the animals caged near the old church while Don Joseph dealt with Rüstem Pasha. A small boy in what looked like billowing pajamas lugged a bucket of water for the horses and gave each of them an apple. My stomach growled.

Serakh brushed a fly from her face. "Tell me your plan if Izabel does not want to go to Belvedere."

"I don't have one yet," I admitted.

Serakh gazed at the sky. Maybe she was praying. "A plan will present itself. Come, let us look at the elephant."

Judging from her smallish ears, head shape, and lack of tusks, the elephant in the pit must have been a gift from India rather than Africa. She was a beauty, clean and healthy-looking. Suleiman the Magnificent probably valued the animals in his menagerie more than the women in his harem now.

A dozen different birds nested and flew in a two-story enclosure containing shrubbery and a fountain. As I touched their delicately wrought cage, something strange moved at the edge of my vision. I turned and blinked.

Several deer herded together in a cage to my left. At least I thought they were deer. In among the brown-branched antlers was one long, golden-yellow horn, curved slightly and pointed at the top. My heart sped up before my brain formulated words.

Jessa's unicorn.

CHAPTER TWENTY-FIVE

I raced to the enclosure and clapped my hands, hoping to scatter the herd so I could distinguish individual animals. Two young bucks raised their antlered heads and skittered away. An elk barely moved. And then a much lighter-colored animal stepped closer. I couldn't help but stare, astonished, at a single, ringed horn thrusting upward from a central spot between the animal's ears.

My pulse surged. I forced myself to shift focus from that magical-looking horn and study the animal itself. This creature resembled an antelope. Humped shoulder. Tufts on its—his—tail.

My heart slowed. *Oryx leucoryx*. An Arabian white oryx. Endangered in the late twentieth century but stable by 2059, according to my ecology lessons. An oryx normally has two horns so perfectly situated that they could look like one if the oryx stood in profile. Maybe this animal had lost a horn in a fight. Unlike antlers, oryx horns didn't grow back. Or maybe he was born with only one horn. A genetic mutation. How common a mutation was that? Common enough that one-horned oryx—unicorns—could have roamed the ancient plains of Arabia?

Another boy appeared by my side. "Would you like to pet Hamza? He has a fierce horn, but he is very gentle."

"I would, yes, please. Has he always had one horn?"

The boy puffed out his chest. "Always. Hamza is a favorite of the sultan, may he live forever."

I placed my hand on the black stripe bisecting the animal's white face from forehead to muzzle. He stomped a foreleg. The boy murmured something, and Hamza calmed. His horn seemed slightly off center, so perhaps there had been another. Or not. I moved to one side and stroked his flank, smooth and luminously white. Logic vanished. All I could think of was jumping on Hamza's back and rising into a cloudless, moonlit night.

"A handsome beast," Serakh said, bringing me back to earth. She placed a coin in the boy's outstretched palm. He bowed and led Hamza away.

"Meryem, they approach from the Gate of Felicity," she said, pointing to the entrance to the harem.

Izabel trudged toward us, pushed along by Don Joseph, who had one hand on her back. She looked chunkier than the last time we'd met, and I realized that she must be wearing extra layers or have hidden something in her clothing.

Serakh and I met them halfway. Don Joseph clamped both hands on Izabel, forcing her to stop. "Is this the one?"

I nodded. Izabel stared at the ground.

"Peace be unto you," Serakh said.

"And unto you peace," Izabel mumbled. As she stood in front of us, Don Joseph pulled the scarf from Izabel's head. He inserted two long, thick fingers into a mass of her deep red curls. "She will do well at Belvedere."

Slimeball. "Perhaps," I said. "Perhaps not." I forced myself to look as if I didn't care either way. "There's a bench by that cypress tree. The child must be seated for a proper reading."

Don Joseph marched Izabel to the bench. I settled myself next to her and made a show of studying her palms. Serakh stayed a few meters away, but close enough that Izabel and I could communicate. Izabel's cheeks were pale. Her lips quivered.

"Trust me to read your true future," I said, winking to show I was on her side.

She frowned. Evidently winks weren't as universal as I'd thought. "Don't worry," I whispered.

While Serakh distracted Don Joseph with questions about jousting and who knows what, I leaned as close to Izabel as I could. "The pasha gave you to Don Joseph to be a servant at the home of his wealthy Jewish family in Galata," I said. "I met the young mistress there. She seems to be kind, but Don Joseph also lives in the house. You don't have to go there if you don't want to."

Izabel looked at the scab at the base of my thumb, where she'd stabbed me when I said I would set her free. "If I do not go with this man, will you throw me out into the street?"

"That's not what I meant about being free. I promise to find a good home for you."

"Where, Lady Meryem?"

Good question. My shoulder twitched. I had no idea. But maybe Izabel did. "If you could do anything, be anyone, what would you want? This is your one chance. Tell me. Please."

"Anything?"

I nodded. "Tell me now before Don Joseph loses his interest in Serakh."

Izabel closed her eyes. The tips of her small fingers were pocked with nicks and scars from her needlework.

A moment later she smiled. "I want to be like Lady Esther, who used to come to the harem. I want to sell beautiful embroidery to fine ladies. I want to wear a silk robe with gold threads. I want to bathe every day in rosewater. I want to…"

Got it. I let out the loudest gasp I could muster. "Don Joseph, you have saved your family from disaster!"

The man himself strode toward us. Serakh followed. Izabel tried to pull her hand away, but I stopped her. Her face paled in fear. I didn't dare reassure her. This had to look convincing.

"Look," I told Don Joseph. My finger traced a crease in the middle of Izabel's right palm from the left edge under her pinky to the space between her first two fingers. "This line of...fertility...ends in the wrong spot."

Don Joseph smiled. "The little wench cannot bear children? Even better."

Wrong. Struggling to keep a straight face, I added, "The girl has spent too long with the eunuch Ayele. She is destined to cause the men around her to lose their manhood. They will no longer be able to perform. The family will have no heirs."

This was a total lie, of course. And I felt sorry for Ayele, who probably was forcibly castrated when he was young, because that would make him a more valuable slave.

Izabel sucked in her breath. Was she genuinely horrified or playing along?

"It would be a sin to take this girl into your household," Serakh added.

I came in for the final blow. "Already you might be contaminated."

He winced. I thought we'd won. But then he said, "Next you will offer to dispose of this little imp." Don Joseph ran his finger down Izabel's cheek. "Unblemished, ivory skin, pleasant features. She will fetch a handsome price."

Now what? My jaw clenched. I took three long seconds to gather my thoughts. Finally I said, "There will be no such sale."

Don Joseph glared at me. "You will keep the child for yourself."

"And ruin my own marriage bed? Certainly not!" I dropped Izabel's hand and stood as tall as I could. I had to be convincing. I had to give Izabel a chance at a decent life.

"Don Joseph, the palm does not lie. The girl's future is linked to Esther Handali, who trades in fine goods. The girl is fated to work for women, live among women, and trade among women. She must not be brought to Belvedere. We will deliver her as a gift to Lady Esther."

Don Joseph grabbed my wrist. He leaned into me, his breath hot and smelling of anise. "We will visit the widow Handali together, much as I dislike that withered old cow who clings to her old ways and thinks she can regain her place at the harem without my influence. You will not cheat me and sell the girl yourself."

My stomach cramped. "Let go of me."

"When I am ready," he growled.

CHAPTER
TWENTY-SIX

Esther Handali was not old, withered, or bovine. A well-dressed servant girl led us to a woman who was about forty, with a round face, dark curly hair, and what my grandmother would call a "full-featured" body. She reminded me of Grandma—proper, polite, and completely in charge.

"What a delightful surprise," Esther said, with only the slightest hint of sarcasm. She sat on a pillow behind a low table strewn with papers. The simple décor looked Turkish, in contrast to the pompous European furnishings at Belvedere. "I am honored by your visit, Don Joseph. What brings you to my humble presence today?"

I liked Esther immediately.

Don Joseph licked his lips, and I thought I detected a crack in his male chauvinist pig attitude. During the coach ride over to the Jewish quarter, he had put Izabel on my side, as far from his codpiece as possible. I indulged in the satisfying belief that he wasn't entirely sure I lied about her impotency-producing powers.

Don Joseph introduced Serakh as a Jewish healer called to Belvedere to tend to La Señora. Serakh curtsied. I did the same when he referred to me as "the healer's companion."

"And this is a Jewish orphan from Salonika," Serakh said. "Her name is Izabel."

Izabel started to curtsy and then seemed to fall into what fairy tales called a swoon. She staggered toward Don Joseph and collapsed, sliding her fingers along his legs before landing facedown on the floor. The performance—I was sure Izabel had faked everything—was so convincing I wanted to applaud.

Don Joseph let out a gurgling noise as if he'd been strangled. Esther thrust a ringed finger at him. "How have I provoked your displeasure that you dare to bring this child here? She is possessed!"

Don Joseph stepped over the fallen Izabel, taking care not to touch her. He bowed and offered his apologies. "She is well-mannered among women, I assure you. I am the one at fault. The girl is skilled in the needle arts. I present her to you as a token of my deep and sincere friendship."

I had to give Don Joseph credit for a diplomatic recovery.

"You are most kind, sir," Esther said, although her face conveyed the opposite. "But I have no need for another worker."

Izabel groaned, whether real or fake this time, I couldn't tell.

"Please give Izabel a chance," I said. "She longs to be in your service."

Serakh put her hand over her heart. "I vow that your kindness will be rewarded."

Esther stood, and I was afraid she was getting ready to dismiss us. Instead she walked to the window and looked out. Ten seconds. Twenty. Izabel didn't move. Don Joseph took a sudden interest in his doublet. Serakh seemed to be an island of serenity. I was a nervous wreck.

By the time Esther turned toward us, my calves had cramped and my feet were throbbing. "Don Joseph, you have done well to bring the child here," she said. "I foresee many years of good relations with the House of Nasi."

A sigh escaped from the prone figure on the floor. My muscle cramp eased. I wondered if Esther had calculated that taking Izabel would improve her business ties with Don Joseph's increasingly influential Sephardic community, or if she simply believed Serakh. In any case, Izabel had a home.

Esther rang a hand bell and gave a coin to the servant girl who appeared so fast that she must have been listening at the door. "Show Don Joseph to his coach," Esther instructed. "Give this to the servant boy for his care of Don Joseph's horses."

A fountain of pleasantries spewed from Don Joseph's lips and Esther's, and then, finally, the slimeball was gone. As soon as we heard the coach leave, Izabel stood up, brushed off her dress, and dropped into the deepest curtsy I'd ever seen.

"Rise, child," Esther said, and Izabel did, rubbing one hand over the other, trembling.

Esther faced Serakh. "You and your companion are healers?"

"We come from the East."

I stifled a smile.

"Can you rid this child of what possesses her?"

"There is no need," Serakh said. "She is possessed only with the good sense to rid herself of Don Joseph."

"I see." Esther studied a ring on her finger. "Izabel. What a lovely name. Can you write it for me, child?"

Izabel stared at the floor. "Yes, venerable lady."

"Come here to my desk." Esther dipped a thin reed, angled and blackened on the edge, into a pot of ink. She handed the reed and a scrap of yellowed paper to Izabel.

Izabel shifted her weight from one foot to the other. "Which alphabet, venerable lady? Shall I write in Arabic or Greek?"

Esther looked as surprised as I was. "Greek," she said.

Izabel bent over the paper in deep concentration, the tip of her tongue sticking out from the corner of her mouth. One long moment later she produced Ιζαβελ.

I wondered if Izabel could read and do math as well.

"Izabel was orphaned after the plague in Salonika," Serakh said, as if that explained everything. "Her brother offered her to the janissaries, who presented her as a gift to the sultan. She is unblemished."

Esther was all smiles. "Give the writing implements back to me now. Are you good with a needle?"

Wiggling out of an outer layer of clothes, Izabel revealed a tapestry bound around her waist with a cotton sash pierced by four silver needles. Each needle was threaded in a different color silk, coiled and held in place with loose stitching. The tapestry was the size of a placemat, intricately embroidered with tulips and carnations arranged in a spiral pattern around a peacock.

Izabel clasped and unclasped her hands while Esther studied the stitching, front and back. "What part of this did you do?"

"All of it, venerable lady. You can ask Ayele. I stitched an even harder one—green with gold and silver threads in tiny square lines. It looks like his talisman."

The servant girl arrived with a tray of dates, pistachios, and white candy that tasted of sugar and rosewater. After she left, we settled ourselves on thick carpets around the table.

Voluble. Another Jessa word. Talkative. Esther laughed and chatted, holding forth as if we were old friends, although she kept looking at Izabel. Evaluating her, I suppose.

"You two young women say you are from the East," she said. "Thus, you have not fled from the peril of the Inquisition. We Jews who have lived here for generations offer hospitality to Jews from places west of our beloved Istanbul, to La Señora and other Sephardim. They often bring great wealth, and we are grateful. But they come with their own traditions, which I fear will smother our ancient ways."

I wondered about the Zarfati family and the Sephardic customs and language they brought to Ottoman Turkey from Spain. I supposed it didn't matter to the sultan where the Jews came from, so long as they paid their taxes and brought their trade and skills to his empire. But apparently it mattered to Esther.

We nibbled and nodded. Izabel snuck three pistachios up her sleeve. Esther coughed. Izabel put the nuts back in the bowl.

Serakh turned to Esther. "May we speak with you in private?"

"Certainly." Esther summoned her servant girl, who whisked Izabel away.

Serakh smoothed her robe. "My companion and I must leave soon, and we trust that Izabel will be a boon to you."

Forget voluble. Esther was all business now. "I can ill afford another mouth to feed. The best that I can promise is that I will provide for Izabel for the next six months while I see whether her handiwork will help to support her."

My stomach tightened. "Only six months?"

Esther thrust both hands out, palms up. "If I can keep her I will. Perhaps the sultan will choose another favorite now that Hürrem Sultan is dead, peace be upon her soul. Perhaps the harem will return to normal and business will improve. You ask for a promise. I give you a perhaps."

"Let it be so," Serakh said.

I was in no position to argue. It's not like I could take Izabel home with me. Still, there was one more thing I wanted to do. "We would like a moment alone with Izabel."

Five minutes later, Izabel and I were in the back garden with the excuse that I was going to read her palm again. Serakh stood next to a nearby laurel shrub.

Izabel held out her palms. "Will they be nice to me here?"

I extracted Gracia's pearl earrings from my sash, placed them in Izabel's right palm, and closed my hand over hers. "However they treat you here, these are for you, in case you ever need them. If you have to leave Lady Esther's protection, use these pearls to buy food and shelter. I don't ever want you forced to live on the streets."

Izabel nodded solemnly. "I will guard these carefully, Lady Meryem. I will remember you always, the way that Ayele remembers the unicorn lady, who gave him a precious talisman."

"The unicorn lady?"

"Yes, Lady Meryem, the lady of your tribe with hair the color of the *hyakinthos* flower."

CHAPTER TWENTY-SEVEN

For one hot second, the whole world narrowed into a tight focus on Izabel's face. *Hyakinthos.* The word sounded so close to *hyacinthus*. As in *Hyacinthus orientalis*. Purple hyacinth. Purple hair. I unwrapped the ends of my scarf from around my neck and let the long silk cloth fall to my shoulders.

Izabel's eyes widened with delight. "Ooooh. May I touch it?"

I stood there, dazed, as she reached up and patted a magenta curl. She squealed when the hair bounced back. "Do all the ladies of your tribe have this hair? Did you come to see the sultan's unicorn? Do you have a magic carpet too?"

"A magic carpet? What are you talking about?"

"Ayele and the unicorn lady. She looked like you."

Jessa? Impossible. But then who was I, standing in this spot on Serakh's *olam*, to say what was possible and what wasn't? I grabbed

Izabel's shoulders. "Tell me exactly what Ayele told you. This is important."

"Ow! You're hurting me!"

"Let go," Serakh ordered. And I did. She crouched beside Izabel and held her hand. "Lady Meryem means no harm. Start at the beginning of the story."

Izabel meandered infuriately through details and asides that made me clench my jaw and pace with impatience. I kept track of the main points.

*Once upon a time...*When Ayele was a young boy, he worked in the sultan's menagerie. A handsome prince and a lady who looked exactly like me flew into the courtyard of the palace on their magic carpet. The lady asked Ayele to fetch the sultan's unicorn. As he did, the earth shook and the animals escaped from their cages. A lion cub attacked the lady and mauled her arm. Ayele chased the cub away and fetched a doctor. The lady gave Ayele a small flat talisman from inside her body. *The end.*

Izabel's eyes gleamed with excitement. "And that's when Ayele knew that she was a magical unicorn lady. Ayele has kept the talisman with him ever since."

My heart thrummed in my throat. "What happened to the unicorn lady after that, Izabel?"

"Nothing."

"What do you mean *nothing*? Where did she go after the doctor fixed her? Did she get on her magic carpet?"

Izabel shrugged. "Ayele didn't tell me."

Serakh touched my arm. "Enough, Meryem. We cannot seek out Ayele—he has the power to do us harm. The story is many years old. There may be no truth to it."

I kneaded the back of my neck. Jessa and I didn't dye our hair magenta until last year, so she couldn't have been the person Ayele saw forty or fifty years ago when he was a boy. Jessa never came home injured like that. Everything was wrong, out of kilter. And yet the woman looked like me and had a passion for unicorns.

"It couldn't have been Jessa, right?"

Serakh cocked her head to one side. "I cannot say. I do not know."

My mind fought for balance. By the time the three of us walked back inside, Izabel had hidden Gracia's pearl earrings in her clothes, and I tried not to look like my world was spinning out of control.

Esther invited us to stay. "You must not be on the streets when the night watchman makes us bank our fires and closes the city gates," she said.

Serakh insisted that we leave.

I hugged Izabel good-bye and she raced away. As the servant girl escorted Serakh and me to the door, I heard Izabel say, "I know seven stitches, venerable lady. Each brings out the beauty of the others. How shall I start?"

In the darkening twilight, Serakh and I navigated a narrow alleyway wedged between a zigzag row of wooden buildings. The air smelled of roasted lamb and raw sewage.

Serakh handed me Gracia's portrait medal. "The coin belongs with your family. Shed the garments of this time and place—the poor will make good use of them."

I grabbed Serakh's hand. "Wait. So you told me that you don't know about Jessa and that she never traveled with you using the blue thread. Could there be a red thread? Or a purple one? Or something else entirely?"

Serakh adjusted the prayer shawl. "I took only blue threads from the many-colored tunic of Joseph, my uncle. Let us cross now, Meryem, and speak of this in the safety of your dwelling."

"I'll be exhausted then," I said. "You said threads. There's more than one?"

Serakh covered my FemForm and prayer shawl with her cloak. "This much I will tell you now. I have taken thirty-six threads from Joseph's tunic. All blue. These threads I have divided and given to the twelve tribes of Israel, the twelve tribes of Ishmael, and to other peoples of the earth. The threads bind us all in righteousness and justice. Your thread comes through the Israelites in the line of Manasseh, a son of Joseph, and through Miryam the prophetess."

"Jessa and I are from the same line, of course. But can't there be another way?"

"Perhaps she travels with another being through the workings of another of the thirty-six threads."

The night watchman's call rang through the streets.

"Meryem, we must go," Serakh said. "I will tell you later."

CHAPTER TWENTY-EIGHT

I sprawled on the couch in the living room, my head pounding. Serakh was right. The trip—or whatever this was—was easier this time, although not by much. She was telling me to rest when I heard *click-click-whirr...za bing!* from the corner of the dining room. We'd woken up the GR-17. Hadn't I put the bot on **IGNORE** for three hours? What time was it now?

If I'd been thinking clearly rather than focusing on the time, I could have told Gryffindor to power down or told Serakh to stand still and let me do the talking. But I wasn't.

Gryffindor put on his best mechanical manners, as he wheeled toward us. "Good morning, Meryem and Unidentified Guest. All of my systems are fully operational. How may I assist you?"

Serakh gasped. She raced across the hall toward the kitchen. Gryffindor swiveled on his flat robotic feet, rebalanced his one-meter-high self, and followed her.

My brain fog lifted. "Gryffindor, stop!"

He did. "I cannot see Unidentified Guest," he informed me. "All of my systems remain fully operational. How may I assist you?"

I dragged my body off the couch and lurched toward the kitchen. That's when Rose's bedroom door opened, revealing Rose in her old bathrobe, with a cascade of unbrushed hair and our stun stick. "What's going on, Meryem? Are you okay?"

"Fine," I said. Which I wasn't. "I can explain." Which I couldn't. Had Gryffindor restarted right after Serakh and I left, which would have been almost the exact time we returned? How long had I been on the couch?

A flash of blue light reflected on the dining room window. Rose didn't seem to notice.

"It's a quarter to five in the morning," she said. "What are you doing down here with your prayer shawl and in your clothes from yesterday? Didn't you sleep at all?"

When? That night in Belvedere five hundred years ago? "I roamed a bit," I said, rubbing my forehead and wishing I could scream, "Come back, Serakh. I need you. I need answers!"

"Gryffindor, go to your corner and power down," Rose instructed. She turned to me, her sympathetic look bringing me to tears. "Your birthday must have been so hard. Plus the anniversary of The Big One is coming up. Resilience Day. Is that it?"

My defenses crumbling, I buried my face in Rose's bathrobe, the way I did when Jessa was away and I was little. "I guess so. Sorry to wake you. I'm going to go upstairs for a couple of hours."

"I'll do breakfast today," Rose said.

I wiped my cheeks with the back of my hand. "No, but thanks. Honestly, Rose, without my routine, how can I get through the day?" I meant that as a joke, only it didn't come out that way.

As I walked upstairs, I was already formulating queries. No way could I sleep. In two hours, I'd appear in the kitchen as my normal self, ready to begin a normal day. I touched Jessa's rug. Its soft woolen fibers caressed my fingertips. A magic carpet? I tripped on the stairs and grabbed the banister to regain my balance. Normal day? Never again.

With the MyCom broken, I unfolded my screen and whispered query after query, careful not to wake my grandmother in the next room. Nearly muted, Aussie Jack answered assorted variations on "Are magic carpets real?" I might as well have queried, "Where is Jessa now?" or "Does God exist?" After slogging through Aussie Jack's responses—he said a lot but told me nothing useful—I hid Gracia's portrait medal in my lobe locket case and eased the frustration knots in my shoulders with a ninety-second hot shower.

On my way down to start the morning routine, I stopped to touch Jessa's rug again. Rose was leaning against the entrance to the kitchen, a smudge of flour on her nose.

"I remember when Jessa brought that back from Turkey," she said. "You were eighteen months old, just weaned, and she was extremely nervous about leaving you in my care for an entire week. I don't blame her."

"Why?" They don't come more solid than Rose.

"We didn't know each other very well then. My English was still shabby and her Russian even shabbier. One time I caught her kissing the rug, but I never learned why. If this house caught fire, she'd have grabbed you first and the rug second."

My stomach twisted. "Did you ever see Jessa take it down? I mean, was it ever missing?"

"Missing? No. I've aired it out several times, and vacuumed it. A rug is a rug. It still gets dusty." Rose motioned me toward the kitchen. As I followed, she said, "I've got about an hour's free time today. Would you like help with your Thursday chicken-goat routine?"

"It's only Thursday?"

Rose smiled. "Thursday, February 20, 2059. All day. So? Goats for me, chickens for you?"

"I'll do both." I needed all the mind-numbing work I could get. After organizing breakfast, I shoved mud muckers over my hiking boots, tuned my earbuds to the primal, otherworldly rhythms of theremin scrag, and headed to Chicken Hacienda. I corralled Tillie, Yetta, and Louise in a temporary enclosure under the pear trees and cleaned every centimeter of their habitat. Still, brain-zaps of Serakh, Izabel, Gracia, Jessa, and magic carpets kept seeping through.

Bandon walked over as I was snapping the eco-plastic roof onto the walls. I unhooked my earbuds.

"Looks like a vintage Lego set," he said. "Need help?"

"Sure." I pointed to a pile of old cotton quilting. "Wipe down the insides of the nesting boxes and fill them with fresh straw."

He nodded and, to his credit, didn't start his usual banter until the enclosure was ready for reoccupancy. "What's next, Farmer Zarfati? Shall we knit hen hats for your feathered friends?"

That deserved the fistful of feed I threw at him.

"Hey, I got you to smile. So, what's next?"

"We muck out the goat shed and clean the feed trough."

"Oh, yeah, fun, fun, fun." He helped me anyway.

After lunch, Bandon took Tillamook for a walk around the block because I told him Tillamook needed the exercise. I was scrubbing the kitchen sink, while Rose counted our canned goods.

"Bandon would shovel goat dreck with a teaspoon to be in your company," she said.

My cheeks grew hot. "He's gay, you know."

"Yes, he told me." Rose finished counting. "He has an *izyuminka*, you know what I mean?" She smiled at the Russian word for raisin and the expression she'd taught me years ago.

"He's got a special something."

"Exactly," she said. "He's worth keeping around."

"What does it take to lift an exclusion order?"

"Meryem, I have no idea."

By mid-afternoon, Bandon-with-the-raisin had had enough work for one day. He announced that he and Ignatius were going out, and he invited me along.

"Another time," I said. "See you at dinner."

After they left, I sat on the bottom step in the front hall. If only Gryffindor hadn't freaked out Serakh. There was still so much I didn't know.

Priscilla and Winslow came home early, which got me off my butt and stopped my brain from spinning. Priscilla showed me my refurbished MyCom. "I couldn't retrieve any of your data," she explained with an apologetic look. "But at least it's fully reconfigured with upgrades, including the latest Query app."

I thanked her and chaperoned Winslow's daily date with Louise. Then, when I was alone again, I used the new MyCom to photograph Jessa's rug. I unhooked the drapery rod from the wall and studied every square centimeter of the rug, front and back, every animal and every stylized flower. I found aqua, teal, violet, but no prayer shawl blue.

Back in Jessa's room I uploaded the rug images to Query. With 89.72 percent accuracy, Aussie Jack pronounced Jessa's rug to be woven in the Oushak style from a region about 250 kilometers southeast of Istanbul in the Asian part of Turkey. The rug was at least a hundred years old and, with 42.65 percent accuracy, as old as the early sixteenth century. Aussie Jack lectured me on antique Oushak carpets, traditional dyeing techniques, and Ghiordes versus Senneh knots. The squiggles along the bottom were too blurry or too complicated for Aussie Jack to decipher, but had a 98.43 percent probability of being Arabic calligraphy. To my questions about the rug's flying capability, likely magical properties, and general aerodynamics, Aussie Jack answered total gibberish, with zippo percent accuracy. Forget it.

I snuck the portrait medal back into the ashbin with the other coin and muddled through dinner and the rest of the evening with an acceptable level of polite conversation—which was easier with Bandon around. Grandma insisted on Trivial Pursuit, and I didn't have the energy to say no. Her team won when she named a major political event of 2048.

"That would be the declaration of Jerusalem as a UN-governed city after the peace agreement between Palestine and Israel," she said. "May 14, 2048, to be exact—one hundred years after the founding of Israel and the day that Mama Two was born."

After checking on the animals, I trudged upstairs and started to get ready for bed. My brain kept spiraling back to Mama Two—a.k.a. Miryam Tikvah—a.k.a. Hope Friis Einhorn, Jessa's grandmother. Why did Jessa name me for her? What was I supposed to do with the prayer shawl now? Would I ever travel with Serakh again?

Auntie An knocked on my unlocked door and then came in uninvited. She sat on my bed and gave me a ScrutinEyes look. "Merry, you can fool my sister and the housekeeper, but you can't fool me. There is an aura about you. I felt it at dinner and twice during the game. Serakh has been here again. Where did she take you?"

CHAPTER
TWENTY-NINE

The last person I wanted in my room was someone who hated practically everything Jessa had done to this house, including moving in right before I was born. I focused on my quilt and said nothing.

Auntie An blew out her breath, a huge exhalation, as if she were clearing the room of invisible demons. "You will tell me when you are ready?"

I rolled my shoulders. That was fair enough. After all, Auntie An was also the one who insisted Serakh would "take me away" in the first place. Now I knew what that meant. And her palmistry had helped Gracia and saved Izabel.

"Yes, I will." I said. I wondered what else she might know. "Since you can sense auras, is there anything special about Jessa's rug downstairs? Anything magical?"

Auntie An sat up straighter. She ran an arthritic finger through her hair and smoothed her caftan. "In all these months you never asked me. Why now? Has Serakh said anything to you about the rug?"

"No," I told her honestly. "I'm just curious. Mr. Nabli told me a folk tale about magic carpets."

She snorted. "Mr. Nabli. I can't imagine what your mother saw in that man. Who knows how much he is charging the estate for his services?"

"Magic carpets, Auntie An?"

Auntie An rested a hand on her collarbone and seemed to stare into space. "Ah, magic carpets. There are so many magic carpet tales from India, Russia, the Arabian Peninsula, even in Judaism. King Solomon's flying rug is one. But in Vietnam? No. I have never believed in something as unnatural as a magic carpet. Unicorns? Perhaps. I let my little sister have her dreams. But magic carpets are not part of the logical order of the universe as revealed through signs and numbers."

Her answer startled me. "And Serakh is part of the logical order of the universe?"

Auntie An exhaled again. "Serakh is real. You know this. You should also know something else, after all these months."

I'd heard enough. "I'm really tired, Auntie An. Let's talk tomorrow."

She ignored me. "I'm older than your grandmother, so I remember more about Vietnam. She won't tell you this, but I will. When Papa One didn't come home, Mama One waited by the door for three days. I begged for food from the neighbors."

Auntie An rubbed her collarbone. "One night many weeks later, a white man came. An American. He wore a soldier's uniform like the one that Papa One had. He brought rice and a live chicken for us and spoke in a kind way. Then he put money on the table. He said that the war was over and he wanted to help our family. Mama One told him she wanted a better life for her children. She bathed us and kissed us and told me to take care of my little sister. She stood with her back to us so she could not see the man take us away. When we came to live in Berkeley, Mama Two wrote to Mama One many times. No answer."

170

"I'm sorry," I said. "But please…"

"I returned to Vietnam in 2010," she continued. "Just me. Ly Tien was burdened with your mother, who was still a toddler. I searched for Mama One but I never found her. I have lost two mothers and two fathers. I know something about waiting and about grief."

Burdened with my mother? "Auntie An…" My stomach cramped. After living under the same roof with The Ladies all these months, and after the crap day I'd had, I needed her to leave me alone.

She wouldn't stop. "We conjure up stories to shield ourselves from the truth. We grasp at every possibility when we lack the proof otherwise. But the time has come for you to see with different eyes, Merry. You know that, don't you?"

I nodded. What else could I do?

"Good. Sleep well," she said, as she headed for my door.

"You too," I said, because Jessa taught me to be polite. But then I couldn't resist adding, "You know The Anthony is ready for habitation again. The mayor announced it a few days ago. I'm sure you are eager to go back home."

Auntie An stiffened, her back toward me. "I did not know," she muttered as she closed the door and left.

Jessa and magic carpets still haunted me the next morning at RescueCommons. I left for the office early so I could search through the database of found objects in the tsunami/coastal inundation zone that might contain traces of DNA. Fibers from rugs, for example.

Mark, the guy from work, was standing by his beat-up Tesla when I reached the parking lot. He waved me over, opened the minivan door, and ushered out his little girl Gemmie and her giraffe.

Gemmie raced over and hugged me, smearing strawberry jelly

on my over-tee and bathing me in the biggest smile I'd seen in months. "Can I come watch you work?"

Mark shook his head. "Gemmie, you know the rules. No children at RescueCommons. You play in the Tesla with Charles, and I'll be out as soon as I can. No fussing."

"I told you, Charles," she said, giving the giraffe a fierce look. Charles didn't move or answer. Maybe his solar-cell eyes no longer functioned to power up his robotics, or an electrical connection was broken inside.

I waited until Mark tucked Gemmie back into the minivan, and then walked with him to the office. "She looks old enough to be in school," I said.

Mark stopped on the stairs. "Technically yes. Practically, not so easy. I don't exactly have Gemmie's health records or a place of residence at the moment."

"I thought the emergency housing plan covers everyone."

"It's complicated," he said. "Anyway, Gemmie and I are managing. We've got plenty of food, and sometimes we sleep at Shander's place."

"Yes, but…"

Mark held up his hand. "Look, Meryem, I'm not interested in a handout. Let's leave it at that."

So I did, although it made me feel uncomfortable. Still, why breach Mark's privacy when Shander seemed okay with the situation and Gemmie seemed to be all right? I settled into my cubicle and started to search through the found objects database.

"Looking for anything in particular?" Mark asked, since we were the only two in the office and wouldn't disturb anyone.

"Textiles," I said. "Pieces of rug actually. Have you logged any?"

"Dozens. Mud is an excellent preservative for textiles." He told me about the old dig at Ozette, on the Washington coast, where the Makah Tribe had discovered textiles preserved for centuries. Then he added, "I didn't mean to snap at you before, Meryem. I've got a lot on my mind, and I'm working my ass off to find a decent place for Gemmie and me. I know you mean well, but just stay off my case, okay?"

"Fine," I said.

Mark went to his cubicle, and I wasted fifteen minutes on the database. Nothing. After the other three volunteers and Shander arrived, I logged into my regular work. I didn't use my earbuds, so I could hear Mark whispering to Gemmie. They were a gluesome twosome, like Jessa and me. I timed each of my breaks so that I could join them for a walk around the block, a game of giraffe hide-and-seek, and a trip to the bathroom in the restaurant next door.

"See you next week," I told Gemmie when my shift was up and I saw her outside. I kissed Charles. "Would you and Charles like another playmate? I have a stuffed unicorn my mother gave me when I was little." Surely Mark couldn't object to that.

Gemmie consulted Charles, who did a happy dance on the dashboard. "Daddy doesn't believe in magic, but we do," Gemmie said.

"Me too," I said.

CHAPTER THIRTY

Grandma accosted me as soon as I got in the front door. "Now that The Anthony has reopened, I have matters to discuss with your Mr. Nabli today."

My Mr. Nabli. As if he belonged to me. "Fine," I said. "Where's Rose?"

"Out somewhere, Merry. I don't keep track of your housekeeper." As if Rose hadn't shopped and cooked and cleaned for her and Auntie An all these months. I escaped to the kitchen and busied myself with crispy cricket mix and a newsfeed on where to get the best hay.

As soon as Mr. Nabli arrived, Grandma materialized from upstairs. "My granddaughter invited me to join you," she said, morphing her insistence into my invitation. After an exchange of pleasantries, she sat quietly while I signed off on the Council lists. I detected only the slightest intake of her breath when I added Jessa's name as among the living.

When we were done, she tapped the table. "Due to circumstances we need not delve into now, I would appreciate a full explanation of Merry's current financial situation. My first responsibility, as you know, is to Merry. I have to look to the future."

Mr. Nabli shifted his papers and I suppose collected his thoughts. He touched the place where I'd added Jessa's name. "As you know, Mrs. Zarfati, there are certain complications with regard to Meryem's mother."

"We'll discuss that another time," Grandma said. I whispered a thank you.

Mr. Nabli cleared his throat. "In that case, let's see. The Chadwicks have informed the Resilience Council that they are moving out this weekend, is that correct?"

No surprise there. "Yes," I said, before Grandma could answer. This was my future too.

Mr. Nabli rolled his pen between his thumb and fingers. "The Council will pay the full credit allowance for the Chadwicks through the end of the month. The Council will also pay for Mr. Rivera for as long as the emergency credit-tenant housing plan is in operation—I'd estimate another month or two at most. Then there's the debt owed to Ms. Kropotkin."

News to me. "What debt?"

Mr. Nabli focused on Grandma. "Ms. Kropotkin's last salary receipt was dated March 1, 2058, right before The Big One. Ms. Kropotkin has not been paid since then. She is entitled to put a lien on this property amounting to a considerable sum for her uncompensated labor. That should be no problem financially, given the life insurance policy and other assets for which Meryem is likely the sole beneficiary."

"Rose has lived with Jessa and me since I can remember," I told him. "She's practically family."

Mr. Nabli shifted into kindergarten teacher mode. "Your grandmother and great aunt are family, Meryem. Your mother employed Ms. Kropotkin just like she would a gardener or a cleaner. Ms. Kropotkin can leave at any time, and you owe her money for the work she's done. I can handle this for you."

"I'll speak to Rose," I told him, which is when I realized I wouldn't tell Rose anything unless she asked. Why would she ever want to leave me? I rubbed the nape of my neck.

"Thank you, Mr. Nabli," Grandma said. "This is very helpful." She shifted into polite conversation mode, talking about the weather (unseasonably warm), construction noise (loud), Auntie An's special toothpaste (Rose didn't buy enough), and the cost of fresh fruit (outrageous). No one mentioned Bandon, who at that moment was defying the exclusion order and feeding his beef addiction at Burgerville. No one mentioned magic carpets, or unicorns, or magenta-haired mothers at Topkapı Palace during the Middle Ages. I glanced at Gryffindor. Suppose I told him to fetch Serakh. Suppose he could. Suppose he did. That would shake things up.

Grandma left, evidently satisfied. After Mr. Nabli collected his papers, I switched to the topic that had been eating at me since I'd heard Izabel's magic carpet story. I showed him the bottom border of Jessa's rug.

"It's Arabic calligraphy, right?"

"I'm impressed," he said.

"Query figured that out," I admitted. "What does it say?"

Mr. Nabli focused his MyCom on the calligraphy and clicked. "It's very stylized, and my Arabic is poor. It's not the usual 'Allah be praised'—I can tell you that much. I'll show it to a colleague."

"So, what I'm wondering is…I know you didn't know Jessa personally, but she must have trusted your firm a lot, and you have contacts in Turkey…" I took a breath. "Are there any folktales about the magical qualities of a rug like this?"

Mr. Nabli didn't laugh or politely inquire about the use of hallucinogenic substances. His eyes softened. "My family is full of stories about magic carpet rides."

I followed him to the front door. "What makes a carpet magical? I mean, is there a special weave? Or a particular thread?"

Mr. Nabli rubbed his chin. "My grandmother used to tell us kids that each of the twelve tribes of Ishmael had a magic carpet. And each carpet had a blue thread woven into the carpet—that's

176

what enabled the carpet to fly through space and across time. Silly notion, but there you have it."

I stepped between Mr. Nabli and the front door, my stomach in knots. "A blue thread?"

Mr. Nabli looked at his MyCom. "It's a long story. Maybe another time."

"What do you know about the blue thread?"

He slung his courier bag over his shoulder and cocked his head to one side.

I blocked his exit and waited, my heart pounding.

"Let's see," he said. "As I recall, the thread came from the cloak of a biblical shepherd named Yusuf—in English, that's Joseph. The Ishmaelites took Yusuf to Egypt to save him from his jealous brothers. I'm sure you know the story of Abraham and his two wives. Hagar gave birth to Ishmael—from which we Muslims trace our ancestors. Sarah had Isaac—from which you Jews trace yours."

"And the cloak?"

"Yusuf's niece thanked the Ishmaelites for saving her uncle by giving each of the twelve tribes a blue thread with magical properties. The magic carpet of my tribe—the Kedarites—is supposed to be handed down through a first-born son named Yusuf."

I stared at the floor, barely able to catch my breath. The niece in Mr. Nabli's story had to be Serakh. When two impossibilities come together, it almost feels like logic.

"And Yusuf Halab, the scientist who was in Manzanita with Jessa, was he a Kedarite? Was he a first-born son? I've tried to locate his family through Query. No luck so far, because of the privacy laws. Would you be able to track them down?"

Mr. Nabli thumbed his MyCom. "Meryem, I'm already late for another appointment." I let him go, and he biked away, leaving me the way Serakh had, with just enough answers to make my questions ache even more.

I was still in the front hall a few minutes later, when Bandon came back from Burgerville. I showed him the calligraphy on Jessa's rug. "Mr. Nabli and I were talking about magic carpets."

Bandon stroked his beard. "Is anybody else home now?"

"Yes. They're upstairs."

"Okay, then. I'll have to be quick about this." He wiped his hands on this pants and then placed his palms against the rug. He hummed softly, his eyes closed, his head bobbing up and down.

"What are you doing?"

"Shh…I need to concentrate."

"On what?"

"Come sit next to me," he said.

Which I did.

He hummed for another minute and reached for my hand. "Why do you think I'm here, Meryem?"

"What?"

"Do you really believe it's a coincidence that I showed up for your sixteenth birthday and found the coin? Think back to the ScrutinEyes feed. What is my full name?"

"Bandon Theodosios Falconer. So?"

"Theodosios. Meaning given to God. That's me. Think about it."

My pulse clicked into double time. Serakh was a magical being, why not Bandon?

"Bandon is a military unit from Byzantium," he reminded me.

My stomach twisted. "Which became Constantinople and then Istanbul. You look so much like a girl I…um…I once knew from that part of the world." I felt my eyes widen. Could Bandon be the link to another blue thread? To Jessa? "I suppose your great-great-great whatever kept falcons for the sultan," I said.

He nodded. "Somebody back then was a famous falconer." While I sat there, struggling to keep calm, Bandon hummed some more and nodded. "I think now is the right time, don't you Meryem?"

I could hardly breathe. Magic had been living right under my nose. "Yes," I whispered.

"Are you ready to free Jessa's carpet from this wall? Are you ready to travel?"

"I am ready."

"Me too." Bandon stood and hitched up his sagging pants. "I have to get my magical feather first, and my invisible cloak, and a peanut butter sandwich. Unicorns love peanut butter."

"What kind of ridiculous…? Bandon!" My whole body shook. "You were breaching me this whole time."

His face got that Winslow-wants-to-play look. "Most definitely. What's a little banter among friends?"

"A little banter? That's completely crude and you know it. Not funny." I clenched my fists and shoved them in my over-tee pockets. How could he betray my trust like that?

Bandon played a tune on his harmonica—something that he said came from a vintage vid called *Star Wars*.

"Come on, Meryem. I mean magic carpets? Really?"

I glared at him.

Then he turned the slightest bit serious. "I'm the unicorn-utopia guy, remember? You're the down-to-earth, save-the-salamander girl."

"Not just salamanders," I said, but I knew what he meant.

"You don't really think this rug is a magic carpet, do you?"

"Of course not," I lied.

"Hey, I'm sorry. You looked like you needed to lighten up after your meeting with Mr. Nabli. Can I offer you crispy cricket mix?"

"Not hungry," I said. "See you at dinner." I trudged upstairs.

By the time I got to Jessa's room for my Friday PerSafe routine, The Ladies were in Grandma's room arguing about something, mostly in Vietnamese. I sat at Jessa's desk, set the PerSafe receiver, and thumbed my personal safety identification code. Jessa seemed as close as the rug in the front hall, and somehow farther away than she'd ever been.

As my fingertips touched the inside of my left forearm, I remembered when I was nine. *Jessa was holding my chin and making funny faces. "Watch me, lovey. You'll feel a sting and then your arm will be numb and you won't feel a thing. That's a brave girl. Now I'll always know where you are and you'll always know where I am."*

I felt the usual ping between the flexor and extensor muscles.

My trips through the *olam* had zapped the MyCom but hadn't damaged my chip, for whatever that was worth. After five seconds, the PerSafe flashed my coordinates and my state of health. At home and with a slightly elevated white blood cell count. A minor infection. Or stress.

I thumbed Jessa's code and waited for the usual message: **NOT RESPONDING. CHECK PSIC AND TRANSMISSION DEVICE.**

And that's the message I got. No magic today, folks. Crap.

I slumped against Jessa's desk, and that's when I focused on Grandma's voice—in English now—shouting at Auntie An. "That's what he told me. The house might legally belong to Meryem now."

Auntie An answered in Vietnamese, her voice high and shrill. Then she switched to English—and I wished she hadn't.

"Who cared for our parents after you married and moved away? Me. I should have gotten this house instead of Jessa, because Mama Two wasn't in her right mind. You know that. After Mama Two died I could have stayed here forever, but then Jessa barged in with her swollen belly and her big plans. You know how I took care of Jessa after the baby was born, but was she grateful? No! Her child drove me away once, and I refuse to let that happen again."

"Don't you push me." Grandma sounded furious. "And don't you ever talk about my daughter and granddaughter like that again. I'll speak to the housekeeper and see what we can work out."

"Forget the damn housekeeper. Speak to your lawyer. I am not going back to The Anthony. This house should be mine. Take Merry to The Anthony and leave me here in peace!"

Grandma switched to Vietnamese. Shouting shifted to crying, and a door slammed.

I buried my head in my hands. That's why Grandma wanted to speak to Mr. Nabli. While I was downstairs asking him about blue threads and magic carpets, she and Auntie An were up here turning my life inside out.

CHAPTER
THIRTY-ONE

I wrapped myself in one of Jessa's shawls, but I couldn't stop shaking. This was my house, my home, wasn't it? I looked out the window to what was left of Jessa's car, stripped of anything salvageable by the night gleaners months ago. Everything was falling apart.

"Merry, we're waiting on you for dinner." Grandma's voice zapped every nerve in my body. "Sorry, I didn't mean to startle you. What on earth are you doing?"

"Nothing. I'm fine. I'll be down in a minute."

Five minutes later, I stood by the dinner table, ready to thumb the image of Shabbat candles for our Friday night blessing. Winslow and Priscilla were eating upstairs. Bandon and Ignatius stood at the table scrubbed and smiling. Even Rose and The Ladies looked relaxed. I was ready to scream.

My mouth and my brain went separate ways. I mumbled through the Shabbat blessings and polite conversation while trying to figure out how to deal with The Ladies' argument. I had to think. Or rather, I had to do something mindless so I didn't have to think, because thinking was driving me crazy.

"Priscilla needs help packing tonight and tomorrow," I said as I passed the bowl of veggie chili to Rose.

Grandma smoothed her napkin and took another slice of challah. "You have other responsibilities tomorrow, Merry."

Bandon started to say something, but Ignatius shook his head. "Not you, sir," he said. Then he turned to Grandma. "Permission to escort you ladies to and from Havurah Shalom?"

Rose touched Ignatius's arm. "They have to leave here by 9:45. That's early for you."

"I'll report for breakfast at oh-nine-hundred hours, Rose."

"Permission granted," Grandma said.

The tiniest smile softened the face of the guy that The Ladies often ignored. "It's an honor to serve," he said.

As soon as I could, I retreated to the third floor and surrounded myself with items in need of wrapping in eco-foam and packing into boxes. I slapped an attentive look on my face while Priscilla talked about acclimating Winslow to the neighborhood and home he hadn't seen in a year. The rhythm of wrapping and packing calmed my nerves.

We'd been working for an hour or so when a rare clap of thunder startled us both. Winslow shrieked, "Mommy!"

"I'd better calm him down. Are you okay here? I might be a while."

"Sure." I swept my arm out over the scattered bits. "I've got plenty to do."

Rain ka-thumped overhead. The room smelled vaguely of peanut butter. I was always safe up here in what used to be my playroom, with Jessa and Rose—sometimes just Rose—standing guard below. Wrap. Pack. Wrap. Pack. A while later, I leaned against the wall, rested my head on a wad of eco-foam, and eased into sleep.

My brain must have conjured up my little kid voice. *Not now,*

Rose. I'm in the middle. Go away. You're not the boss of me. I don't want to. I don't want to.

My voice morphed into Winslow's. "I don't want to. I don't want to."

Blinking awake, I peeled eco-foam from my cheek and pulled off the quilt Priscilla must have covered me with during the night. Light shone through the window. I followed Winslow's voice into Priscilla's room. He stood in his underwear, his arms flailing. "I don't want to. I don't want to."

"Winslow refuses to put on his clothes," Priscilla explained. "He doesn't want to leave Louise."

Here was one thing I could manage. "Since it's such a special day, I could bring Louise upstairs here to watch you finish packing."

Winslow stopped flailing.

"But only if you put on your..." I paused and looked at Priscilla, who held up his brown KidForm. "But only if you put on your brown KidForm, Winslow. Louise is partial to brown."

Winslow frowned. "What does partial mean?"

"Partial." My voice echoed Jessa's. "That's another good vocabulary word. Do you want to hear a story about the word partial?"

"No. I want Louise."

I laughed. "Got it. In this case partial means that Louise really likes brown. While you get dressed, I'll get her from Chicken Hacienda."

Winslow reached for his KidForm.

I thumbed the time on my way downstairs. 7:32. "Sorry I'm late," I told Rose. "I have to get Louise to avert a toddler meltdown."

Louise craned her neck in surprise when I took her egg, some feed, and her chicken self into the house. I wiped her golden-brown feathers with an old rag and fluffed up the backside bushiness that Buff Orpingtons featured. When we got to the third floor, a fully dressed Winslow was hopping from one foot to another, barely containing his excitement.

Two hours later, six e-trikes with box trailers had navigated their way down what was left of our street and stopped in front of the house. An exhausted Louise joined Tillie and Yetta at Chicken Hacienda. After everything was loaded and ready, I gave a tearful Winslow a hard-boiled egg with Louise's name on it.

"Zank you," he said, without Priscilla's prompting.

"You take care of yourself," Priscilla told me, giving me a quick embrace and her contact info. "It's been hard for you, I know."

I bit my lip. Later, I lugged our box of Sweeper Swarms up to the central charger on the third floor and sent them scurrying over every horizontal surface. One Sweeper puked up a tiny shield from one of Winslow's Mighty Microbots. I put the warrior shield in my pocket, as if it could protect me.

I came armed at dinner that night with the warrior shield and another mind-numbing activity. All I needed was a break in the conversation. The Ladies were tag-teaming about Purim, which was coming up in a few days.

"Purim might remind you of Mardi Gras," Auntie An told Bandon, while I dissected a Brussels sprout. "It's a good excuse to put on a costume and party. The Purim story is different, since it's based on Near Eastern mythology and celebrates saving the Jews in ancient Shushan, but the rowdiness factor is the same."

"We'll make *shamlias*," Rose added. "It's basically fried dough."

"You'll like them," Grandma said. "My Aron gave us an old Turkish-Jewish recipe from Izmir. Jessa adored *shamlias*."

I remembered one Purim party from when I was five. *Grandpa was singing and laughing, his fake beard peeling away from his chin. He suddenly started to cry, and then so did I, because I thought I had done something wrong. Jessa explained later that when he lived in*

Istanbul, he went to Shabbat services one day and something horrible happened. His crying had nothing to do with me. Purim lost a lot of its fun after that. It wasn't until years later, after Grandpa had died and I asked Query, that I learned Aron Zarfati was one of the few Jews to survive the terrorist shooting at Istanbul's Neve Shalom Synagogue in 1986. He was seventeen.

"Meryem likes them too," Rose said. "We've made *shamlias* every year, even when Jessa was away. Well, but not last year of course."

I shifted topics. "Let's repaint the third floor rooms," I said, hoping I sounded enthusiastic. "With the Chadwicks gone, it's the perfect time."

Rose passed the Brussels sprouts to Ignatius. "We just painted those rooms three years ago."

"We might as well give it a fresh new look, Rose," I said. "We can afford paint, can't we?"

"Oh, I'm sure we can," Grandma said. "What a good idea. Pick out your favorite color, Meryem." She patted Bandon's hand. "You'll help, won't you?"

He nodded, his mouth stuffed with dinner.

Rose shrugged. She gave me a look I'd seen a dozen times in the months since The Ladies had arrived: I pick my battles. Something felt odd, though. Grandma usually complained about "unnecessary" expenses, which I suppose this was. She complained about my working too hard, which sometimes I guess I did. I wished I'd kept my mouth shut.

Sunday morning, Bandon and I set out for Deuce Hardware. He turtled his head in his hoodie, and I wondered if he worried about bringing the Council down on our heads again. This whole bit with Calantha Corps was unfair.

"What does it take to lift the exclusion order?" I asked as we ambled along.

"Beats me," he said. "It would be great to set up headquarters in Portland instead of out by Gales Creek. Got a magic formula to make that happen?"

"I'm fresh out of magic," I said, which was so true it hurt. I ran my hands across the damp needles of an old rosemary bush overseeing the debris stack on the corner of 17th and Lovejoy. I rubbed the tips of my fingers together, breathed in the pungent scent, and offered my fingertips to Bandon. "Take a whiff."

Bandon cupped my hands and brought my fingers toward his nose. A misty drizzle softened the world around us. I said nothing and he said nothing, and for that moment it felt so good to have a friend again, the way it used to be before they moved away.

Which is when the dogs started barking.

First two, then another. And another. My body tensed. I thumbed the MyCom's alert system. Nothing.

"Are you okay?"

A slow unwinding along my spine left a shudder in its wake. "Last year, before the warning sirens, the dogs barked. The dogs knew first. This time it's just a dog fight."

I expected Bandon to resort to a dose of banter. He didn't. Instead, he held my hand all the way to the store. We lugged the CaseinCoat home and unearthed painting supplies from the basement. I'd bought light ochre and an off-white for the trim, the best of the few choices we had with paint in short supply.

I thought I'd feel good easing into the rhythm of the work. I tried. I smiled at Ignatius, who barely spoke but looked happy, especially when Rose smoothed his shirt for no obvious reason. I sang along with Bandon's sea shanties. At Rose's instigation, I told the story about when I was little, and Jessa explained that boisterous meant rowdy, and I insisted that girls who were rowdy should be called "girlsterous."

"Jessa added 'girlsterous' to our vocabulary," Rose said, beaming at me. "I made a note in my Russian-English dictionary."

I laughed along with the rest of them, but I couldn't help thinking about Grandma's enthusiasm for redoing the third floor.

Painting these rooms had been my idea—another time-consuming, mind-numbing chore. Now I was making it even easier for them to stick me up on the third floor, or, worse still, to send me to live with my grandmother at The Anthony and rent the third floor to someone else.

CHAPTER
THIRTY-TWO

While we were cleaning up in the third-floor bathroom, I asked Rose if The Ladies had said anything to her about moving back to The Anthony.

"Not yet," she said. "Give it a couple more weeks until their neighbors are back."

"Suppose they don't want to leave?"

Rose frowned. "Then you'll nudge them out the door, okay? Ever so gently."

"It's not up to me, Rose."

She wiped a splotch of paint from her cheek and laughed. "Well, it's certainly not up to me. I'm just the housekeeper, remember? The painting was a fun break today. Thanks."

And that was it. End of discussion. I managed dinner and a particularly boring game of Trivial Pursuit before I collapsed into bed that night and slept until the MyCom dinged 6:15. The air was still fresh and the neighborhood quiet enough to hear birdsong. When I got downstairs, Bandon and Gryffindor were playing chess in the dining room.

The housebot noticed me before Bandon did. "Good morning, Meryem. I am entertaining Bandon with a game of chess. All of my systems are fully operational. How may I assist you?"

"Good morning, Gryffindor," I said. "I do not need assistance."

Bandon barely smiled. I expected him to make a joke about being fully operational too, but he didn't.

"See you in the kitchen when you're done," I said. "I'm starting millet and squash stew for lunch. Rose should be down soon to make biscuits."

He nodded and got back to the game.

A few minutes later, Gryffindor announced. "Checkmate." Bandon slouched into the kitchen.

"You seem pensive," I told him. Pensive. Thoughtful. A good Jessa word.

He reached for a piece of pear leather. "Hey, you know I'm having a fine time here, but there's Calantha Corps work to be done, and I should go do it. You know me. Utopia awaits. I can't hide in your house forever."

"You're not hiding."

"Right. I'm goat sitting. Anyway, I'm going out after breakfast to meet with a couple of citizen action folks."

"Is that safe?"

"Safe enough. They are not part of the DC Six, and the compliance officers are tied up looking for people stealing construction material. Want to come along?"

I shook my head. Bandon needed alone time. Or maybe I needed to get used to him not being around. "Too much housework."

Ever since The Big One, Monday had been my best day. A week's worth of chores awaited me, with Rose and EduComps and RescueCommons to help me stay focused and keep me afloat. This Monday felt different. I couldn't settle into anything like a mindless routine. I rooted around in the storage closet on the third floor and unearthed the stuffed unicorn Jessa bought for me back when I still shared my mother's belief that they might have been real. The mane was still bright white and the horn sparkled. I stroked its back, waiting for memories of Jessa to well up inside me, but the unicorn seemed to belong to Gemmie already.

Bandon was still gone by dinner, and Ignatius didn't show up either. That left The Ladies and me—the new family, as Grandma put it—plus Rose. Jessa was so absent from the table that I felt her presence deep inside my heart. Rose brought up the toothpaste mystery again.

"Surely we can afford toothpaste," Auntie An grumped. "Why do you insist on keeping track of every tube?"

Rose folded her napkin. "I'm not keeping track. It's just that it's nearly impossible to find that brand of toothpaste these days, and you seem to go through it so fast."

Grandma said something to Auntie An in Vietnamese. Auntie An argued back, her voice rising. Grandma buttered her roll and turned to me. "I remember when you used to visit Grandpa and me when you were little. You loved feeding the ducks at Tanner Springs Park. We had such fun. It's so good to be together under one roof."

Rose picked at a stain on her jumpsuit.

I fiddled with my lobe locket. "They were great times," I said, trying to keep my voice steady. I loved my grandmother, even if I didn't want The Ladies in my face on a daily basis. After Grandpa died and Auntie An moved in with Grandma, we visited The Ladies every couple of weeks, and that was plenty. Now was the perfect time to talk about moving, wasn't it?

My breath came faster. I fought to stay in control. "You must miss your friends at The Anthony, Grandma. When are you and Auntie An planning to move back there?"

"The Anthony is a building without a soul," Auntie An said. "Not like here." She thrust her fork at me. "How many years have you lived in this house?"

"Sixteen," I said.

"And your grandmother? How many years did she?"

"Well...um..."

"You have no idea, child."

"An Chau, stop it," Grandma warned.

Auntie An spat back something in Vietnamese.

Grandma shook her head.

"Eight," Auntie An said. "Only eight, not counting since The Big One. Eight years from the time we moved here in 1990 until your grandmother married Aron and left. She has no attachment here, Merry. But me? How many years has this house been my home?"

Before I could guess, she said, "Fifty-five," stabbing the air twice. "Fifty-five years. I took care of my parents in this house until they died. I took care of you here when you were born, until Jessa chased me away."

Rose pushed back her chair and stood. "This is unfair and uncalled for. Jessa's not here to defend herself."

"Precisely," Grandma said, her face pinched with fatigue and sadness. "That's the reality of the situation. Jessa is no longer here."

The air grew thick with silence.

I curled my fist. My pulse thundered in my neck. I tried to find the right combination of Jessa's vocabulary words to express my anger and pain. And fear. All I could do was storm into the kitchen, scrape the rest of my dinner into the digester, and retreat outside to the safety of Munchkina and the chickens.

I could have taken the next hour to think things through, to sort out my blue-thread-magic-carpet world and my here-and-now reality. Did it matter? I couldn't find Jessa in either place. I could have concentrated on another mind-numbing project at Chicken Hacienda. Instead I sat on the ground by the chickens and let the tears roll until I was tapped out.

When I came back inside, Rose and Ignatius were sitting at the dining room table, laughing like old friends and playing poker.

I couldn't hide my surprise.

Rose practically glowed. "We've been playing poker on and off for a month now. Ignatius here usually wins. He's great company when The Ladies aren't around. Want to join us?"

"No thanks." I started for the back stairs.

"Wait up," Rose said. "Let's get you something to eat. You hardly had dinner."

We reconvened in front of the fridge. "I'm so sorry about The Ladies and this house business," she said.

I rolled my eyes, not wanting to talk about that again. "What's with you and Ignatius?"

Rose smoothed her jumpsuit, which is when I noticed she'd changed into a fresh one after dinner and she was wearing the silver bracelet she kept for special occasions. "I'm forty-one, Meryem. I'm not getting any younger. You won't be needing me much longer."

I remembered Mr. Nabli's revelation about Rose's lien and her right to leave. My heart twisted. "I'll need you forever. You know that, don't you? Ignatius is a sweet guy, but he's sixty-four. You can't be serious about him."

Rose extracted two non-alcoholic beers from the fridge. "He's good company. Anyway, I don't plan to leave any time soon." Rose waved a bottle at me. "Let's talk later. I'm on a winning streak."

That made one of us.

CHAPTER
THIRTY-THREE

During the night, the fear that I'd never see Jessa alive again—here or elsewhere in the *olam*—had taken root inside my guts. It germinated, sprouting spiny vines that strangled me slowly, slowly, slowly, while I made Tuesday's breakfast because Rose was vid-voicing her grief counselor.

"The counseling service has a vid-voice opening this afternoon, if you're interested," she told me afterward.

I shook my head. "Too busy. I've got RescueCommons."

"That's only two hours, Meryem."

"Yes, but then I'm working with Bandon in the basement today."

"Fine," she said, sounding too much like me.

The five-block walk to RescueCommons did little to improve my mood, despite the much-needed spring shower. Mark's minivan was gone. Shander told me that Mark had to take Gemmie somewhere and would be back later.

I gave Gemmie's unicorn to Shander for safekeeping. "How long have they been living in the Tesla?"

"A day would be too long," ze said.

"No, I really don't mean to breach Mark's privacy, but there's a little girl at stake. I'm worried about Izabel…I mean Gemmie."

"Mark lost his home before The Big One," ze said. "When he lost his job, he couldn't manage the rent. You know, Meryem, there were plenty of people living in cars and vans before the quake. Particularly people of color. We still have a long way to go in this community."

"I know. But why doesn't he get help from the Resilience Council? I have three people living in my house as credit tenants."

Shander sighed. "Suffice it to say there are difficulties. The main stumbling block is that Gemmie is perhaps not Mark's biological daughter, and her biological mother is out of the picture." Ze touched my shoulder. "I've said too much already. Time to get to work."

For the next two hours, minus the breaks, I examined drone images of a site near Coos Bay, logging geo-coordinates and the date and time each image was taken. Nothing of interest turned up, not even a beer can.

At the end of my shift, Shander parked me in front of Stuart Miltson's photo by the front door. Stuart Miltson, a.k.a. Miracle Man, was the guy that RescueCommons discovered by searching a sextillion drone images of the Coast Range. No one had reported him missing. No one had counted him among the dead or the living. He was simply found dazed, emaciated, but alive, after five months alone in Cummins Creek Wilderness.

"Stay brave, Meryem," Shander said. "All will be as it should in the fullness of time."

The fullness of time was taking way too long.

Rose's note on the kitchen table announced that she and The Ladies were at the doctor's—something about Auntie An's knee—and Bandon and Ignatius were getting shelf braces at Deuce Hardware. I grabbed a bag of crispy cricket mix and stretched out on the couch for a minibreak. Shander's words floated through my brain. All will be as it should be in the fullness of time.

Which is how it came to me. Time. I'd been logging times for months now. Not just places, but times too. The spiny vines began to loosen their grip two minutes later, as I curled up in the Jessa nest and queried.

Izabel's story about the unicorn lady came down to this: Ayele was a boy during a quake that hit Istanbul hard enough to destroy a lion's cage at Topkapı Palace. I had the geo-coordinates for the place; all I needed was the time. I'd seen Ayele—he was certainly at least as old as Rose, if not older. How many strong quakes could have struck that region during Ayele's boyhood?

Query deluged me with hits, most of them irrelevant, but an hour later I linked to an old British book called *Earthquakes in the Mediterranean and Middle East: A Multidisciplinary Study of Seismicity up to 1900*. The book was organized chronologically.

And there it was. September 10, 1509. Sea of Marmara—the body of water that bordered the southern shore of Istanbul opposite the Golden Horn. Other sources cited the quake as the Lesser Judgment Day. A European primary source from 1510 noted the quake's destruction of the "house wherein the lions are enclosed." The book's author concluded that this was near "Aya Sofia, where the Sultans' menagerie was housed."

Excellent! Everything fit. Ayele would have been a boy in 1509. The lions had gotten loose. Aya Sofia was only a few meters away from the church that Serakh and I had stood in front of inside the walls of Topkapı. All I had to do now was find a way to get to this exact spot on the *olam*. Jessa had to be there. Absolutely.

I snuggled deeper into the Jessa nest, certain that Aussie Jack had given me all I needed to know—except when Serakh would return. And now she would because I had the final piece of the puzzle, the complete entry in the log. I was ready, just like with the prayer shawl and Gracia's portrait medal. Somehow she'd know.

My certainty overflowed into the next day. With new energy, I whipped through the morning chores, weeded the garden, hung out with Munchkina and the chickens, and nailed another EduComps lecture.

"You deserve a break, friend," Bandon told me. "Let's go to Couch Park." He rhymed Couch with ouch, so I said, "If you want to mix with us natives, remember that Couch Street and Couch Park aren't pronounced like the piece of furniture. It's *kooch*, rhymes with pooch."

"Got it," he said. "So, how about we grab some grub, a blanket, and a thermos of vintage 2059 filtered water? Let's spend a couple hours doing nothing."

"That does sound appealing," I said. "Let's do no grub and forty-five minutes."

"An hour with two peanut butter sandwiches for me and edible but disgusting insects for you."

"Crispy cricket mix is not disgusting."

"Deal?" He gave me his want-to-play look.

"Deal."

It had rained the night before. Now the sun was shining, making this perfect sweater weather. The grass smelled fresh. We spread the blanket next to one of the big tulip trees. Bandon pulled off his shoes, revealing socks of a dubious gray color, threadbare at the heels.

"Ah, that's better," he said. "Your turn. This is a picnic."

I couldn't say no without looking like a yutz, so I loosened the laces and put my boots next to his. The two pairs looked comfortable together, his big and slouchy, mine sturdy and small. We sat against the tree and stretched our legs. Bandon extracted his harmonica and played a sweet, lazy tune I didn't know.

A few minutes later, he reached down and pulled off his socks. Tiny reddish blond hairs sprouted near the joint on his big toes.

Bandon grinned. "I show you mine, you show me yours."

"What?"

He reached for my socks. "Feet, my friend. Ten little piggies basking in the sun."

I shifted my hips and sat with my feet tucked safely away.

The next thing I knew, he was marching back and forth on the blanket in protest mode, pretending to hold a sign. "Free the Portland Ten," he chanted, over and over.

My cheeks burned. An old guy lounging on the grass about five meters away stared at us in apparent amusement. I tugged on Bandon's pant leg, which made his jeans ride even lower. Wrong move.

Bandon stopped in mid-protest. "So, will you free the Portland Ten or do I have to take aggressive measures?"

Honesty bubbled up. "Nine," I said.

He sat next to me, questions clouding his face.

"Phalanges 2 on my right foot is a prosthesis. My feet got cut and infected after The Big One. Glass."

"Do they still hurt?"

"Sometimes, when I'm not careful. They look horrid, Bandon."

"How bad can they be?"

"Bad."

"Now I definitely want to see them."

I remembered Serakh's reaction when she saw my feet at Belvedere. I needed her now. Why wasn't she coming? What was taking her so long?

"Meryem, your feet?"

I blinked. Couch Park. With Bandon. Here and now. I took off my socks.

Silence.

Then, "That's pretty impressive scarring, Meryem. The one by your right instep looks like Harry Potter's lightning bolt. My dad was a Harry Potter fan, like your mom." He handed me my crispy cricket mix. "Now we feast."

The sunshine felt good on my feet after all these months. I munched my mix and let time ease by. Bandon ate a sandwich.

It was a beautiful day to be outside, especially because I had a decent inside to return to every night, and not a minivan. "Bandon, you know the place where I volunteer—RescueCommons?"

"Yup."

"Well, there's a guy—Mark—who works there, and he lives in his minivan with his little girl Gemmie. There's got to be something I can do to help."

"In the short run or the long run?"

"Both."

He ran his fingers through his hair. "In the long run, good luck. All you have to do you is get Mayor Hammilason to stop congratulating himself on Portland's recovering from The Big One and to start getting serious about reliable and consistent programs for affordable housing."

"Such as?"

Bandon reached for another sandwich. "Don't get me started, Meryem. Calantha Corps has implemented scores of programs that work in other cities. The DC Six had that one lousy meeting in September, when I admit things got out of hand, and the powers that be in Portland have shut us out."

I folded up my crispy cricket bag. "I wonder if maybe in the short run, Mark and Gemmie could stay on the third floor like the Chadwicks did. The Ladies would probably have a fit."

"So? From what I hear their condo is ready to reopen. They'll be moving out soon. The house belongs to you," he said. "You're the boss."

Which was so not true.

CHAPTER
THIRTY-FOUR

Shamlias are easy. Make dough. Roll dough paper-thin and shape into braids folded in half. Fry dough. Sprinkle dough with cinnamon and sugar. Devour. Rose and I made *shamlias* the next day. We'd made them together since forever; how could I not make them now?

I followed the Purim tradition of giving to the poor—this time taking *shamlias* and hard-boiled eggs to the food pantry at William Temple House a few blocks away. But I refused to go to Havurah Shalom's Purim party—I couldn't bear it without Jessa—and The Ladies stayed home too. Instead, they made a big fuss over Bandon, who showed up at dinner dressed as Queen Esther, the Jewish heroine of the Purim story. The guy had guts, and I must admit he did liven up the evening.

"I am the most beautiful Jew in all of Persia," he said, waltzing around in Rose's tights and best apron, plus two of Auntie An's long silk scarves. Auntie An laughed so hard I thought she'd pee in her pants. Ignatius ate almost as many *shamlias* as Bandon, and we all seemed to bliss out on carb overload.

Bandon and I gave *shamlia* leftovers to Tillamook and Munchkina. "Got any more Jewish holidays coming up?" he asked, scratching at his tights.

"Passover," I said.

"Great! I know that one. The exodus from Egypt, right?" Bandon burst into song. "Go down, Moses! Way down in Egypt's land. Tell ole Pha-a-a-roah...to let my people...go!" Off key. "Not bad, if I say so myself," he said.

Munchkina bleated.

"Stick to the harmonica," I said.

He laughed. "The *shamlias* were stupendous. Invite me back next year."

"You expect to be in Oregon that long?"

Bandon draped one of his scarves around my neck. "I like Oregon," he said. "And I like you, friend."

"Yeah, well, you'd probably like Mark even more," I said, reminding my hormones to settle down.

His eyebrows danced.

Maybe it was talking about Passover, which reminded me of Serakh washing my hands at Belvedere. Maybe it was the *shamlias*, which reminded me of Jessa. Serakh and Jessa. Both of them gone. I woke in the night, threw back the covers, clapped on the light, and retrieved the prayer shawl I'd put in Jessa's top drawer.

I sat in Jessa's chair, wrapped the blue thread around my finger, and whispered into the darkness. "Serakh, it's Meryem. Wherever you are, whenever you are, come for me now. Please. I have the time coordinates. I have to see my mother. Even if it's just to say good-bye."

An hour later, I was still sitting, waiting, surrounded by Jessa's things. Jessa seemed to be fading. Even her scent was leaching away after all these months.

I put my useless shawl away and collected Jessa's bottle of lotion from the bathroom. Somehow the two little tubes that Bandon, Rose, and Ignatius had gotten me for my birthday didn't have quite the same smell. Sitting back in bed, I cradled her bottle in my hand and studied all the claims for its goodness stamped on the label. All natural botanicals. Non-GMO. Fair trade. Organic. Where did it say open at your own risk?

I squeezed a precious dollop of honey-orange lotion on my left index finger and put the bottle on the end table. I touched my thumb to that finger and slowly glided my thumb across the rest of the fingertips on my left hand. Then I put all my fingertips together in a prayerful pose with Jessa's scent locked inside.

I brought my hands to my nose and I breathed in Jessa.

I inhaled again.

Still not enough.

I rummaged in Jessa's closet until I found the faded woolen sweater she claimed had traces of my baby barf in its fibers. I breathed in the sweater's smell and then put the sweater on the bed, padding the Jessa nest. I breathed the Jessa scent that clung to her memorabilia hoodie, the one she no longer wore in public but couldn't throw away. That too went on the Jessa nest. Next a pair of her hand-knitted socks with holes in the heels. Then the FemForm she usually wore to the lab. And her lab coat.

I couldn't stop. The Jessa nest grew and grew. Scarves, shawls, over-tees, nightgowns, caftans, lingerie. I collected clothes from dresser drawers, hangers, and storage boxes. Clothes and more clothes—Jessa had worn them all. If only I could extract her essence from each garment and piece my mother back together.

My foot slipped on a felted hat that had escaped to the floor. I grabbed the bed quilt for support. The quilt shook loose from it moorings. Jessa's clothes slid on top of me—a smothering motherly hug as I lay on the floor. I gathered her clothes in my arms and heard a low moan escape from my throat. The moan grew until it erupted into a keening I couldn't stop.

Then Grandma had her arms around me. "Oh, my sweet baby. My sweet baby. Finally. It's okay, Merry, let it out, let it go."

And I did, until there was no sound left. Exhausted, I rested against Grandma's heart and listened to her blood-thrum.

"There. That's better. Shall we clean up this mess now?"

I shook my head.

Grandma rested her hand on my knee. "Merry, would you like to stay with me in my room?"

"Yes," I whispered. "I can't face tonight alone."

The sweet, creamy smell of cardamom and butter drew me out of the swamp that had passed for sleep. I blinked open my eyes to Grandma sitting on the bed with a bowl of millet under my nose.

"Time to wake up, sleepyhead. Have your breakfast while it's hot. Bandon collected the eggs this morning. He played 'Old MacDonald' on his harmonica for the animals. That young man marches to a different drummer."

I rolled on my side. "What time is it?"

Grandma put the bowl on her desk. "I brought you your toothbrush and towel in case you want to wash up in the hall bathroom. And a change of clothes, hiking boots, and your MyCom, of course."

She opened the curtains. Full sunlight, a bad sign. "Rose managed quite well without you this morning. You needed your rest. I told her to let RescueCommons know that you weren't coming in today."

Crud. "Grandma, I do important work there." I thumbed the time. 9:37. With luck I'd be only half an hour late.

"Merry, it is my responsibility to…" I didn't hear the rest, because I'd grabbed the bowl and my things and closeted myself in the hall bathroom. I vid-voiced Shander that I was coming in after all. "In the fullness of time," I joked. "Sorry I overslept."

202

Eight minutes later, I was out the door. I took a shortcut through the narrow alley between Kearney and Lovejoy, one I usually avoided because of rats. Two women huddled by a dumpster halfway down the alley. It took me a moment to realize that one of them was Auntie An.

CHAPTER
THIRTY-FIVE

Before I had a chance to formulate a coherent sentence, Auntie An planted herself between me and the other woman.

"What are you doing here? You should be at RescueCommons by now. Why did you follow me? Who sent you here? This is none of your business."

Her voice was high and shrill, and underneath all that verbiage she looked genuinely frightened. What happened to my great aunt was definitely my business. I took her hands in mine and tried to steady her. Whatever this was, I had my MyCom and could send out an alarm if I had to.

"I overslept this morning," I told her as calmly as I could. "I was taking a shortcut to work. Tell me what's going on. Are you okay?"

The lilt of an Asian language rose from behind her. Auntie An kept her eyes on me as she answered in kind. Her fear had faded. She slipped back into English. "I am surprised your mother never made you learn Chinese," she said. "I will teach it to you. Now listen to me. When I introduce you to Mrs. Liú, keep quiet and bow to show respect."

I did as I was told. The woman behind Auntie An looked half my size and five times my age. She wore a large woolen shawl layered over baggy plaid pants and a torn over-tee that read OREGON DUCKS. I smiled out of politeness. She smiled back, revealing a few long, yellowed teeth in a gaping mouth.

There was more Chinese, more smiling, more bowing, and then Mrs. Liú thrust a hand in her pants pocket and fished out a familiar-looking tube of toothpaste.

Auntie An sucked in her breath, said something in Chinese, told me in English to bow again—which I did—and escorted me down the alley. "You are to say nothing about the toothpaste. Do I make myself clear? Mrs. Liú should not have shown it to you."

"Fine," I said.

But Auntie An wasn't done. "Ly Tien and I have known Mrs. Liú for years, because she always appeared at The Anthony on recycling day. She refuses to leave the streets, poor woman. She likes the taste of fennel toothpaste, and so I see that she always has some. It's a treat."

"Your friend eats toothpaste?"

Auntie An shook her head. "Mrs. Liú is not my friend, she is a neighbor. I make sure there is no fluoride in it, so she doesn't get sick. It's not up to a housekeeper to judge. If I put the toothpaste on the shopping list, she should buy it and not ask questions."

"All this is about toothpaste?"

Auntie An puffed up. "All this is about honor and respect."

I wasn't about to argue. Now wasn't the time to get into what Rose should or should not do. I gave Auntie An a perfunctory peck on the cheek and left.

Mark was waiting for me on the front steps. "Shander said you'd be here soon and ze wasn't going to let me get to work until I talked to you, so here goes." No preliminary hello.

He patted the step for me to sit next to him. "What do you think of my sending Gemmie to Manitoba to live with my sister?"

"Pardon?" I was still trying to organize my brain around Mrs. Liú and her toothpaste.

"Janine—that's my sister—Janine's willing, and she's got four kids, so what's one more? The Tesla is a terrible place to raise a kid, but if I go to social services for help, I'm afraid I'll lose her. Gemmie's mother disappeared when Gemmie was fifteen months old. We weren't married, so…"

Mark tossed a stone from one hand to the other. "What do you think? Should I ship my little girl off to Manitoba until I can stitch my life back together?"

I hugged my knees. No one had ever asked my advice for something this big. "Manitoba, Canada? What does Shander say?"

Mark chucked the stone at an innocent maple. "Shander says I need your perspective because you've met Gemmie, and you live in a house without your parents. Ze also says ze's looking for a permanent place for Gemmie and me, but who knows how long that might take."

I couldn't remember if I'd told Shander about the Chadwicks leaving and space becoming available on the third floor. Maybe that was another reason ze had Mark talk to me. I took a breath. "Does Gemmie know your sister?"

"Never set eyes on her."

I let the silence between us stretch for about ten seconds, which seems short until you watch every second of waiting take its toll on someone's face. I needed that time to decide if Rose and I could manage. And The Ladies complicated things. This was more than buying special toothpaste.

Finally, I said, "I might be able to arrange for you and Gemmie to stay on the third floor of my place. The people who lived there were a mother and son, and they liked it a lot, at least the little boy did. There are only five of us now, plus a guest who'll be gone in another week or so. And two of us might be leaving soon. Maybe three. You'd have your own bathroom. We have enough credits to give you meals too."

Mark stared at the ground around our feet. "I don't take

handouts, remember? Besides, Gemmie doesn't like being around a lot of other people. It wouldn't work."

"How do you know that? Gemmie likes me. Charles like me."

"Thanks, okay? But no thanks."

I followed Mark up the stairs. "Gemmie needs you. Think about it. Is she in the Tesla? I'd like to say hi."

"She's staying at a friend's place today," he said. "She's got a cough."

I insisted that Mark give me his contact coordinates, which he did. "I think you'd really like the house," I said. "Gemmie could play with my goat and chickens."

Mark's face turned stormy. "Lay off. I already said no."

After he left, I sat on the steps another minute. By the time I went inside, I'd resolved to square things with Rose and try to convince Mark the next time we met.

I was logging drone images of the Reedsport area when Shander touched my shoulder. I popped my earbuds. "Collection duty," ze said. My stomach cramped.

I shook hands with a woman carrying something the size of an orange wrapped in eco-foam.

"Thanks for coming," I said, feeling the opposite. "Please follow me."

I got an extra screen and ushered us into the walk-in closet that now served as our collection room. Two stools, one table, one lamp, one box of tissues.

The woman signed the release forms, and we got started on the part I dreaded: forensic sample and story. "I'm going to be logging anything that might be relevant," I explained. "How may we help you?"

The woman's name was Elsie Chumway, born and raised in Beaverton. So was her daughter, Rebecca, twenty-one next month. Elsie reached for a tissue.

"You haven't seen Rebecca since The Big One," I prompted.

"Since 2057, actually, Ms...."

"Please call me Meryem." Shander instructed us to use first

names during interviews, to put people at ease and at least appear to be helpful.

"Elsie," she said.

I smiled.

She sighed.

I waited for her to start the story I didn't want to hear, because I hurt too much already.

Elsie reached for a tissue. "Rebecca did her national service year at the NOAA labs in Newport."

I wondered why a government agency like the National Oceanic and Atmospheric Administration hadn't asked Rebecca for a DNA profile, but I didn't ask. Instead I listened and logged.

"We saw her less and less, a vid-voice every so often, and she came home for the Christmas before The Big One. We lost the house to the quake, and it's taken us months to get back on our feet. I wasn't going to bother you, because I know you are so busy with the emergency, and Rebecca never was one for staying in touch."

"What do you have for us, Elsie?"

She unwrapped a pocket-sized brush with several strands of hair coiled around the bristles.

I silently thanked Jessa for having a DNA profile done before she got pregnant—it made matching a lot easier. I recited the official speech about the forensics lab and databases. I explained privacy constraints and all the bureaucratic hoops that RescueCommons jumps through with state and federal regulations. I showed Elsie where to tap the screen and what to sign. We stood and shook hands, and then, because it felt right, I hugged her.

"Ardmore says—Ardmore's my partner—anyway, Ardmore says we should stop waiting and start living again. The world is full of people who still need love and care. But it's hard."

I handed her another tissue. "I understand," I said, taking another tissue for myself and escorting Elsie to the door.

My shift ended with no change in the missing persons list and no objects of interest on the drone images. As I walked home, I couldn't help thinking about Mark and Gemmie. And Mrs. Liú.

I rubbed the tiny bump left on my hand by Izabel's embroidery needle, and remembered how terrified she was of living on the streets—or dying there—like Calantha.

That Ardmore guy was right. There was plenty to do besides waiting, which is what I'd been doing for months, waiting and looking at casualty lists and specks on drone vids. Jessa was…well, she wasn't in Portland with me now. Gemmie was, though. And giving her that old stuffed unicorn wasn't nearly enough. What was I thinking? Maybe Bandon could persuade Mark to board with us on the third floor, or to find some other place where Gemmie would be sheltered and secure. Where she could have a home. Maybe I could join Calantha Corps and work with Bandon—if it weren't for his ridiculous exclusion order.

CHAPTER THIRTY-SIX

Mr. Nabli was all smiles when he showed up that afternoon. "My colleague decoded the calligraphy on Jessa's rug," he said. "There are two intertwined words—Jessa and Meryem."

Jessa. Meryem. That made sense. I thought I'd get all mushy, but, oddly, the only emotion welling up was curiosity. Maybe I was tapped out. "So it's a new rug?"

"The calligraphy is an overlay on a much older weave. My colleague was surprised that your mother would have defaced a museum-quality textile."

I thought of Izabel's unicorn lady. "There's a lot about Jessa I don't know," I said. Then I got down to business. "How long am I your ward?"

"That depends," he said. "It's possible that your grandmother might sue for custody, given the circumstances." Mr. Nabli put down his pen and leaned across the table. "Are you dissatisfied with the current arrangement, Meryem?"

"No," I said. "Honestly, you've given me more freedom than my grandmother would have." I cleared my throat. "What happens if I sign the death papers and Jessa turns up the next day?"

Mr. Nabli gave me such a sympathetic look that I had to turn away. Maybe I wasn't tapped out after all.

"Hypothetically," I added.

Mr. Nabli cleared his throat. "The situation might be complicated for a while, but eventually the house would revert to your mother unless you contested the reversion. And there'd be an insurance issue."

"Are you authorized to pay Rose her back salary?"

"That's also complicated. It would be easier after we know the contents of certain documents."

"Right." I bit my lip and reached for Mr. Nabli's papers. As usual, the Council had listed The Ladies, Rose, and me as the current non-credit occupants of 732-NW19-97209. For months now I had added Jessa's name. This time, I didn't.

Mr. Nabli touched my hand. "Brave girl," he said.

I took a breath. "How well do you know members of the Resilience Council?"

"I have some influence there. One of the members was with my law firm, and we're still good friends. The mayor in fact."

"Excellent," I said, managing to keep my voice steady. "Then I'm ready to sign the death papers on one condition."

His eyebrows arched. "And that is?"

I shifted to the most authoritative face I could muster. "The Council lifts the exclusion order on all members of the DC Six, including Bandon Falconer."

I set my jaw and prepared to argue. Why would they care about Jessa's death papers? Still, it was the only bargaining chip I had.

Mr. Nabli folded his hands and shifted to a neutral look that he probably mastered in law school. His voice was as noncommittal as his face. "Interesting. What, precisely, is the connection between your survivorship documents and the presence of Calantha Corps in Portland?"

I sidestepped the question. "Bandon says that the September incident with that Council meeting was a mistake. Besides, we have an opportunity to…um…to continue to improve how we live together. Calantha Corps deserves a chance to tell us their ideas. It's only fair."

Mr. Nabli started thumbing his MyCom. "Give me a moment."

I drank a glass of water in the kitchen to steady my nerves and then came back in the dining room, trying to look casual, trying not to hover.

Six minutes later, he said, "The Council hasn't filed any formal violation notices against Calantha Corps in at least the past 180 days. I'll see what I can do."

I decided to say nothing to Bandon about my exclusion order plans, because I didn't want to get his hopes up. Hope isn't always a great thing to have. Hope can also drive you crazy.

I went about my business as if this were a normal Friday. After the Shabbat blessings at dinner, Bandon reported that he and Ignatius had made stellar progress on the basement shelves.

Then Auntie An tapped her water glass with her fork.

"I have an announcement," she said.

I thought it would be about the toothpaste and Mrs. Liú. I was wrong.

"Bandon says that there is enough paint left over to cover one wall of the bedroom I am in now. This is an auspicious moment to change rooms. I am the oldest and the one who often needs a bathroom at night. I will move into Jessa's bedroom suite."

Grandma said something in Vietnamese.

Auntie An rolled her eyes. "I *suggest* the *possibility* that I move into Jessa's bedroom suite," she said. "My *little sister* will stay where she is. Merry, you should sleep in the bedroom I have now. It was Miriam Josefsohn's room more than a hundred years ago. And it was the room that Mama Two used as her study and sewing room when we moved here from Berkeley. It's perfect for you. The room of the Miriams. Good karma."

I didn't want to give up Jessa's room, even after my meltdown. Still Auntie An made sense about needing the bathroom. I herded peas from one side of my plate to the other. "This seems like a lot of work for the short time you'll still be here."

Grandma cleared her throat. "We might be staying on for a bit longer," she said. "And the room could use some freshening up, don't you think?"

"It's up to Rose," I said. "The room Auntie An is in now used to be Rose's before The Big One."

"Let's not worry about which room I get," Rose said. She stole a quick look at Ignatius.

That's when I knew. Rose had had enough. She was leaving. My lungs deflated.

"It's settled then," Grandma said.

Rose said, "Let's start tomorrow." My heart stopped.

Ignatius escorted The Ladies to and from services Saturday morning again, while Bandon and Rose reorganized the rooms and I escaped outside to care for the animals and work in the garden. Rose stopped by as I was putting in a row of Swiss chard. "Which of your things do you want from the storage closet upstairs? I thought I'd sort that out so it's ready when you switch rooms."

I buried three nugget-looking seeds. "Nothing." I didn't dare ask Rose about leaving. I wasn't ready for her answer.

"There's plenty of space in your new bedroom. Meryem, look at me. That's better. Surely you want something from the storage closet. What about that Turkish shawl Jessa gave you a couple of years ago? You used to wear it all the time."

I wiped my nose with the back of my hand. "Maybe later," I said. After she left, I remembered the two items I had to keep with me. I followed Rose inside and tried the knob on Jessa's bedroom door. Unlocked.

All of Jessa's personal things had been put away. One of Auntie An's caftans and two of her numerology books lay on the edge of the bed like an invasive species. The quilt was different, the pillows were arranged wrong, the bed was made with Rose's hospital corner precision, the Jessa nest had been completely destroyed.

I fought the urge to throw up. I tried to remind myself that this room belonged to Auntie An's mother before it belonged to mine. It was only one room in a big old house.

No good. I still felt sick. I rescued Jessa's bottle of honey-orange lotion and her baby barf sweater in under thirty seconds. They'd live with me.

When I went downstairs again, The Ladies seemed waiting to gang up on me.

"Rabbi Judith has planned a healing and memorial service for next Saturday morning," Grandma said. "She's hoping that everyone in the congregation will attend."

Auntie An smiled. "Everyone."

"It's a gathering of the whole congregation to support each other as we get ready for Resilience Day next Sunday," Grandma added.

I nodded.

Grandma sighed. "I need you to be by my side at services, Merry. You lost your mother. I lost my daughter. You knew Jessa for fifteen years. I knew her for fifty. I expect that you will come."

"Fine." Which wasn't a yes, but she left it at that. Knowing Grandma, I'd keep hearing about that service until I agreed to go.

The Saturday afternoon activity of choice for everyone except me turned out to be finishing the bedroom shifts and painting that one wall in the Miriam Josefsohn room. I pitched in because Rose insisted.

Ignatius and Bandon had to move the heavy wooden armoire that had been in this room since forever. Rose joked that everything shook in the house during The Big One, except this armoire.

"What have we here?" Bandon said, when they'd finally pushed the armoire away from the wall. A piece of paper that resembled one of Grandma's playing cards was wedged into a decorative molding at the bottom corner of the armoire. Bandon held up the card by its edges like you would an old photo. Yellowing cardboard. Faded blue ink. Definitely vintage. The card had a blue rose, probably for Portland, the Rose City. Underneath were the words:

"JUSTICE, JUSTICE SHALT THOU PURSUE"

—*DEUT.* 16:20

VOTE YES ON AMENDMENT 1

The biblical phrase in Hebrew was *tzedek, tzedek tirdof*—the words on my prayer shawl. I wiped my hands on a paint cloth and studied the card, then showed it to Rose and The Ladies. Auntie An wasn't sure what Amendment 1 meant, but Grandma knew exactly.

"Miriam Josefsohn printed this for the 1912 election," she said, nesting the card in her hands as you would a newborn chick. "It's a suffrage card, urging men to give Oregon women the right to vote. Did you know this was here, Rose?"

Rose shook her head.

Auntie An beamed at me. "See? I knew this room was meant for you when you turned sixteen. All the years we lived in this house and only now does the card reveal itself—the card made by another Miriam, who slept in this room so long ago. That Miriam wore the justice prayer shawl with the blue thread, and then Mama Two, and now you. The card is definitely a message for our Meryem." She turned to Grandma. "Don't you agree?"

"I never argue with my older sister," Grandma said.

Stifling a snort, I put the suffrage card in my over-tee pocket. "Let's get this over with. I still have to tend to Munchkina."

I stayed in Grandma's room again that night, to let the paint fumes die out in my new place. She snored lightly, her mouth falling open, her breath sour. I woke once in the darkness. Grandma rolled on her side and called out, "Jessa?"

I kissed Grandma's cheek. "Shhhh…" I said. "Go back to sleep."

She did, but I couldn't. The suffrage card kept nagging at me. Auntie An, for all her craziness, had been right about Serakh. Was she right about the suffrage card being meant for me? Did the card's appearance mean that Serakh would come back soon?

215

Nothing magical or mystical happened the next day. I did the usual Sunday routine. Thanks to Bandon, I was in a halfway decent mood.

At dinner, Rose raised her glass of water and proposed a toast to Tillamook.

Grandma looked up from her cucumber salad. "Is Munchkina pregnant?"

"Possibly. We won't know for a while. In the meantime, Ignatius and I have been advertising Tillamook's stud services. We had two appointments today and there are four more scheduled for this week. You'd be surprised at how many credits Tillamook's services are worth."

Bandon punched the air. "Go, goat!"

"One of our customers has offered to buy Tillamook for 375 credits," Rose continued. "I told her I'd have to check with you."

Bandon slathered peanut butter on bread, preparing the first of his postdinner sandwiches. "I borrowed Tillamook from a guy who knows a guy, so I'll ask and let you know." He looked at me and stroked his beard. "If they don't want him back at Gales Creek, how about we split the credits? Half to you for Tillamook's upkeep. Half to Calantha Corps for our projects."

I took a sip of water. "How about zip for Tillamook's upkeep, since we get the benefit of his stud services for free? Calantha Corps gets it all."

Bandon shifted into mock-surrender mode. "I won't argue. Thanks!"

Grandma wiped her mouth with her napkin. "That's an excellent idea, Meryem. Your Auntie An and I are considering ways to help the homeless people in our midst as well. We'll let you know our plans soon. How do you like sleeping in Miriam Josefsohn's room?"

"Fine," I said, still my all-purpose four-letter word of choice. The bedroom didn't feel like mine, but then the rest of the house hardly felt like mine now either.

First thing Monday morning, I got a message from Mr. Nabli that was anything but fine. "Vid-voice me when convenient after 11:30," it read. "Council refuses to lift exclusion order."

CHAPTER THIRTY-SEVEN

By the time I stormed downstairs to help with breakfast, I was furious. At the Council. At Mr. Nabli. At Mayor Hammilason, whose voice was emanating from the ridiculous hand-crank emergency radio that Rose still listened to for postquake updates.

"The water and sewage system has been completely restored this past week in Pacific City," the mayor said. "This significant step brings us closer to allowing nonemergency travel to the tsunami/coastal inundation zone."

"He sounds like he's running for governor instead of taking care of people in his own city," I mumbled. I yanked a container of eggs from the fridge. "He sounds like a pompous ass."

Rose, who seemed to be in it's-a-beautiful-day mode, turned off the radio. "What's with you this morning?"

I told her.

She cradled a mug of tea. "That's too bad. Calantha Corps is a worthy organization."

"Exactly. Mr. Nabli doesn't like Bandon anyway."

Rose took a sip. "Oh? You don't think he tried hard enough to convince the mayor. Now what?"

I smacked the eggs, emptied their contents into a mixing bowl, and hurled shells into the digester. "Nothing. I have a sextillion things to do around here."

"Bandon helps with the housework," she said. "So that's a sextillion minus a bunch. Meryem, you missed the digester that time."

I cleaned the mess, downed breakfast, and left Rose to deal with everyone else. No way could I face Bandon with the bad news. Instead I cleaned every centimeter of the goat shed and wiped down Munchkina until she glowed. The chickens got a personal grooming from beak to claw. I worked up a satisfying sweat sawing off a dying branch on one of the pear trees and rewarded myself with an extra forty-five seconds in the shower. By 11:30, I was ready to sound civil when I vid-voiced Mr. Nabli.

I stretched out on the bed in the Miriam Josefsohn room. Her suffrage card leaned against my lobe locket box. Justice, justice shalt thou pursue. Vote yes on Amendment 1. Maybe Mr. Nabli had done his best to convince the mayor, or not. Had I?

"Hello, Meryem." Mr. Nabli looked relaxed.

I decided to shake up his day. "I need to give this one more try," I said, hoping he couldn't hear the shakiness in my voice. "I have to meet with the mayor."

"Let's see what I can do," he said, without a trace of surprise. "I told Joule you wouldn't give up that easily, judging from how you've been about your mother. Give me a minute to access his calendar."

"You know the mayor that well?"

Mr. Nabli ignored me. "Nothing for today, tomorrow, or Wednesday. How about Thursday at 9:20?"

I rubbed my forehead. "Um…sure."

"He'll be at FEMA headquarters at the Heathman Hotel. Shall I pick you up?"

"I'll meet you there."

Mr. Nabli narrowed his eyes, giving me his authoritative lawyer look. "Under no circumstances is Mr. Falconer to come with you, Meryem. You'll have to handle this yourself. We're on the mayor's calendar for twenty minutes. You can vid-voice me as late as seven Thursday morning if you wish to cancel. Understood?"

My shoulder twitched. "I understand."

I thumbed off, my mood alternating between "yes!" and "yikes!" Now all I needed was a crash course in Calantha Corps projects, the prequake state of homelessness in Portland, and solid proposals for temporary shelter and permanent housing in the future. All that and whatever else it took to make Mayor Hammilason change his mind in twenty minutes.

I pounced on Bandon when he showed up for lunch. "I'm meeting with the mayor this Thursday morning to ask him to lift the exclusion order and to start working with Calantha Corps."

For once, Bandon ignored the food in front of him. "You what? Stupendous!" He played a fanfare on his harmonica. Then he got serious. "How did you manage this, Meryem? You're not telling me something."

I explained that Mr. Nabli was the mayor's friend and that he was doing this as a favor to me. No way was I going to tell Bandon about the death papers agreement—too personal.

Bandon seemed satisfied. "You'll be great," he assured me. "I'll give you the results of fourteen Calantha Corps projects across the country since 2050, plus info-streams on affordable housing successes in New York City, Baltimore, and Los Angeles. You'll have plenty of material."

By dinner, I knew the basics about homelessness in Portland before The Big One—how the situation had improved in the 2030s and 2040s, with the job boom in the alternative energy sector, but had gotten worse in the past ten years. I understood the essentials of the shelter-in-school program in Boston and the housing voucher program in Minneapolis. We downloaded Bandon's Calanthagram to my device, and Bandon showed me how to set

219

up the holography laser. "Let Calantha do most of the talking," he advised. "It's a really convincing performance."

During dinner, The Ladies and even Rose peppered me with suggestions, strategies, and statistics. Ignatius kept quiet, but his smile spoke volumes. I had graduated into the ranks of the good guys.

Grandma pressed her hands on the table. "Since we're talking about homelessness, I have a proposal to make. An Chau and I are considering leasing my condo at a deep discount to Havurah Shalom. The congregation would then use the condo to provide transitional housing and support services to a homeless family. We'd call it Aron's Place."

Aron's Place. Grandpa. I remembered his face-wrinkling smile, silly jokes, and the way his whiskers tickled me when he kissed my cheek. Aron Zarfati, a young immigrant in search of a new home in America, then a real estate businessman here, and finally someone whose wealth enabled his family to provide a home for others.

"Great," I said, and I meant it. "It's the perfect way to honor Grandpa." I tore my dinner roll in half. "But you must miss your friends. Will you be looking for a place in your old neighborhood?" As soon as the question flew out of my mouth, I knew the answer.

"Our friends will visit us here," Auntie An said. "We will never have to move again."

CHAPTER
THIRTY-EIGHT

I swallowed hard, took a sip of water, and swallowed again. How could I say anything bad about Aron's Place? "It's awfully crowded here," I added. Dumb excuse.

"We'll manage, Merry," Grandma said. "It's a temporary inconvenience." Meaning, I suppose, that Bandon would be leaving soon, and then Ignatius, and finally Rose.

I took another sip. "You could have asked me first."

Grandma patted my hand. "I suppose we should have, but we knew you wouldn't mind. Aron's Place is still in the planning stage because we're not even sure who owns this house."

I felt my eyes widen. "What? I own it. Mr. Nabli told me so."

Grandma wiped the corners of her mouth with her napkin. "It's nothing for you to worry about. My lawyers will be speaking with Mr. Nabli."

"Trivial Pursuit time," Rose announced, her Russian accent

thickening the way it often did when she was stressed. "Ladies and Meryem against Ignatius, Bandon, and me."

I wasn't ready to play games. "What do you mean I wouldn't mind? Aron's Place is one thing. But this house belongs to Jessa and me. I was born here."

Auntie An glared at me. "This house should be mine. I earned it. I cared for it and for the people who lived here until the day they died."

Grandma said something in Vietnamese and reached for Auntie An's hand. Auntie An shook her head and strode out of the dining room.

"Let's talk about Aron's Place another time," Grandma said. "Rose, I'd like a cup of tea."

"I'll get it," I said, escaping to the kitchen. Grandma followed me. Her tiny hands grasped my shoulders. "You know I'll do what's best for you, don't you, Merry? Even if the house reverts to your Auntie An. We're family. I was hesitating about Aron's Place, but when I saw that suffrage card about pursuing justice, I knew I should do my part. And then, when you were feeling terrible about staying in your mother's room…We should stay together, here, in this house, whether it belongs to your Auntie An or you. Don't you agree?"

I bit my lip. I couldn't tell my grandmother her living here with me made Jessa feel farther and farther way. I couldn't say I didn't want the full-time responsibility for caring for two elderly women, day in and day out. I didn't want a new family. I wanted the old one.

The best I could do was, "I understand."

"Good girl," she said.

Hours later, still awake, I wrapped myself in my quilt and curled up on a bed so different from the Jessa nest that my soul ached. It was my fault that I had flung Jessa's clothes all over the place and wound up sleeping in my grandmother's room and started this whole bedroom switch. I tried not to think about what would happen when Rose left, because she was leaving me, it was only a matter of time. Would I waste night after night with The Ladies playing Trivial Pursuit?

Staring at the ceiling, I remembered asking Jessa what trivial meant. I was six or seven.

"You mean from Grandma's Trivial Pursuit game, lovey?"

"Uh-huh." I snuggled next to her on the couch.

Her eyes got sparkly. "Are you ready for a vocabulary story?"

"As good as pumpernickel?" I giggled. Pumpernickel came from words that meant devil's fart.

Jessa kissed the top of my head. "Not quite, but you'll like this one too. Trivial means it's about trivia. Take the word apart, lovey. 'Tri' is the same as in tricycle, remember? And triangle. So it means?... Three— you're right! And via is a Latin word for road. Trivia tells the story of where three roads meet, meaning a very public place. It means something that's common and not important."

She squeezed me tight, smothering me in honey orange. "There's nothing trivial about the gluesome twosome."

I grabbed my socks, hiking boots, and sweater. One place in this house still belonged to Jessa and me. I climbed the back stairs to the third floor, opened the pull-down stairs, and stepped out onto the eco-roof.

Stars pierced the dark from light years away. From forever. The *olam.*

I wanted to rise. I wanted to lift up and float. I wanted my own magic carpet to glide me to a palace of magical reasoning where Jessa would kiss the top of my head again and wrap me in her honey-orange scent.

Instead, I sank to my knees in *Sedum spurium*—dragon's blood. The gravity of Jessa's long absence dragged at my bones, and a new fear threatened to crush me flat. Serakh was my only way into the magic I needed to pursue Jessa now that I had figured out when and where I might see her again. But what if Serakh never came back? What if our tri-via, our three roads in time and space— Serakh's, Jessa's, and mine—would never cross? I closed my eyes and imagined dragon's blood seeping up through my knees, infusing me with a magical antidote to loneliness and loss.

"Miss Meryem?"

It took me a moment to realize that the voice had come from the world outside of my head. I opened my eyes and there he was, solid, standing by the hatch to the third floor.

"Ignatius, how did you know I was up here?" I asked.

"I am a light sleeper," he said.

It wasn't until we were sitting on the edge of Priscilla's bare bed surrounded by the emptiness of the third floor that either of us spoke again.

"Miss Meryem," he said, "do you have a situation?" Scarred and buckled flesh covered the top half of his right arm. His sweatpants slouched over his hips, his feet lay buried in unlaced combat boots. He stared at the floor.

Silence passed between us, and then suddenly I needed to say it out loud. "I...I do have a situation. It's not really about The Ladies or this house. It's about my mother."

A tiny nod. "Rose informed me when I moved in that you believe she is missing in action."

The back of my eyes felt full, but no tears came. "I look for bits of her twice a week at RescueCommons," I said. "I can't let Jessa be gone. I don't know how to be without my mother."

Another nod. "My men were my family. I see the faces of the ones that died and the ones still missing. I still wait. You don't want to be like me. You need to stand down."

Predawn light seeped through the windows. We sat there, Ignatius in his combat boots, me in my hiking boots. "I'm not ready to be alone," I told him.

Neither of us moved. Ignatius smelled of witch hazel and sweat. I wanted him to put his arm around me in a grandfatherly, comforting way, but I didn't dare ask.

"What time do you report for kitchen duty, Miss Meryem?"

"At 7:30. It's Tuesday, so I'm in charge of breakfast, because Rose has a counseling session."

"Catch some shut-eye. I'll wake you at oh-seven-hundred hours. I'll know 'cause that's when the construction noise starts. You're safe with me, elsewise Rose wouldn't have let me stay."

I leaned my head against his shoulder and closed my eyes.

After Ignatius woke me, I got myself into work mode and made breakfast. Rose came into the kitchen as I was scraping tofu bacon bits into the digester.

"Love you," she said. She enveloped me in a hug so long and strong that I knew Ignatius had told her about what had happened. "I had a very helpful session," she said. "Counseling is the best thing I've done for myself and this family since The Big One. Grieving is hard work, Meryem. But it's worth it."

"Mmmm," I said, concentrating on wiping the kitchen counter. Tuesdays we avoided discussing Rose's sessions with Dr. What's-Her-Face.

"Which is why I found a short vid-voice slot for you for tomorrow afternoon at four."

Breakfast threatened to come back up. "You told me you'd never do that. You promised."

"The session is only for fifteen minutes, and it's with the same woman I use. Shanaya Kaur. Do this for me, Meryem. Do this for all the times that Jessa left you in my care."

I planted my hands on my hips and faced her. "This is a total breach, Rose, and you know it. Unfair!"

Rose shook her head. "Jessa entrusted you to me since you could barely walk. I nursed you through a broken arm and that horrible flare-up of scarlet fever we all thought would never hit the States again. I brought you through The Big One, and I'll be damned if I'm going to let you face all this feeling alone."

Rose looked so smug, as if she were going to stay forever. "Alone is right," I said. "I've watched you and Ignatius. Now you won't tell me where you'll be sleeping, and you're into clean jumpsuits and silver bracelets, and playing poker with him, and Mr. Nabli says they're going to lift the emergency any day now, and Jessa owes you a ton of money."

"Meryem."

My head felt ready to erupt. "Don't you Meryem me. I have eyes, Rose. I'm sixteen. I'm not your employer's merry little girl anymore. As soon as the estate is settled, you and Ignatius are going to waltz out of here and live happily ever after. Grandma and Auntie An will take over this house and my life. And then they'll die and I'll really be alone."

Rose's mouth opened and closed and opened and closed. Nothing came out. She shook her head.

"I don't want your stupid counselor," I yelled. "I want my mother back! And if I can't have Jessa, then I sure as hell don't need you to count the days until you collect your back pay and leave me."

I grabbed my hoodie and stormed out into the rain.

CHAPTER
THIRTY-NINE

By the time I reached RescueCommons, my anger had barely started to fizzle. Mark was locking his wreck of a Tesla. No sign of Gemmie or Charles. I intercepted him by the front steps. "You didn't send her off to your sister's, did you?"

"Not yet." He avoided looking at me, his polyplaits a mess, his usually clean shirt stained with what looked like sriracha sauce.

I grabbed his arm. "Listen. Just listen, okay?"

He said nothing.

I took a breath and tried to explain it the way Jessa would have. "Hebrew is based on three-letter roots, so it's easy to see how words are connected," I told him. "There's the word *tzedek*, which means justice. And there's *tzedakah*, which sort of means charity, about doing a righteous and charitable act. The link here is that charity shouldn't be like coins tossed to people without looking at them. Charity is like justice. Both the person who gives charity and the person who accepts charity help to spread justice. Maybe it doesn't matter where acts of charity end and acts of justice begin. Maybe that's how the world is supposed to work."

Mark shook his head.

"Staying with me, even for a little while, is *tzedek-tzedakah*. Gemmie deserves that. You deserve that. I deserve that."

He pulled away. "What's the Hebrew word for principle, Lady Bountiful? My family taught me you don't take hand-outs, and you don't feed the lie that black people would rather live on welfare than work."

I reached out to him. "You don't understand. This isn't about those old lies and how things look. This is about taking care of Gemmie."

He thrust a finger at me. "You think you're being so kind and just, and then Gemmie gets sucked into the system, and then some bureaucratic jerk is going to say Gemmie isn't my daughter, and then they'll take her away."

Mark turned and strode toward the minivan.

I followed him. "I don't know the Hebrew words for pride and stupidity either," I shouted to his back. "Or for fear. It's not going to happen like that."

Mark's shoulders slumped. "You sound like Shander. You think you can snap your fingers and magically change the way things are."

I started to walk toward him. "It's one step at a time. I get it. Believe me. Please, Mark. All I'm asking is that…"

I didn't finish the sentence. The Tesla had wheezed into operation, and Mark was gone.

Shander had left for a meeting downtown and no one else was on my shift then, so it was just me and the routine. When my two hours were up, I slogged home defeated. I could keep three chickens in their hacienda, but I had no idea how to help a little girl live with her father—or whoever he was—in a better place than their car.

Bandon met me in the kitchen with an official-looking white envelope. "This is from Rose," he said, his voice somber. "She and Ignatius and The Ladies are out. I'll be around if you want to talk."

Barely keeping it together in front of Bandon, I retreated to the

Miriam Josefsohn room and sat on the floor with the envelope in my lap. Rose sometimes wrote letters to me when Jessa was away and we had arguments, when she said I was being impossible and she insisted on some specific "arrangement" until Jessa got back. She used to say we would be clearer about the "arrangement" when she wrote it down. No way was this going to be good.

Bandon played the harmonica in Ignatius's room, leaving the door open to the hall. Ten minutes later I'd worked up the guts to open the envelope and extract two pieces of paper.

My hands shook as I read the first document, an e-printed one directing Mr. Nabli to give to Ignatius—in the form of housing and food credits—half of the debt that Jessa's estate owed to Rose. I stared at the ceiling. Rose was getting ready to leave.

Bandon's zippy tune turned my stomach. I closed my door and sank to the floor again, steeling myself to read the "arrangement" I expected would be in the second document—a handwritten letter on beige stationery I didn't know we had.

4 March 2059

Dear Meryem,

You mean the world to me. Sometime in the future, you will want a family of your own. Until then I hope to have a place in this house and in your heart. Ignatius and I are very fond of each other. We would like to spend more time together, but we are taking things one step at a time.

I plan to be here with you as long as you want me to stay. You must know by now, as I have felt since The Big One, that Jessa has passed away. She will never return to us. I ask you, as someone who cherishes you, to keep the appointment with the grief counselor tomorrow.

All my love,

Rose

I leaned against the bed and let wave after wave of relief wash over me. When I heard the front door open, I took the stairs two at a time. "Oh, Rose." My voice collapsed in my throat.

"Shhh, it's all right. Ignatius would like mashed sweet potatoes tonight. We still have some sweet potatoes, don't we?"

I checked and we did. I added sour cream, cardamom, black pepper, and nutmeg in honor of the occasion. Ignatius ate two helpings. Bandon, to my complete shock, had none, the first time since we'd met that he'd turned away food, not counting crispy cricket mix. He didn't like sweet potatoes.

"Blessed are the underconsumers for they shall reduce global warming," he said. "But not by much." Same old bantering Bandon.

Wednesday we met on the third floor, where there was lots of space and relative quiet. I was sitting on Priscilla's bed, while Bandon paced in lecture mode. "Portland can benefit from the experience in Cleveland, Ohio, where Calantha Corps has implemented the rapid-rehousing program with resounding success. The key to this program is knowing landlords who have units available for immediate occupancy," he said. "The key is also providing financial services, such as the tenant's security deposit."

I stood and stretched. "Let's stop talking about housing for now. What worries me is what the mayor and the Resilience Council think about Calantha Corps itself and especially the DC Six."

He kept pacing. "It's your job to convince them we're a respectable organization with an impressive track record. Tell them the facts, Meryem. We've done a lot for other cities. We can do the same for Portland."

"That's not what I mean," I told him. "When I used the

ScrutinEyes on you, the criminal matrix showed three convictions from a couple of years ago. Vandalism. Disturbing the peace. How do I explain those?"

"Good question." Bandon stroked his beard. "I forgot you zuckered me. The Council probably has that information too. FEMA for sure. Shit."

I rubbed the back of my neck. "I'll tell them you'll make sure Calantha Corps won't disrupt any more meetings or do anything disruptive."

Bandon shook his head. "The Corps doesn't operate like that. I'm influential, but not a dictator. Six of us came out here from national headquarters, not just me. I don't want you to guarantee what I can't deliver. Concentrate on the good we can do—our program ideas."

"It won't work."

He stood still, finally, his eyes soft and kind. "Meryem, look. It won't be your fault if the mayor insists on continuing his asinine exclusion order. I'll head back to Gales Creek and we'll keep in touch. Got it?" He looked at his MyCom. "Now it's almost time to vid-voice Rose's counselor. Rose would kill me if I made you late."

Before I had a chance to tell him that I could tell time and didn't need reminding, he pretended to strangle himself as he staggered toward the stairs. "Oh, no! Death by therapist!"

Which, oddly, made me feel better. At one minute to four, I thumbed the connection.

CHAPTER FORTY

"Hello, Meryem." The counselor's dulcet tone bordered on saccharine, but her face was far from sweet. A scar snaked from the left side of her forehead across the bridge of her nose to the upper part of her right cheek. An artificial visual device took the place of her right eyeball. Her skin was slightly lighter than mine, her hair hidden by a headscarf.

I shuddered.

"I'm Dr. What's-Her-Face," she said. And she laughed.

Then she said nothing.

And I said nothing.

And she said nothing.

Finally I said, "A guy I know lives with his little girl in his old minivan. He asked me if he should send her to live with his sister in Manitoba."

We talked about Mark and Gemmie. I downloaded links she gave me for Mark, and afterward I felt I could pass along some solid advice.

"Thanks," I said, when the session was ending.

"I hope things work out for Mark," she said. "By the way, Meryem, grief isn't just about death. We also mourn for the missing. Good-bye for now." She thumbed off before I had a chance to answer.

That familiar ache grew in my chest—the dark, hollow ache from not saying good-bye to Jessa that last time because I was mad. And Jessa knew it. That's how I left it between us. That's how I severed our lifelines.

I'd never talk to Dr. Kaur about that last vid-voice with Jessa. Never. Or maybe not for a very long time.

Back in the kitchen later, I answered Rose's questioning look with, "I made a half-hour appointment for next week. Wednesday at 3:30."

"Good idea," she said, leaving it at that.

Bandon was all excited at dinner that night, singing my praises as the defender of the homeless and the arbiter of reason who would bring Calantha Corps to the good citizens of Portland.

Auntie An raised her glass of water in my honor. "You are pursuing justice."

Grandma, ever the history teacher, lectured Bandon on the Free Speech Movement protests on the Berkley campus in 1964. "My American mother, Hope Friis, occupied Sproul Hall nearly a century ago," she told him. "During the 1950s and 60s, there were many sit-ins for racial justice. Peaceful protest is woven into our political fabric."

"I haven't accomplished anything yet," I said, feeling ridiculous about all this attention. "I can't even get a colleague of mine at RescueCommons to find a decent place. He and his daughter live in his minivan."

I repeated the story I'd told Dr. Kaur about Mark and Gemmie. Even as I explained what Dr. Kaur recommended, I knew Mark wasn't about to "take charity," as he put it. Was this the best we could do for his little girl? Freeing her to become a servant in some wealthy Jewish household?

My shoulder twitched. Wrong girl. Gemmie, not Izabel. But still. What if the mayor met Gemmie? What if I could show him how Calantha Corps programs would benefit her directly?

"Excuse me," I said, dropping my spoon on my plate and leaving the table. "I've got something that can't wait."

I thumbed Mark's contact coordinates. Nothing. Nothing. Then finally an audio link.

"You won't take no for an answer," he said.

"Look Mark, I need a favor from you. Please. Don't thumb off. I'd like Gemmie to spend tomorrow morning with me. Can I pick her up around 8:30?"

"What for?"

"I…um…there's a meeting that…"

"Meryem, I'm in the middle of something here. Gemmie is staying with Shander tonight. If ze says it's okay, then it's okay."

My idea was definitely okay with Shander when we vid-voiced a moment later. "Gemmie has been through a lot worse, and she'd enjoy a trip to the Heathman. The mayor won't know what hit him."

"What do you mean?"

Shander laughed. "She's irresistible. Cute little girl with a winning smile." Then ze switched to serious. "You're showing the mayor a poster child for homelessness, the image that makes it easy to be compassionate. Don't get me wrong, Meryem. I'd do the same."

I thought of Mrs. Liú in the alley and Ignatius when he first showed up with his credit-tenant voucher. Shander was right. Gemmie was my version of Calantha—and it was my job to convince the Council to work with Calantha Corp. I had to make the meeting count.

The next morning, I walked five blocks to Everett, the closest rubble-free street fully open to traffic. Shander's car pulled to the curb and blinked at me. Its occupants were eating doughnuts.

"We saved one for you," Gemmie said, her lips purpled by blueberry filling. "We decided you like the plain kind."

Shander handed me a napkin and smiled. "The least messy,"

ze said. "You hop in the front while I finish braiding Gemmie's polyplaits."

I studied the dashboard. "Shander?"

"The GPS location is already set. Just press the reenter traffic button."

The car joined the queue heading down Everett. A light rain was falling. Charles rested on the dashboard. I nibbled on the doughnut and tried to find a center of calm in the thoughts roiling inside. What possessed me to bring a six-year-old and her stuffed giraffe to meet with the mayor of Portland? Maybe the mayor didn't even like kids. Gemmie looked sweet and clean in a freshly laundered KidForm and over-tee. She was wearing tights for the first time since we'd met, and her Klogs had been wiped down. I frowned. For a girl who lived in a minivan, shouldn't she look more rumpled?

We slowed at the temporary bridge over the 405 and rode into the Pearl District, which looked nearly back to normal. Some construction company was always building there. Then we stopped for the light at 9th and Everett, where the National Guard had taken over the hotel, and Portland seemed under siege. We crossed the North Park Blocks crowded with water filtration dispensaries and temporary studios from the art college, and then we turned right onto Broadway.

I took a centering breath. About a dozen blocks to go. I rehearsed Bandon's instructions for setting up the Calanthagram and reviewed prequake statistics for homelessness in the Portland area. I'd start out with the January 9, 2058 count that showed 5,000 people on the streets or in temporary shelter, including 1,500 women, 540 veterans, and 713 children under the age of eighteen. Or was it 713 veterans and 540 children? I took another breath. Shit. I was losing it.

"Shander, I can't do this."

"You'll be fine, Meryem." Ze kissed the top of Gemmie's head. "You've got Charles and Gemmie. Let them do the talking."

I'd been to the Heathman Hotel several times for lunch, although none of Jessa's visitors ever stayed there. Too spendy. Even though the place was built before The Ladies were born, the hotel's seismic retrofit had withstood The Big One better than most of Portland's government buildings. Only the large metal overhang at the entrance was gone. The FEMA team and some other officials got to camp out in a place with a good restaurant and private bathrooms.

The hotel's GR-17, dressed in an English Beefeater costume, greeted us with "Welcome to the Heathman. How may I assist you?"

Gemmie squealed in delight. She was all for a giraffe-doorbot conversation—although Charles's robotics weren't working—but there wasn't time. Mr. Nabli walked across the lobby, with its high ceilings, marble floors, overstuffed chairs, and a gilt-flecked mural covering an entire wall. Not as elegant as Topkapı, of course. I slipped into that blue-thread world for a nanosecond and blinked myself back. Portland, 2059. Got it.

After Mr. Nabli and Shander shook hands, Mr. Nabli cleared us with the guard by the registration desk. "The Council is meeting with FEMA officials in the conference rooms," Mr. Nabli explained. "Mayor Hammilason can give you twenty minutes in his office suite."

Shander settled into an overstuffed chair. "I'll wait down here and catch up on my reading," ze said with a take-it-easy smile. "You tell Charles to behave."

By the time we got to the mayor's suite, my palms were sweaty and my mouth dry. "Joule Hammilason is a decent guy," Mr. Nabli said as he knocked on the mayor's door. "He won't bite. Just don't expect that he'll lift the exclusion order."

My mouth turned sour.

The mayor looked larger in person than I'd expected. He wore a cowboy shirt and jeans, as usual, but had traded in his polyplaits for a ponytail. He smiled and waved us into a huge suite. A kitchen and office area occupied one section of the room, and low tables, couches, and chairs nestled by a fireplace on the opposite wall. The room smelled of furniture polish and fresh coffee. "Good to meet you, Ms. Zarfati. May I call you Meryem? Please call me Joule."

I nodded, familiar with the first-name technique from RescueCommons. Still, I didn't feel any more at ease.

"Adnan said you were bringing a guest." He squatted next to Gemmie. "What's your name, sweetie?"

Gemmie stopped staring at her surroundings long enough to thrust her giraffe at the mayor. "Charles doesn't like you to call me sweetie. If you try to give me candy, he'll report you to my dad."

I winced. So much for letting Gemmie do the talking. "This is Gemmie Albermarle and her companion, Charles," I explained. "Gemmie lives with her father in a battered up Tesla minivan."

The mayor stood and took two paces back. "It's a pleasure to meet you, Gemmie," he said, his face in neutral. No response to hearing she lived on the streets. Instead, he looked at his MyCom. "Shall we get started?"

Gemmie took off her Klogs and plunked herself down on the couch, next to Charles and Mr. Nabli. "This is way fancier than Shander's place," she told us. "Don't worry. I know how to behave." Mr. Nabli grinned. Charles looked unsure.

I unpacked my projection pad on the mayor's writing table, closed the drapes, uploaded the Calanthagram, and adjusted the audio. Within seconds a half-meter high holographic image of a girl in an outsized overcoat hovered over the table.

"My name is Calantha Broadwell," it said, although of course the image was an avatar of the real girl. "I'm seven years old, and I share a cardboard box with my dad near the baseball stadium in Baltimore, Maryland. By the time you see this, I will be dead."

The mayor cut the feed. "I'm not interested in canned presentations by Calantha Corps. What else do you have to offer?"

Gemmie propelled herself from the couch and tugged on my sleeve. "Charles has to go to the bathroom. Now."

"Meryem is busy right now," Mr. Nabli said. "Come with me." He took Gemmie's hand, and they left for the adjoining bedroom.

That left one annoyed-looking mayor and me, staring across the writing table from each other. I opened the drapes. "As of January 9, 2058, there were…"

He held up his hand and finished my sentence. "…nearly five thousand people on the streets or in temporary shelters in the Portland metropolitan area. I don't mean to interrupt, Meryem, but let's not waste the next thirteen minutes on statistics."

I wished I could escape to the bathroom too.

"It's complicated," he said. "As much as I'd like to, I can't guarantee that every Portlander is appropriately sheltered—including little girls and their stuffed giraffes."

"Why not?" The question burst from my lips. I must have sounded juvenile, and I knew there were people like Mrs. Liú who would be hard to help, but Gemmie?

"These are people," I added, raising my voice a notch. "Flesh and blood people."

The mayor crossed his arms and leaned against the table. "Now, Meryem, let's be reasonable. I understand that you want the Council to lift the exclusion order for the DC Six, including Mr. Falconer. And I sympathize with you."

"I appreciate that," I said, although I doubted his sympathy. "And under the First Amendment…"

He smiled as he interrupted me again. "I'm a lawyer. I know a lot about First Amendment rights of free speech and assembly. I also know that I am acting completely within my authority under our ongoing state of emergency."

Pompous ass. He didn't have to keep interrupting me. Even Don Joseph had better manners. "Hiding behind emergency powers is a breach of justice," I said. There. That didn't sound stupid.

Joule arched his eyebrows. "Justice?" He looked at his MyCom again. "An 8.9 earthquake isn't concerned with justice. Or due process or equal protection. The Big One didn't play fair. Now it's my responsibility to pick up the pieces. So let me ask you this, Meryem: With all the challenges Portland faces now, why should we allow a group of outside activists and opportunists to take advantage of our misfortune in order to push their own agenda? Give me something practical about having Calantha Corps here at this time. What's in it for Portland?"

CHAPTER FORTY-ONE

"What's in it for Portland?" I had an urge to call forth a flash of blue light and rematerialize next to the Calanthagram—not that I could, really. Still, I so wanted to stun the man who was fiddling with his MyCom again. I wanted him awestruck, as the embattled pursuers of justice for homeless people entered Portland, spreading decent shelter and affordable housing for all.

Instead, I said, "That's a good question." I hugged myself. If I were back in Istanbul with Don Joseph, I could have pulled off an impressive prophecy, thanks to Aussie Jack. "I can't predict the future," I said, stating the obvious.

Which is when I realized I could use the past. I knew a lot about medieval Istanbul and Ottoman culture, thanks to Jessa, Grandpa Aron, Aussie Jack, and my own travels. It was worth a try.

"But then neither can you…Joule." I stepped toward him. "Let's talk about life in Istanbul under the Ottoman sultans." That was vague enough, and that was all I needed. "You have a lot in common with them."

He looked up, a scowl invading his face. I took a breath. Now at least I had his attention. I slipped into the wide-eyed story-telling mode I used with Winslow. I had only a few minutes left, and I was going to use every second. "Istanbul was a walled city, and there were rules about what you could do inside those walls, just like our urban growth boundary."

The mayor creased his forehead. "There's no comparison. The sultans were despotic rulers. I'm a democratically elected mayor."

"Of course, they weren't elected," I said. "But these sultans acted in ways to help their people. They regulated the price of meat so that all but the poorest could afford to eat it at least once a week. They built public bathhouses. Their nightwatchmen patrolled the streets to keep them safe. Istanbul had places where poor travelers could get food and shelter." I didn't bother to add that all of this wouldn't have helped slave girls like Izabel.

I took a step closer. "Istanbul sits on active fault lines. The sultans even organized work crews to repair the city every time earthquakes struck there. Doesn't this sound familiar?"

"Well, since you put it that way, I…"

"But…" It was my turn to interrupt. "But the Ottoman sultans had a major flaw. Their empire became weaker and weaker because everyone in Topkapı Palace did the sultan's bidding. Tens of thousands of people. The sultans decided which people would advise them, which people they'd do business with, which people they'd allow to stay in Istanbul, and which people wound up with their heads on a pike." The thought of the straw-stuffed heads I'd seen with Serakh still turned my stomach.

The mayor frowned. "It's an exclusion order, not a death sentence."

"Not so different," I persisted, pacing in front of him, my head throbbing. "Calantha Corps might be able to help you, if you heard what they had to say instead of worrying that they might disrupt the smooth functioning of who knows what. You are using your emergency powers to close yourself off from people who might have solutions that your closed circle of advisors didn't think of. If you drop the exclusion order and meet with the DC Six, you might discover something beneficial for yourself and, more importantly, something beneficial for the rest of us."

I pointed my finger at his nose. "And that, Joule, is what's in it for Portland."

The mayor narrowed his eyes. I felt ill, but I refused to look away.

Gemmie raced toward me from the other room. "Two beds," she exclaimed. "And sooooo many pillows. Guess how many."

Her timing couldn't have been worse.

"Four," I said, breaking eye contact with the mayor.

"Eight! Including the fat sausage kind. Mr. Nabli let me snuggle into every single one, didn't you, Mr. Nabli?"

He stood by the door to the next room holding the stuffed giraffe under his arm. "Charles prefers the softer pillows," he said.

Gemmie raced back, grabbed Charles, and marched over to the mayor. "Who sleeps in that room?"

He smiled down at her. "I do sometimes."

"Just you?"

"Just me."

To my surprise, and apparently the mayor's, she curtsied. Where did she learn that? "Charles and I promise to be very, very good, and very, very quiet if you let Daddy and us sleep in the other bed," Gemmie said, her voice tottering between persuasion and whine. "Daddy hardly snores, and when he does, all you do is roll him over on his side and he stops. Just this once. Just for tonight, okay?"

I bit back tears and said nothing.

The mayor looked at Mr. Nabli, who shrugged and waved his hand toward me. "An impressive team, Joule."

The mayor rubbed his forehead. He ran his fingers through his hair and headed for the door to the hall. "I really must get to that meeting with FEMA and the other Council members. Adnan, would you please see the front desk and my press secretary about getting a room for tonight for Gemmie and her father?"

Charles zoomed into the air and landed upside down by the fireplace. Gemmie captured the mayor in a hug surrounded by more thank yous than I could count. I couldn't help feeling that I'd failed and that this night in the hotel was a consolation prize. But then the mayor turned back toward me.

"Give me a single for-instance, Meryem. I'd like one example of what you or Calantha Corps might suggest for the homeless community in Portland under our present circumstances."

"Absolutely," I said, stalling. The only thing I could think of was the situation I'd been living with for months. "Keep the voluntary credit-tenant program after the state of emergency is over. That… um…that would use existing housing units and cost less than other alternatives. You might be surprised at the number of people who want to keep their current arrangements."

He arched his eyebrows. "Interesting."

Mr. Nabli made that half-snort, half-chuckle so familiar to me from his Friday visits. "That's all you're going to say? Interesting?"

The mayor frowned. "You know me, Adnan. I don't rush into things."

"You'll hear by noon," Mr. Nabli told me. "Joule will ask a few trusted colleagues for a sanity check, run his ideas by FEMA, make a decision, and stick to it."

We were walking down the three flights of stairs to the lobby. Charles somersaulted most of the way, apparently unharmed. "Do you think they'll lift the exclusion order?"

Mr. Nabli touched my back. "I think you made the best case you could, Meryem. Politics interferes with equitable and just governance even in the best of times, which these aren't. That's the world we live in. Can I get you anything before my next appointment?"

I shook my head.

"Vid-voice me when you hear," he said. "I'll see you tomorrow afternoon as usual."

Shander greeted us in the lobby, heard what happened, and pronounced the meeting a complete success. "I doubt that Mark will accept the mayor's offer," ze said. "But it's worth booking a room." Mr. Nabli saw to the details while the Beefeater bot entertained Gemmie and Charles.

The smell of vinegar assaulted me as soon as I walked in our front door. Gryffindor was washing the dining room windows, which required more supervision than greeting people and giraffes at the Heathman. "He keeps missing the upper left-hand corner," Rose told me. She put Gryffindor on pause. "How'd it go with the mayor?"

"I don't know yet. Probably not well. Where's Bandon?"

"Working in the basement with Ignatius. Bandon did a decent job with the chickens this morning. I hope he gets to stay. Meryem, what's wrong?"

Now that the meeting was over, all I could do was wait. After all these months of waiting for Jessa, I should have been an expert, but still, that suspended feeling never got easier. I sank into a dining room chair and rested my head in my hands.

"You'll be here tomorrow with Mr. Nabli, won't you?"

Rose rubbed my shoulders. "I plan to. There's nothing else on the schedule. Why?"

The words squeezed out of my mouth. "I had an agreement with Mr. Nabli, and he kept his end of the bargain. No matter what the mayor decides, I am going to keep mine."

I managed to lift my head and look at Rose, her face creased with concern. "I'm signing the papers tomorrow. Jessa's. The death papers."

"Oh, my dear Meryem." She blinked away tears. "Do you want to invite The Ladies?"

I touched my fingertips together, forming the old one-to-one sign, which was supposed to make her smile but only got her more weepy. "Just you and me," I whispered. "One-to-one."

We lingered there, with her hands on my shoulders, until I said,

"I'm going to change my clothes and clean out the goat shed that doesn't really need cleaning."

"Good idea," she said.

The text came an hour later. **"Exclusion order lifted. Can you and Falconer meet with me Tuesday @10:40? Joules."** No vidvoice, which was good, because I looked a mess.

I hugged Munchkina and ran inside.

Rose was having tea in the kitchen. I tugged off my mud muckers and announced, "We did it. No exclusion order."

Rose beamed. "Excellent! I knew you could do it. Bandon's in the basement with Ignatius."

"Bring out the jelly beans," I told her as I headed for the basement door. "Let's party!"

When Bandon heard the news, he hoisted me off the floor and twirled me around. "The Queen of Calantha Corps," he whooped. "You are the best." Ignatius saluted.

Lunch consisted of salad with jelly beans on the side, plus crispy cricket mix for me. Grandma toasted Bandon with her glass of water, and Auntie An gave him one of her antiquated high fives. Bandon played song requests on the harmonica, and I almost forgot about Mr. Nabli coming the next day.

CHAPTER FORTY-TWO

For the past eight months I had volunteered at RescueCommons every Tuesday and Friday morning, and I wasn't about to stop now. Shander reported that Mark and Gemmie did stay at the Heathman and that Mark had vid-voiced he was taking the day off.

Shander congratulated me on getting the mayor to lift the exclusion order and on my work on the Rebecca Chumway case. "Forensics got a match with bone fragments near Seaside. That's closure for one more family."

A chill climbed my back and lodged in my heart. Closure is such a horrid word. Rebecca was dead.

"The Chumway girl wasn't on our official list, so we've still got eighty-four missing. I'd like to get down to eighty-one before they defund us. Eighty-one is such a magical number." Shander sounded like Auntie An.

Three hours later, when Mr. Nabli showed up dressed for a funeral, my heart nearly froze. He set out the usual credit-tenant papers, and I dealt with those first. Rose sat next to me, her hair brushed into the French twist she wore on special occasions. She'd replaced her usual jumpsuit with a woolen skirt and matching sweater set, and she wore her silver bracelet. I'd purposely worn my everyday FemForm and over-tee, telling myself it would be easier that way. It wasn't. I felt shabby.

Mr. Nabli opened the death papers folder while I instructed Gryffindor to play the last movement of Rimsky-Korsakov's *Scheherazade*, one of Jessa's favorite pieces of classical music. We kept discussion to a minimum while I scrawled my name again and again on documents he explained. I tuned out the explanations and nodded when I thought a nod was required. I expected to cry. I didn't. Neither did Rose.

Afterward Mr. Nabli said, "My condolences, Meryem. As we say in Islam, 'Surely we belong to Allah and to Him shall we return.'"

"Thank you," I said, handing him his pen. If Jessa, by some miracle, was still alive, then none of this mattered. But for now, I was doing the right thing.

And then there was one more thing that suddenly felt so right that I could hardly breathe. "Wait here," I told them and headed for the basement.

When I returned with the leather pouch, Rose was telling Mr. Nabli about the provision she'd made for giving Ignatius part of her back pay. I brushed ash from my hair and answered Rose's puzzled look with, "McPherson. I'll explain later." Then I opened the pouch and deposited two coins on the table.

"My great-grandmother gave these to Jessa," I told Mr. Nabli. "Aren't they mine now?"

"They are yours." He didn't explain and I didn't ask.

I put the silver coin in Rose's hand. "This one is for you. I don't know how valuable it is, but I'm sure Mr. Nabli can get it appraised and find a buyer."

Mr. Nabli nodded. "I can certainly handle that, Ms. Kropotkin."

Rose put her hand to her mouth. "Meryem, don't. This is a family heirloom."

"You are practically my second mother, Rose," I said. "Mama Two!"

That got her to smile.

"And I'll still pay you after you finish suing me for back wages," I said, trying for some of Bandon's banter.

Rose managed a laugh. She flicked her wrist at me, barely connecting with my forearm.

I handed Gracia's portrait medal to Mr. Nabli. "I know more about this one," I said, and I gave him a few facts. "As my lawyer, can you sell this and put the proceeds in some sort of fund for Gemmie?"

He fiddled with his pen. "Are you sure?"

"Absolutely. I thought I'd need it for...another little girl. Izabel. I don't. But I can still use it to redeem...that's not the right word. Anyway, I'm sure it's supposed to help Gemmie now."

"Consider it done." Which was how Jessa's funeral ended, unexpectedly wrapping me in a warmth that lasted through Friday night dinner with The Ladies. Bandon hummed along with the Shabbat prayers and played the harmonica later. Rose told stories about Jessa and me. After that visit to the roof, I couldn't bear another game of Trivial Pursuit, so instead I went through the storage closet and got some things for my new room.

Still, reporting for memorial services Saturday morning was harder than I thought. I'd left my prayer shawl at home—wearing one wasn't a requirement, and it reminded me that Serakh was probably gone forever. Winslow's warrior shield had found its way into my pocket.

Grandma and Auntie An guided me to a row near the back of the sanctuary. People crowded in around us, packing the small sanctuary so tightly that after fifteen minutes I escaped to the bathroom for breathing space. A woman interrupted my hand washing to tell me how sorry she was about Jessa.

"Thank you," I managed, stifling the urge to walk out the main doors instead of going back to my seat. Half an hour later we were into the Torah reading, which meant I could sit quietly for a while and pretend I was following along. The weekly portion—this one was *Tetzaveh*—came from the Book of Exodus. It dealt with priestly robes and building the tabernacle in the desert, and it was several chapters after the portion I'd read when I became a bat mitzvah. Mine had been *Yitro*, and I got to read the verses that included the Ten Commandments.

Listening to ancient verses about silver, copper, and precious jewels, my mind shifted to Topkapı Palace, to Izabel, and to the word opulence. Lavish display of wealth. A perfect Jessa word. *"Opulence comes from opus, lovey. It's the Latin word for work. Lots of work goes into making something opulent."* I wondered why people didn't work less on opulence and more on helping ordinary people.

The service droned on. We stood, and sat, and stood, and sat again. I stared out the windows. Then Grandma squeezed my hand, returning my focus to Rabbi Judith, who was reading the names of all those "who died this week and at this time in years past." In alphabetical order. "Joshua Abramson, Georgette Blum-Cisneros…"

I shoved my free hand into my pocket and wrapped my fingers around Winslow's warrior shield. By the time the rabbi got to "Sarah Posner Raine, Elliott Simon," the shield was digging into my palm, making a place for the pain in my heart.

"…Jessa Einhorn Zarfati."

Rabbi Judith asked for the mourners to rise. As I stood, I saw Auntie An clasp hands with Grandma. Grandma dabbed at her eyes with a handkerchief. Auntie An let her own tears fall. The Ladies recited the words I couldn't, even though I knew the *kaddish* by heart. When the rest of the congregation chorused "amen" I whispered, "I love you." I couldn't say good-bye.

Bandon, Rose, and Ignatius were waiting in the drizzle outside with our umbrellas. Ignatius held out his arm for Auntie An. Rose got Grandma.

"Falconer Fetching Service," Bandon said in a mechanical voice, offering me the crook of his elbow. "Good afternoon, Meryem. I am fully operational. How may I assist you?"

I nested my arm in his. "You've been spending too much time with Gryffindor."

"Got you to smile," he said.

Rose had already prepared lunch. While I nibbled on quinoa and cucumber salad, Grandma explained to Bandon that she wouldn't be lighting the twenty-four-hour *yahrzeit* candle commemorating the anniversary of the death of a family member.

"It's a custom but not required by Jewish law," she told him. "We'll forego a memorial candle under the circumstances."

Grandma didn't say whether this was for Auntie An's benefit, because she was afraid of fire after The Big One, or for mine.

I sought asylum at Chicken Hacienda. Yetta was favoring one leg. I removed a pebble wedged near her metatarsal fold. She burrowed into my heavy work sweater, friendlier than usual, her black feathers matching the regrowth under all my magenta. Afterward I retreated to my room and listened to theremin scrag. Bandon let me be. So did everyone else. That's what I wanted—or needed—I didn't know which. It didn't matter.

Jessa visited in my dreams that night. She wore her baby barf sweater and was surfing a wild gray ocean on a sleek black coffin. Her skin shimmered with neon-colored fish scales. Two large garnets sparkled in her eye sockets. She told me not to be afraid.

"Afraid of what?" I asked.

She didn't answer.

CHAPTER
FORTY-THREE

Sunday morning Shander made it easy to stay home and avoid the crowds at the Resilience Day celebration. Ze vid-voiced me while I was making breakfast.

"Mark just told me that he's meeting someone about housing today, and he wants me to come along," Shander explained. "Any chance you could take care of Gemmie for a while? I'm sorry to foist this on you, but I couldn't think of anyone else she and Mark would trust."

I practically kissed the MyCom.

Later, after the house emptied out, Shander and company triggered the Sentry Mat. Mark handed me a bouquet of lavender that he'd probably picked from the yard down the street.

"I really appreciate your taking care of Gemmie," he told me. "There's this new transitional housing unit nearby, and I think I have a chance of being selected. They have rules about going to school or getting a job. There's rent, even though it's really low, so it's not charity, which is great. But it's a two-year commitment."

I put the lavender in a vase of water and asked whether they wanted to stay for lunch. "We've got biscuits from this morning, and I'm sure there's lentil soup in the fridge."

Gemmie snuggled against Mark. "Don't you have doughnuts?"

"We can go to the store and get some later," I told her. "Would you like that?"

Gemmie shook her head. "I want to go with my dad."

Mark lifted Charles from her arms. "We agreed, Gemmie, remember? Charles wants to stay here."

Gemmie grabbed at the giraffe. "He does not!"

Mark reached over her to give Charles to me, which is when Gemmie tugged on one of the giraffe's legs and a seam opened in Charles's chest.

Gemmie wailed. She clutched the giraffe to her chest, fell in a heap at Mark's feet, and sobbed. Mark stood there, looking close to tears.

"I can fix the rip," I told them. "Rose keeps a sewing kit around somewhere."

"More than that needs fixing," Shander said. Ze put a hand on Mark's shoulder. "Gemmie needs you today. It would be her home too."

One glass of water and one trip to the bathroom later, Gemmie went with Mark—the gluesome twosome. She placed Charles in my arms, after assuring him that I would tend to his injuries, that it wouldn't hurt, and that he didn't have to go to the emergency room. "I'll be back for you," she said and kissed his furry face. "You know I always come back."

Quiet enveloped me as I sat at the kitchen table with biscuits and a bowl of soup. Charles rested against the emergency radio that Rose still kept on the counter. I remembered waking up under the table, unable to feel my feet, and Rose telling me everything was going to be all right. A lie, of course, but she must have wanted to believe it then too. How could Jessa leave and not come back?

251

I put my spoon down, unable to manage another sip, and returned the rest of the soup to the fridge. The kitchen smelled of Rose's baking, the way it often did since I was little. "The Resilence Day kitchen," I told Charles. "As good as before The Big One. As if nothing has changed."

Charles put his solemn face next to mine. "Everything has changed," I imagined him saying.

I got Rose's sewing kit and sprawled on my bed. The blue thread in her kit was a decent match for Charles's furry chest. I took out a small pair of scissors, cut a length of blue thread, then threaded a sturdy needle, pinned the seam closed, and took my first stitch, tucking the end inside.

My mind was on my sewing, which is why I didn't notice right away.

"Peace be unto you, Meryem," she said, standing in the hall by my open door.

I sat there, stunned and silent. Drowning.

She walked toward me. "The One guides me to you again. I do not know why."

My fingers slid along the new stitch in Charles.

A strand of white hair fell across her face. "I believed the intertwining was at an end, and yet something is left undone."

A bubble of hope brought me to the surface. I took a breath. I found my voice. "Yes. Exactly. Time."

My heart thudded. Maybe I was wrong about the three paths—Jessa's, Serakh's, and mine—never coming together. Maybe this was my chance to make things right.

I put Charles on the bed beside me and held out my hands toward Serakh. "We missed one infobit before—the right time. Izabel told us that Jessa was in Istanbul during a large earthquake, remember? That has to be the one on September 10, 1509. So now we've got the where and the when. We'll figure out the magic carpet part when we get there."

"You are thinking with your heart," Serakh said. "Izabel relates a tale she heard as a child from her master when he was a child."

I nearly laughed. Here was this magical creature reminding me about logic. "Yes, but still. Or maybe we're supposed to go to Manzanita right before the tsunami. I have those geo-coordinates and the exact date and time."

I wrapped her hands in mine. "One minute with my mother. That's all I'm asking. One more minute."

Serakh let out a long, shaky breath. "We will go where we are sent."

CHAPTER
FORTY-FOUR

I opened my eyes to a Mediterranean cypress whose delicate evergreen leaves framed a dreary sky. My head was in Serakh's lap, my muscles in spasm, my feet tingling.

Before I could ask, Serakh said. "We are in Istanbul, partway up a hill from the water we crossed to get to Belvedere."

"When? Is it 1509?"

"We will know soon. A woman walks toward us."

Serakh helped me to stand. She gave me her large outer robe to tent over my prayer shawl, clothes, and hair. Tombstones rose at odd angles under the trees. Beyond them, I saw a mosque and the city walls.

The woman's headscarf, loose trousers, and flowing robes marked her as someone from Ottoman times. She stopped several meters in front of us and dropped into a deep curtsy.

"Peace be unto you," she said, as if she expected us.

"And unto you peace," Serakh answered.

Judging from the woman's milky complexion, blue-gray eyes, and the strands of red hair escaping from her headscarf, she could have been Bandon's twin sister born five hundred years apart. Her pearl earrings looked familiar.

"Izabel?"

The woman's face creased into a smile. "I have kept faith with you in these ten years since you saved me, Lady Meryem. Every day I utter prayers of thanksgiving. I feed the poor and needy in your name. I shelter a young girl for your sake."

Gone was the feisty girl who pretended to be possessed. I rubbed my temples. This was 1569, not 1509. Why?

Serakh put her palms together and bowed slightly. "Why have you sent for us?"

Izabel put her hand to her throat. "It is you who have called me," she said. "Lady Esther told me to keep watch by Ayele's grave today and to speak the truth."

We sat on a bench near the cypress, and Izabel began, her eyes wide and bright as she recounted her success with Lady Esther, the needlework she stitched for wealthy patrons, and her betrothal and marriage to a Sephardic Jew in the spice trade. "Yakob is gentle with me," she said. "We are very happy, although it has been six months and I am still without child."

Izabel raised her eyebrows.

"That story I told Don Joseph about you is not true," I assured her. I wished I could say she'd have children, but then I didn't really know.

Relief softened her face. "Even my brother does well now," she added. "Habib is one of the best falconers for the sultan." Izabel clasped and unclasped her hands. "I cared for Ayele in his last illness."

I couldn't believe it. Ayele? The man who would have sold her to the highest bidder as soon as her body was worth more than her embroidery? "He gave you to Don Joseph," I said.

Izabel folded her hands. "This is true. But Ayele was kind in his own manner. I choose to remember him that way. I returned the kindness when he lost his position and had no one to protect him. In his final moments, he gave me his talisman and told me that he could not rise to heaven while his soul was burdened with a false tale."

My shoulder twitched. Was this why we were here? To find out that everything about Jessa was a lie? Still, I smiled encouragement.

Serakh nodded. "You are here by his grave today to speak the truth?"

Izabel smoothed her robe. "Ayele labored in the sultan's menagerie, as I told you those many years ago. But he did not have the honor of caring for the sultan's lions. He was responsible for the health of a peacock."

"And the unicorn lady?"

"Ayele did meet her on Lesser Judgment Day, Lady Meryem."

"The 1509 earthquake?"

"I think that is the right year."

A fierce wind gusted up from the Bosporus. I shivered. "Tell me about the unicorn lady."

Izabel's hands fluttered. "She floated in on a magic carpet with her prince. I have never seen such a wonder, but Ayele said it was so. She asked to see the sultan's unicorn. The menagerie usually holds such a creature. Then the earth shook. A block of stone fell on the prince's leg, pinning him to the ground. A lion—a young one—did attack the unicorn lady, and men came to trap the lion. They led the lion away. The prince yelled to them to save the unicorn lady, but they did not listen to him. The unicorn lady withdrew the talisman from her arm and gave it to Ayele. She told him to fetch a doctor. All that part is true."

"And then?"

"You will not be angry, Lady Meryem?"

"We must hear all of the story," Serakh said before I could answer.

Izabel sighed. "They lifted the stone and carried the prince away. Ayele ran for help, but they caught him. They beat him for leaving the peacock. When he returned later, the unicorn lady was gone. So was the prince. So was the magic carpet."

I stared at Izabel. "They left her to die?"

Izabel looked away. "Please understand. The unicorn lady had the appearance of a mere woman. They did not know her worth. The peacock was valuable."

"The *peacock* was valuable?" I fought to keep my voice steady. "She's bleeding out, and they're worried about the *damn peacock*?"

Serakh touched my shoulder. "Meryem."

A deep roar rose from the cemetery. The bench shook.

"Move behind the tree," Serakh shouted. The ground rolled and shifted. One second. Two. Fear jacked my heartbeats to triple time.

A moment later, the earth stopped shifting. We waited under the cypress. No aftershocks, at least not yet. My breath slowed.

A turban-shaped stone rolled past, tumbling down the hill toward the water.

Izabel fell to her knees. "I beg of you, Lady Meryem, do not be angry with Ayele. He was only a boy." Then she scrambled uphill. By the time we caught up with her, making our way through more of a garden than a cemetery, Izabel was fussing over a tall, thin headstone topped with a turban much like the one that had rolled away.

"Lady Meryem, I am grateful to you for sparing Ayele's marker," Izabel said. "I paid for his burial." Izabel's fingers traced the script on Ayele's headstone.

The wind died down. The sky cleared.

"I'm not angry," I told her.

Izabel looked skeptical. "You will not cause the earth to rumble again?"

Serakh leaned close and whispered, "She believes you caused this, Meryem. Let it be so. She will not believe otherwise."

I patted the headstone. "Ayele is safe."

Izabel hugged herself and stared at the ground. There was something more.

"Lady Meryem pursues justice," Serakh said. "As with you, she is generous and kind."

Izabel reached under her cloak and extracted a small tapestry pouch, richly embroidered with the name Ιζαβελ. "Ayele kept the talisman upon his person because he feared that a *jinn* might try to spirit it away. When the angel of death was upon him, Ayele gave the talisman to me. I put it in this cloth embroidered with my name on it to protect the talisman from the *jinn*."

She took a breath. "This belongs to you, Lady Meryem. I feel that in my heart. If Ayele had seen you without your veil, he would have known you were of the same tribe as the unicorn lady. Perhaps he would have given the talisman to you. Now he will be at peace."

Izabel placed the pouch on my outstretched palm. I closed my fingers around the pouch and brought my fist to my lips.

Serakh put her hands over Izabel's head. "May The One bless you and keep you," she said.

I answered, "Amen."

Izabel's face glowed in the afternoon sun. She curtsied once more. "I must see to my husband," she said. "Peace be unto you."

"And unto you peace," Serakh and I answered.

Izabel disappeared down a path shaded by an Oriental plane tree. That's when I started to shake. Every Friday for months I had searched the ether for this bit of circuitry that was once inside Jessa, and now I couldn't bring myself to open the pouch.

Closing my eyes, I breathed in the goat smell that clung to Serakh. I wondered whether Munchkina was pregnant, which seemed like such a trivial thing to think about at a time like this.

"Keep your eyes closed," Serakh said. "I am taking you back."

I felt the blue thread. Light flashed behind my eyelids.

We're going home. Mommy and me.

CHAPTER FORTY-FIVE

Serakh must have guided me to the chair in my room. I grabbed her sleeve. "Jessa's chip?"

"I worried that you might drop Izabel's pouch. I carried it across." She opened the pouch and pressed the thin medal square into my hand. The corners nested into the flesh at the base of my fingers. Safe.

Dazed and aching, I stared at the chip. The ones we had were outdated models. No memory. No capacity to store health status or geolocation while in a person's body let alone with the bio-connection severed. Jessa's chip could tell me nothing.

"So she was there. And then she left. Do you think she returned to Manzanita and…died…there?" *Died.* The word seared the inside of my mouth. "Do you think my mother is dead?"

Serakh kissed my forehead. "Your mother is gone. Perhaps she will return. It is not in my power to know. Izabel has given you a part of your mother that you can touch and remember. You are bound in a love that will bring you pain and comfort all the days of your life."

The gluesome twosome, I thought. Silver etchings on the chip caught the fading light. "Couldn't I have seen her one last time?" I closed my hand over the chip. "I miss her so much."

"Meryem, I must not linger. Let us not part without saying good-bye."

My eyes were drawn to the swath of sky framed by my window. I heard Jessa again. *"Hundreds of years ago, life was more precarious than it is now, lovey. Precarious. That means uncertain, in someone else's hands. So when people parted from each other they said, 'God be with ye' and that became godbwye and that became good-bye."*

Then it dawned on me. "You have even less control over your life than I do."

Serakh shrugged a simple, human, Bandon-type shrug. "Who among us has control? What matters is what we choose to pursue and how we act along the way. Now, shall I help you to stand or do you wish to remain in the chair?"

"Help me up."

I willed my leg muscles to keep me vertical. I held her close. Then I drew back and stood on my own.

"Until perhaps," I told her.

"Until perhaps," she said. "Peace be unto you."

"And unto you peace." I closed my eyes, knowing that when I opened them Serakh would be gone.

In the quiet that followed, I eased Jessa's chip from my hand. I nested it in Izabel's pouch and slid the pouch underneath the top of my FemForm. Charles seemed to need a reassuring cuddle, so I held him in my arms. We stood together looking out the window for I don't know how long. Then I put Charles back on my pillow, retrieved my MyCom, set it to audio only, and thumbed Priscilla. I told her about the warrior shield, and she said not to bother giving it back.

"Winslow is into the Dancing Teeth Family now," she told me.

I asked about her tattoo and later thumbed the contact she gave me.

"Dermal Dreams. Mary Jane speaking. How may I assist you?"

GR-17 or human? "I'd like an implant appointment for tomorrow," I said.

"What is the nature of the implant?"

"My mother's PerSafe chip. I want to keep it next to my heart."

The voice turned human. "Oh, that's lovely. I'll make time for you. Are you interested in a tattoo as well?"

Which is when I realized I was. "A unicorn. And a salamander."

"What a unique combination," she said. "We'll talk about that when I see you."

We settled on a time. I thumbed off, wrapped Izabel's pouch in my prayer shawl, and put them in the armoire.

Next came Charles. I slipped the warrior shield inside and sewed him up with Rose's plain blue thread. Seven stitches. Nothing magical. Sometimes that's all you need.

After I cut the thread, the scissors stayed in my hand. Without thinking, I grabbed a clump of hair two finger-widths from my scalp.

Snip.

The fistful of long magenta strands that came away had a tiny trace of my natural black on the ends. Two finger widths was the right height to cut away all the magenta and to start over with what little was left of just me.

Snip. Snip.

Later I stuffed the severed curls inside a pillowcase and knotted the top. The magenta dye we'd used was made from botanicals—henna and indigo mostly. Izabel might have recognized the formula. The hair would make perfect nesting material.

I was on my way downstairs to the backyard when the Sentry Mat signaled the return of my housemates. I could have made a dash outside through the kitchen. Instead, I sat on the stairs by Jessa's rug and waited.

Auntie An saw me first. Her eyebrows threatened to fly off her head. "What have you done to your beautiful hair? It will take years to grow back!"

Grandma came up behind her. "You look lovely, Merry. It's not that much shorter than mine."

Auntie An muttered something in Vietnamese. Grandma stiffened. She studied me in the grandmotherly ScrutinEyes way that made me itch.

"I'm fine," I said.

She rolled her eyes.

Ignatius nodded approvingly. "Longer than mine," he joked.

Rose was Rose. "It's a bit uneven in the back," she said. "I'll fix that later." She liked my recycling plan.

"You're gorgeous!" Bandon told me.

"And I wasn't before?" Two can banter.

"Before you were perfect in purple. Now you are elegant in ebony."

The tiniest bit of allrightness bubbled up inside me. Allrightness. Not an authentic Jessa vocabulary word. Still, I liked it.

I was getting dinner organized with Rose when Mark arrived. "Nice buzz," he said, nodding toward my hair. "Gemmie's conked out at Shander's. She thanks you for the unicorn. We've had long day, but I think I closed the deal."

I sat Mark by the nutriculture wall, served him a cup of coffee and a biscuit that had miraculously survived since breakfast, and retrieved Charles. He grabbed the giraffe by his tail—Gemmie would have been appalled—and thanked me for sewing the rip.

"Charles should heal nicely," I said. When I saw Gemmie again, I'd tell her about Charles's new protective powers, the kind of magic I thought Mark wouldn't understand. "What happened with the housing?"

"It's worth jumping through all their hoops for Gemmie's sake," he told me. "Definitely not charity. There are a lot of work requirements and stuff I have to do for Gemmie to make sure we won't be separated. It's a two-year lease unless I find better housing before then."

I pinched a radish off the wall. "Where is this place?"

"In the Pearl District—would you believe it? A two-bedroom unit in some fancy condo. We move in May first. Have you heard of Havurah Shalom?"

I don't flush as visibly as some, so I probably looked calmer than I was. I nibbled the radish, needing a minute to collect myself. I knew where this was going. "I went there a lot when I was little," I said. "Not so much any more."

"Oh. I didn't know you were Jewish. Nice folks. I'm their beta tester for a new program. It's called 'Aron's Place.'"

"That sounds great," I said. My shoulder twitched. I wondered whether the book of fairy tales that Grandpa used to read to me would still be on the bookshelf there. "I hope everything works out."

As soon as Mark left, I shared the news with Rose.

"Your grandfather was a good man," she said, collecting the coffee cup and plate from me. "He'd be proud of you. I see you took Jessa's lotion and that old sweater to your new room. Is there anything else you want from Jessa's room? I tidy up after your Auntie An in there every day."

Jessa's room. That's the way it would always be for Rose and me. I wondered if Auntie An thought of it as her parents' room. "Which bedroom are you going to take now?"

She washed and dried the dishes, then wiped her hands on her apron. "I'll stay in the library. Fix it up a little, now that The Ladies are staying. That's the most practical. Ignatius is happy where he is, and I'd rather keep a room to myself without marching up and down to the third floor."

"We could offer the third floor to Bandon as a temporary headquarters for Calantha Corps," I said as I put the dishes away. "Do you think The Ladies would mind?"

She smiled. "Probably not. They'll be delighted to know about Mark and Gemmie moving into Aron's Place."

I leaned against the counter and stared at the space under the kitchen table. "I miss her so much, Rose."

"I do too," she said.

"What really happened between Jessa and Auntie An? Why did Jessa get the house and Auntie An have to leave?"

Rose leaned against the counter next to me. "Honestly, Meryem, I have no idea. An Chau was gone by the time your mother hired me. We'll never know the whole story. Are you okay with The Ladies staying?"

I took a breath. "Grandma's doing the right thing with Aron's Place, and you're staying here until forever. Okay, semi-forever. Plus Auntie An loves this house." I ran my hand over tuffs of hair on my head. "She'll teach me Chinese. Mandarin, I think. It should be fun. Oh, and I've solved the toothpaste mystery."

Rose turned to me. "Do tell."

"Auntie An gives the toothpaste to a homeless woman. She's been doing it for years, apparently. It's a sort of tradition."

"Why didn't she just tell me?"

I shrugged. "Why does Auntie An do anything?"

Rose sighed. "Anyway, knowing Mandarin wouldn't hurt when you apply to college. In another year or so you'll be off to who knows where, and then who knows what will happen next. That's life."

Life. I contemplated telling Rose I had to do some chore or other. Instead I stuck to the absolute truth. "Life feels wobbly," I told her. "I'm going outside."

Reds and purples canopied what was left of the West Hills. The soothing sounds of a construction-free Sunday enveloped the backyard. I'd finished draping the pear trees with strands of magenta hair, and I'd added hair to the bushes at the edge of the side yard, the roof of the goat shed, and assorted vegetation surrounding Chicken Hacienda. The air had turned cooler, the sky deepening to blue gray. A half moon was waxing toward full. Still, I wasn't ready to go inside and join the rest of them.

I looked at the goat shed and thought about Munchkina, who was probably pregnant. And Chewsette, who was gone. And Serakh, who might never come back.

I'd always thought Jessa would come back, come home. Now I

didn't know where she was, or when she was, or if she was. When I heard the back door open, I breathed in the last of my solitude.

"Falconer Fetching Service," Bandon said. "This sweater is from your grandmother. The tofu roll-up is from Rose. You were smart to miss dinner, Meryem. The Ladies proposed hiring a carnivorous cook. Rose was ready to breathe fire. Wanna talk?"

"Not especially."

He grinned. "Got you to anyway."

I rolled my eyes.

"In case you might be interested, the mayor gave a decent speech for Resilience Day today. Listen to this clip." Bandon thumbed his MyCom.

Joule's voice filled the air: "In the coming weeks, the Resilience Council and Calantha Corps will work together to keep Portland progressive. Our first project will be to extend the credit-tenant program indefinitely. We in this great city can do more than settle for life as it was before The Big One. We can be more than resilient. We can be better. And we will."

The clip ended in mid-applause.

"You've got the magic touch, Meryem," he said. "I contacted the mayor after the speech, and we're still meeting at 10:40 Tuesday morning at the Heathman. So, what do you think? Are you ready to save the world?"

I slung Grandma's sweater over my shoulder and gave half of the roll-up to Bandon.

"I'll see what I can do," I said. I tucked my arm into the crook of Bandon's elbow, the way I had after the memorial service. I guided my free hand to my heart. Now the sliver of circuitry that had lived in my mother would become part of me, along with every single moment of our time together.

"God be with ye, Jessa." I whispered. "God be with ye."

La Chica Medal
© The Jewish Museum, New York

AUTHOR'S NOTE

Seven Stitches joins the past with the future and weaves together facts, folklore, and assorted bits of fantasy. For those of you interested in what's real, Query is a good place to start. Everything that Query conveys to Meryem—with I think two exceptions—is true. This includes information on unicorns, magic carpets, earthquakes, the Sephardic Jews in the sixteenth-century, and the *la chica* portrait medal. The exceptions? Calantha Corps comes from my imagination. So does Aron Zarfati, who is Meryem's Turkish grandfather. Although Istanbul's Neve Shalom synagogue was attacked in 1986, my character could not have been among the survivors.

Among the characters in the story are real members of the Nasi family, which included Doña Gracia Nasi, the sixteenth-century widow of one of Europe's wealthiest spice traders. The *Seven Stitches* incidents never happened, of course, but you can learn much more about the family in Andrée Aelion Brook's nonfiction work, *The Woman who Defied Kings*. The portrait medal in the story is part of the collection in the Jewish Museum in New York City.

Esther Handali is loosely based on a Jewish woman by that

name who traded with the women of the harem. Her fictional concerns were justified. The Nasi family and other newly immigrating Sephardic Jews (*Sepharad* is Hebrew for Spain) would transform much of Jewish culture in Istanbul, eclipsing the language and traditions of Jews who had settled there centuries earlier. Had Meryem asked about Esther, Query would have added information that Esther returned to favor at the palace but later wound up with her head on a pike. If Meryem had known, she might not have left Izabel in Esther's care. I decided not to tell her.

Incidentally, the Hebrew word for France is *Tzarfat*, from which I derived Aron's family name Zarfati. In my story, Aron's Jewish family comes to Turkey from Spain but spends time in France. Mr. Nabli's Muslim family travels to Turkey from the Palestinian city of Nablus, also the biblical site of Shechem.

The Query references to Serakh and to the justice quote in this story are accurate. She is the basis of many legends, although the blue thread story is my own. She travels the *olam*, which in Hebrew connotes both the universe and eternity.

The Ladies (An Chau and Ly Tien) are based on accounts of children born to black American soldiers and Vietnamese women during and after the Vietnam War. According to Trin Yarborough, author of *Surviving Twice: Amerasian Children of the Vietnam War*, an estimated one hundred thousand so-called Amerasian children were conceived or born during the US involvement in Vietnam.

Homelessness—don't get me started! Estimates vary, but it's a fair guess that three million people experience homelessness in the United States every year. The "point-in-time" January 28, 2015, count of homelessness in the Portland, Oregon, greater metropolitan area showed nearly four thousand people without permanent shelter that night and an estimated twelve thousand living in overcrowded or unsafe conditions. The fictional Aron's Place is loosely drawn from Micah House, founded by members of Temple Micah in Washington, DC, and part of the "One Congregation—One Home" initiative of Lutheran minister John Steinbruck.

The Eliseus Project is based on current efforts to "resurrect" the passenger pigeon, Tasmanian wolf, woolly mammoth, and other species. According to Project Passenger Pigeon, these birds went from an estimated five billion in North America in 1800 to zero on September 1, 1914. I haven't heard of research on unicorns. If you have, let me know. RescueCommons is based on CrisisCommons and similar organizations that are part of the Digital Humanitarian Network (DHN). Since 2012, the DHN has used its resources to aid in natural disaster relief, the ebola epidemic, assistance to refugees, and other instances where crowd sourcing provides vital information.

Meryem's house closely resembles one on NW 19th Avenue and Johnson Street in Portland, Oregon. The real structure features an ashbin with the McPherson cover, dumbwaiters, two internal staircases (only one of which leads to the servants' quarters on the third floor), and a large safe in the paneling on the first floor. To my knowledge, there is nothing inside the McPherson ashbin but ash.

Finally, to earthquakes. The 1509 quake in Istanbul is real. Quotes in the story come from *Earthquakes in the Mediterranean and Middle East: A Multidisciplinary Study of Seismicity up to 1900*, by Nicholas Ambraseys. The Pacific Northwest is due—some say overdue—for a megaquake in the Cascadia subduction zone. I based the level of destruction and postquake environment on several books and articles and on the Oregon Resilience Plan (available for download). We have gone from "if" to "when." In this story, The Big One takes place on March 9, 2058 at 4:47 in the afternoon, Greenwich Mean Time. The rest is…not yet history.

ACKNOWLEDGMENTS

A writer writes. This writer—fortunately—does not write alone. *Seven Stitches* took shape with the guidance and encouragement of past and current members of my writer's critique group, Viva Scriva: Addie Boswell, Melissa Dalton, Amber J. Keyser, Sabina Rascol, Elizabeth Rusch, Sara Ryan, and Nicole Schreiber. An early version of the manuscript benefitted from Per Henningsgaard's editing class at Portland State University (PSU). The book's excellent team at Ooligan Press encouraged and guided me through revision after revision, for which I am profoundly grateful.

Birol Yesilada, the director of PSU's Center for Turkish Studies, offered context and contacts for my trip to Istanbul in 2013, when *Seven Stitches* was known only as "Book 3." I am particularly grateful for help from historian Naim Güleryüz, at that time president of Istanbul's Jewish Museum, and from archaeologist Bilge Ar, who pulled back the modern metropolis to reveal sixteenth century buildings and an ancient Jewish cemetery.

Seven Stitches became a better book thanks to Devin Naar, the Isaac Alhadeff Professor of Sephardic Studies at the University of Washington, and to Aron Hasson, founder of the Jewish Museum of Rhodes. My thanks goes to Jeffrey Kilmer (of Kilmer, Voorhees & Laurick, P.C.) for his hospitality and for the grand tour of the firm's headquarters, which I featured as the home of Miriam Josefsohn in *Blue Thread* and Meryem Einhorn Zarfati in *Seven Stitches*. Thanks also to Serguei Goncharenko, a graduate of Moscow University, for his help with Rose.

A writer lives. This writer—fortunately—has a supportive family. My husband Michael shares his life not only with my imaginary characters, but also now with a certain blue giraffe. Thanks, Mike. Thanks to our son Ben, an extraordinary engineer, who shaped my ideas about future technology, and to our son Keith, whose own writing inspires me and who helped me to keep my perspective. Three grandsons—Samuel, Jonah, and Milo—feed my imagination and bring me tons of love. I've written you three into this book. Let me know when you figure out how.

ABOUT THE AUTHOR

Barbara Gundle

Ruth Tenzer Feldman is the author of two young adult novels including *The Ninth Day* and *Blue Thread*, which won the Leslie Bradshaw Award for Young Adult Literature and is listed by the American Library Association as one of the best feminist books for young readers. Ruth has written ten nonfiction books for children and young adults, such as *The Fall of Constantinople*, and she has written numerous articles related to science and history. Feldman lives in Portland, Oregon.

OOLIGAN PRESS

Ooligan Press is a student-run publishing house rooted in the rich literary culture of the Pacific Northwest. Founded in 2001 as part of Portland State University's Department of English, Ooligan is dedicated to the art and craft of publishing. Students pursuing master's degrees in book publishing staff the press in an apprenticeship program under the guidance of a core faculty of publishing professionals.

Project Managers
Alyssa Gnall
Julie Swearingen

Acquisitions
Molly KB Hunt
Bess Pallares
Emily Einolander
Emily Goldman
Cora Wigen

Design
Ryan Brewer
Leigh Thomas
Cade Hoover
Andrea McDonald

Digital
Emily Einolander
Cora Wigen
Stephanie Argy

Marketing
Dory Athey
Jordana Beh

Social Media
Alan Scott Holley
Elizabeth Nunes

Editing
Olenka Burgess
Megan Doyle
Whitney Edmunds
Nicholas Shea
Michele Ford
Jordana Beh
Alyssa Gnall
Emily Goldman
Rachel Lulich
Lisa Hein
Vi La Bianca
Frances Kane
Camilla Ruth Kaplan
Amanda Matteo
Andrea McDonald

COLOPHON

This book is set in Adobe Caslon Pro, designed by Carol Twombly for Adobe in 1990. A revival of William Caslon's original specimen pages from the mid-1700s, it is an elegant typeface with many variations. The titles are set in Futura Std, a digital version of Paul Renner's original twentieth-century designs. Its versatility in condensed forms makes it especially appealing for this text.